FROM "RED INK"

COMPOUNDING HIS TERROR WAS A DERANGED cackle echoing in his mind at how foolishly he'd blown his cover. How he'd tripped himself up in an unnecessary lie.

Isaac needed to get the hell out of there before anyone figured out who he really was, and what he was really after.

FROM "THE DEVIL'S DELINQUENTS"

WITHIN MOMENTS, NATALIE'S CONVULSIONS CEASE AND her body sags, her chin drooping to her chest. She stays that way, breathing deeply.

"Are you okay?" Cal asks.

"I felt him," she mutters and lifts her head. Her lips have widened into a gratified, post-orgasmic smile. "He reached out to my soul and took me down into his dominion. I felt his utter, infinite power. I was helpless. And then he laid his hands on me. All over me. I experienced pleasures beyond pain. Burning ecstasy. I never wanted it to end. I wanted to serve him forever."

"Cool," Derry says.

FROM "A MANY SPLENDID THING"

A BRANCH SNAPPED NEARBY, STARTLING ME. I spun around to see what it was, dropping Pete's corpse into a pile of fallen leaves and brambles. I expected to see another person there and was wracking my mind for an excuse to explain the human-shaped blanket I was lugging. To my relief, it turned out to be a squirrel jumping between trees.

MURDER
IN
MONTAGUE
FALLS

NOIR-INSPIRED NOVELLAS BY
RUSS COLCHAMIRO,
SAWNEY HATTON
& PATRICK THOMAS

CRAZY 8 PRESS

ACKNOWLEDGMENTS

RUSS COLCHAMIRO dedicates *Red Ink* to his oldest friend, historian Kevin Draper, who, once upon a time, was out there, too, delivering newspapers along the suburban streets, back when young teens were allowed to do such things—with the time to dream up wild and dangerous stories that would last long into the night. And thanks to Jonathan Butler for advising on the police elements of *Red Ink*, to Alex Shvartsman for the Russian translations, and to Dayton Ward and Sawney Hatton, who gave valuable edits and feedback along the way.

SAWNEY HATTON would especially like to thank Dr. Emily E.F. Philbrick for all her love, support, and feedback, as well as longtime friend and author-in-crime Russ Colchamiro, along with Sheri White, Edward Swing, Tony Carroll, Caroline Miller, Sonora Taylor, and the other members of the Weird & Wondrous Writing group. As lonely an endeavor as writing can be, no writer writes entirely alone.

PATRICK THOMAS would like to thank John French for his support, encouragement, and technical expertise and advice for *A Many Splendid Thing* as well as most other things. Special thanks to Jessi Perry for coming up with the science experiment used in this story.

CONTENTS

RED INK

BY RUSS COLCHAMIRO

CHAPTER 1

An infrared scope cut through the suburban tree line.

Perched on a high-angle branch in the neighbor's spruce tree, Isaac could see her through the living room window, six houses away.

The M21 semi-automatic sniper rifle with fiberglass stock and 20-round box magazine was snug against his shoulder.

One bullet. One body.

Though camouflaged within a thicket of evergreen leaves, he had a clean shot. "Come on," he whispered, his eye against the scope. "Give me the signal."

In perfect synchronicity, Isaac's earpiece crackled. *"Target confirmed. Kill shot approved."*

His adrenaline spiked, anticipating the moment. Happened every time. Snipers embrace that liminal stasis, the precious seconds between about-to-pull-the-trigger and squeezing off the fatal round. Between before and after. Between life and death. The ultimate rush.

But he'd been trained to control his emotions, to focus on the task at hand. To stay cool.

Finger coiled around the trigger, Isaac held the piney aroma in his lungs, then let it out slow. Cleansing his body. Freeing his mind. "Here we go," he said, barely a whisper. "Here... we..."

An autumn breeze whistled across the rooftops then, swaying the branches. Ruining the shot.

Damn.

He'd have to get in close.

Isaac fitted the rifle in its black leather pouch, descended the spruce, then stashed the weapon in the bushes.

From behind a hedgerow of small juniper trees he slipped out to the sidewalk along Sycamore Lane, deceptively fertile ground for a lethal operative.

After years working the territory, he had examined the terrain, studied the minutiae.

He'd memorized license plates. Knew the distances between telephone poles, tree lines, and street lamps.

Which residents mowed their lawns and who hired landscapers.

Which houses sported mailboxes and which had mail slots. Chimney or no. Free-standing or attached garages, or single door or double.

Which neighbors ate in front of the TV.

Who yelled the loudest at their kids. Who drank whiskey or vodka. Who smoked. Who cheated on their wives. Or husbands.

In short, he knew the neighborhood. He knew the grid.

Despite the placid suburb, all he saw were access points, escape routes, and potential targets.

So as he had done every Thursday night, he walked, innocently it seemed, up to the front door.

Only this time he adjusted the ASP .9 mm handgun in the back of his blue-jeans waistband, concealed by his blue denim jacket.

That custom pistol, with its shortened barrel, double-magazine pouch, clear Lexan grip, and Guttersnipe sight system, had saved his life time and again.

Isaac rapped his knuckles on the front door, white with black trim. "Collect," he said, as if it were the secret knock.

After a moment of shuffled movements from within the two-story cottage, the door opened. "Hi, Isaac," Mrs. McGuire said.

"Hey, Mrs. McGuire. Nice to see you."

To the untrained eye, Isaac Fuller was just the neighborhood paperboy. He stood just five-foot-six with shaggy brown hair, an oblong face, and a mild case of acne.

Some found him to be a halfway decent kid whose family had fallen on hard times. To others he was a strange, hard-to-read loser who wouldn't amount to jack shit, if he amounted to anything at all.

But as an elite spy and assassin, trained by the Agency, that's exactly what he wanted people to see. What he wanted them to believe.

Recruited at an early age, Isaac and his fellow spooks were the Agency's best chance to help President Reagan fight back against the Russians.

Those commie red bastards had planted their own sleeper agents throughout America, posing *as* Americans, hiding in plain sight, living next door, plotting to undermine the United States in every way they could. They wanted us to become commie red bastards just like them.

And what better way for America to spy on the spies than with a spy of their own. One who nobody notices. A fourteen-year-old kid, a freshman at Van Buren High School.

Looks aside, he wasn't one to trifle with. If he had your number, your time was up.

Standing in the porchlight, he eyed Mrs. McGuire, an attractive woman with short brown hair in a bob cut, diamond stud earrings, and perfectly manicured eyebrows, her sweet perfume dancing on the breeze. He'd long suspected her. Now he knew for sure.

"So it was you," Isaac whispered what he'd only meant to think.

Mrs. McGuire offered a puzzled smile as her orange-and-white cat tiptoed along the sill inside the living room window. "What was me?"

"Oh, it's nothing," Isaac said, improvising to cover up his mistake. A rare slip. "I thought I saw you come out of the salon the other day on Essex Avenue. Jensen's, I think. Your hair. It looks great."

Mrs. McGuire blushed a little. "Oh. You're very sweet. Thank you for noticing."

Isaac winked at her, the gun pressed up against his back. "I just call 'em like I see 'em."

And I see you, you commie bitch. I've got a bullet with your name on it. Right between the eyes.

Isaac reached behind him. In his mind's eye he saw himself do the deed.

She extends her left hand to give me the money. I reach for it with my own left, so that our arms crisscross. Only I bypass her hand and take the inside of the left elbow. Pull her in close. Then with my right hand, I remove my gun, stick it in her gut. Pull the trigger three times fast. Pop-pop-pop. I ease her to the floor. Shut the door with both of us inside. Kill the husband, too. Can't have witnesses. Even if he's innocent, he's collateral damage. Open the door again, say thanks and goodnight in case any neighbors overhear. Close the door behind me, then go about my way, finish my collections. Just like always. Let the clean-up crew take care of the bodies.

As predicted, Mrs. McGuire handed him the money. "Here you go," she said.

About to lean in, primed to transact his deadly business, Isaac's earpiece crackled once more. *"Stand down. Kill shot revoked. Abort."*

Isaac quick-looked to his getaway vehicle, a silver-framed Piranha with multi-tread tires, black rubber hand grips, and a milk crate fastened to the handlebars with metal clamps. On the surface, it was just a run-of-the-mill dirt bike.

But the boys in the tech department had equipped it with weapons of every kind. An assassin's machine.

Isaac grinned, nodded, releasing a breath through pursed lips. Behind his back, he unbound the grip on his handgun.

"Thanks," he said to Mrs. McGuire, in the most authentic, genial voice he could muster. "I'll see you next week."

And when I do, it'll be the last time we meet.

"Get home safe," Mrs. McGuire said.

She closed the front door, unaware of just how close she'd come to being killed. Or that he'd already planted an XD5 self-contained electronic covert listening device and long-range camera on her gray-shingled roof to surveil her movements.

Always collecting data, Isaac recorded the transaction in his little green collection book—17 Sycamore Lane was paid up.

Plus a check mark in the right-hand column, meaning: *Target secured.*

Check mark with a circle around it meant: *Target eliminated.*

And so it went, Isaac knocking on doors or ringing doorbells, keeping his cover intact. He did the same on the next block,

Mulberry Lane, and wrapped up on Greenfield Street. By the time he finished collecting, he'd caught up with 22 of the 37 houses on his route.

Percentage-wise, Thursdays were the best nights. A school night. He'd head back out again Friday and Saturday night. Anybody he missed by then he'd get next week.

Back home, Isaac parked his Piranha in the garage, against the old wood cabinets and next to the lawnmower. He went inside his house and hung his jacket on the wall-mounted coat rack between the closet and a row of framed family photos.

He navigated the narrow hallway, waving hi to his mom, who was in bed watching *Dynasty*, while his dad was out, just driving around. He did that a lot. He didn't used to.

Isaac leaned against the kitchen sink, standard procedure after working his territory, scrubbing the newsprint from his hands and from underneath his fingernails, the cheap ink practically embedded in his flesh.

He poured himself a glass of milk, went down to the basement, dug out his secret stash of peanut M&Ms, then sat at the folding bridge table on the matted red carpet. He counted his loot, and updated his surveillance log for the Agency.

Finally able to decompress, the phone rang, jolting his heart rate, his face flush. Because he knew who it was.

"Hey," Dani Larsson said from the other end of the phone, on the other side of town. "How'd you make out?"

"Still counting," Isaac answered, and with his tongue dislodged a chocolate clump from his back teeth. It cost Isaac $2.05 to purchase a seven-day package of *The Daily Ledger* from the publisher, with the retail price to customers set at $2.75. Collecting an average of $3.50, tip included, meant a decent little profit. "About eighty-five and change."

"Better than last week," Dani said, strumming on her guitar. She hadn't gotten the hang of it yet, but he could at least recognize the opening verse of "Have You Ever Seen the Rain." She sang, too. Hesitant, but in key. "But let me guess. You were out doing the superspy game on your route. Catch any Russians?"

"Hey!" Isaac said as he spread out the various coins, isolating the quarters, dimes, and nickels into separate piles. "Not so loud. You'll blow my cover."

"Oh, please," Dani giggled. Isaac could almost hear her eyes rolling at him as she leaned back on her bed, draped in her Benetton sweatshirt. "So who was it tonight? Ms. Jenkins? Mr. Urlect? Ms. Gagne? She'd totally deserve it."

"Mrs. McGuire," he said.

"Aww. But she's so nice."

"I bet you say that about all the Russian spies. But that's how they getcha. They smile and give you cookies and pretend to really like you... then wham-o! They bring the entire Russian army right down on your head."

"Wham-o?" Dani said.

"Yeah," Isaac said. "Wham-o."

Dani chuckled. "Aren't you getting a little old to be a fake secret agent? It was fun when we were like, ten. But we're in high school now. Let the actual spies do the dirty work. Just sayin'."

"I'll make you a deal," Isaac said, the phone cradled between his left shoulder and his ear. "You stop lip syncing *Like a Virgin* into your hairbrush, in your underwear"— his heart spiked again when he said *underwear*, tiptoeing into flirt territory—"and I'll stop pretending I'm James Bond."

Isaac wasn't delusional.

He knew he wasn't a spy. He didn't have a gun, rocket launcher, or exploding fountain pen. And he didn't report to a secret Agency.

But for someone on his own as much as he was, out on his route every day, year-round, with nothing but time on his hands, it was fun to fantasize. A way to kill time.

A little wish fulfillment, he figured, never hurt anyone.

It was just a game.

"Shut up," Dani said in that cute girly teasing kind of way that confused and excited him in ways he wasn't entirely sure how to reconcile. Isaac wanted to kiss her, even though he'd never said the words out loud.

"No, you shut up," he retorted playfully.

Dani changed the subject. "Hey. Speaking of Ms. Gagne. You get your money? She owes you, what... two weeks by now?"

"Yep. Something like that."

"That's kinda weird for her, right? Maybe it's 'cause she retired," Dani said. "Good thing she did. She wouldn't've been able to handle my wicked French skills. They're *la bombe!*"

"Oh," Isaac said with a smirk, "you'd *bombe* all right."

"Yeah, whatever, spy boy. I'm going to bed."

Isaac turned all the bills he'd collected—mostly singles, with a few fives and a ten mixed in—to face the same way.

Dani was right, though.

As cheap as Ms. Gagne was—she never left more than a twenty-five-cent tip—in the last year and a half she had never missed even a single week.

Every Thursday, Isaac was sure to find, in the small black mailbox mounted on the brick face next to her front door, a white envelope marked with only a single word—*Paperboy*—handwritten in script. And now she was behind on her payments.

Oh, well. It would keep.

Worn down from the day, Isaac popped another handful of M&Ms into his mouth, eager to head up to his room and close the door. He and his pal Ronnie Campbell had swiped a stack of *Playboy* magazines Ronnie's dad had tied up in the garage and intended to throw away.

"Oh, I just realized!" Dani said as she plucked the top string on her guitar. "*Night Court* is on. Wanna watch? Dan is so funny!"

Isaac loved watching TV with Dani on the phone, the 13-inch Zenith just feet away from him. It was their way of being together, sharing a moment, when they weren't able to be in the same room. In some ways, it was their best together time of all.

"Maybe next time," he said, already dreaming of Miss July 1983. "But I've got reading to do."

CHAPTER 2

ONE ADVANTAGE OF BEING A PAPERBOY was having loads of time between houses to read the comic strips, sports pages, and, most import to Isaac, movie reviews and showtimes.

Police Academy, Revenge of the Nerds, Gremlins, Indiana Jones and the Temple of Doom, The Karate Kid, Star Trek III, The Last Star Fighter, and, he admitted only to Dani, *The Muppets Take Manhattan,* made it a banner year movie-wise.

And some new horror movie called *A Nightmare on Elm Street* was coming out soon. Sounded cool.

Yet as an occupational hazard—they were right in front of him—Isaac also saw the newspaper headlines. He didn't always understand what they meant or care enough to investigate further, but it was impossible to ignore that turmoil was raging across the world.

Those Russian commie bastards had pulled out of the summer Olympics while waging war in Afghanistan. Ronald Reagan was stockpiling enough nukes to incinerate the entire planet at least ten times over, because... why take any chances?

Ethiopians were becoming emaciated through famine while Americans seemed to get fatter, lazier, and dumber by the day.

And gay guys were dying by the truckload from a new horrible disease called AIDs and were thus declared an enemy of the people, a plague against humanity.

Grown-up problems, Isaac thought, yet he knew someday they'd be his problems too.

Maybe they already were.

THE FOLLOWING WEDNESDAY afternoon was mild for mid-October, 66 degrees, but the leaves had started to change.

Isaac leaned his dirt bike against the white oak tree in front of Ms. Gagne's house, where he would wrap up his first round of deliveries.

He took seven copies of the *Ledger*, left one paper each in the mailbox or between the screen and front door at 21 and 23 Sycamore, crossed the street, then hit 22, 20, and 18.

He finally crossed back once more, his last delivery at Ms. Gagne's house, number 17, a small brick house with a hickory brown door.

Isaac folded the paper cylindrically, placing it on the two hooks beneath the mailbox. He was about to hop down the short stoop and finish his route when he remembered that Ms. Gagne still owed him money, now three weeks overdue.

Ms. Gagne was a lot of things—cold, exacting, impatient— but she had always paid on time. It was only since she retired in June, just a few months back, that she had started to fall behind.

Isaac hadn't put a whole lot of thought into it because she always made good.

Even though it was a day earlier than usual for collections, he rang the bell and knocked on the door, just to be sure. No go.

Sure, it was possible Ms. Gagne was actually home and ducking him—Mr. Jankowski at 37 Sycamore had pulled that nonsense on him last year—but it was far more likely she wasn't home, or, at her advanced age, couldn't hear him knocking.

Figuring he had nothing to lose, Isaac leaned on the black metal rail bolted into the brick stoop and the front of house. With his gut against the rail, he stood up on tiptoes to glance through the living room window.

Isaac had developed his mythical spy world over many years.

His alter ego was a lethal weapon, a ninja, a master of language and disguise, with tactical brilliance, who got the jobs done that no other spy in their right mind would attempt on their own.

A teenaged James Bond.

He'd gone on missions in his own neighborhood, across the U.S., and to more countries than he could remember.

He'd stolen secret plans and intercepted foreign messages.

He'd been in bombings, gun battles, and knife attacks. He'd

killed many enemy spies and had been injured several times himself, sometimes quite badly, with the scars to prove it.

He'd seen his share of blood.

So much blood—well, fantasy blood—that he didn't initially trust himself when he saw Ms. Gagne.

On the floor, face up, eyes open.

And a murky red puddle oozing from the back of her head.

"Holy shit."

Isaac righted himself and looked around. His bicycle was where he left it, propped against the white oak, with three dozen papers in the milk crate.

Shielding his psyche from the shock of a dead body—and someone he knew—Isaac scanned the neighborhood, anchoring himself to the familiar.

The black paved street and gray curb. Mrs. McGuire's cat stalking a robin.

The setting sun casting a faint glow on red and orange leaves.

Halloween decorations adorning neighbors' doors and windows.

Heart racing, he curled his lips and squeezed his eyes shut so hard his head shook.

Eyes open again, more hesitant this time, he leaned over the rail… slowly… and once more peeked through the window.

The hardwood floor was dark stained, and inside the house only a single-bulb lamp on a console table gave any illumination.

The sun was also setting earlier, the sky an ashen purple, so maybe he wasn't seeing clearly.

But there she was—Ms. Gagne—in a pool of her own blood.

The sight horrified him, like being chucked in front of a speeding train.

Until he saw a pair of brown loafers.

They stepped over the body, avoiding the blood.

With his fingers still clenched around the railing, Isaac immediately fell down the steps, nearly yanking his arm from the socket.

Struggling to breathe, he darted for his bike, which nearly toppled over as he grabbed it. The weight of the newspapers forced the milk crate, and thus the handlebars, toward the ground, taking the bike and him with it.

His right hand caught between the crate and the bike's cross-bar, scraping the skin from the front of his hand.

He scrambled off the bike and straightened the handlebars, pushing the Piranha forward until he had it balanced and under control.

With his undelivered papers in the crate—the top copy sprinkled with drops of his blood—Isaac pedaled away as fast as his feet could take him.

CHAPTER 3

THE EARLY EVENING AIR RIPPED AT Isaac's throat like a jackal mauling its prey. Adrenaline alone powered him down the block and around the corner.

Through sheer instinct he headed home.

But as the black tires of his silver bike ate up Greenfield Street, just a block from his house, he realized—*What if the killer saw me? What if he knows who I am? And where I live and how to find me and what if I'm next and...?*

Not so much thinking as fleeing, he instead made a sharp left on Coral Turnpike, heading in the opposite direction of his house, through the intersection and past the Getty gas station.

He continued along the woods, which encircled the Montague Falls reservoir, a notorious hangout for delinquent teens.

It was only after he rode by Fenmore, Merkel, and Benson—three parallel side streets, dead-ending at the woods—did he start to slow down.

Like a deflated tire, air leaked out of him.

Cars motored by in both directions, passing under the train trestle ahead. It intersected with Silver Peak Way, the town's main artery. The lanes were long and wide.

And the light changed quick.

Like a child terrified to look under his bed, Isaac studied the road, as if the monster chasing him would evaporate into dust as long as their eyes never met.

But Isaac was convinced that if he could get to the other side, as if Silver Peak Way was some sort of magical threshold, he'd be safe, evading Ms. Gagne's killer.

He pedaled beneath the railroad trestle—it was creepy under there, especially at night—damp and smelling of oil, mold, and vomit.

Ahead of the changing light Isaac made a break for it, cutting off a white '72 Lincoln, and raced through the intersection. A barrage of horns blared at him as he dodged a green four-door Ford and a red pick-up truck.

Upon making it south across Silver Peak Way, he pulled into the Mobil gas station parking lot, three gas pumps unattended beneath a brightly lit, white-and-blue steel canopy.

Nearly out of breath, Isaac scanned the suburban sprawl, praying he was safe enough to rest a minute and check for his attacker.

He squinted into the haze, the distant sun disappearing below the woods and into the mouth of darkness.

Lining Silver Peak way neon signs alighted roadside retailers—an auto parts dealer, pizzeria, realtor, framing shop, nail salon, hardware store, dry cleaner, massage parlor, Greek diner, and a New Age bookstore, the owner of which was rumored to possess a demon fetus in a jar of formaldehyde.

"You barely made it," a man croaked—a deep, evil voice. "That's a lot of blood."

Isaac turned his head, his chest drawn tight.

Standing over him was a gas attendant in a gray jumpsuit with his name patch, Fred, stitched on the chest in red script letters. Fred wore a Mobil baseball cap, tipped down over the straited crow's feet branching out from the corners of his eyes.

"You gotta be more careful, kid. You don't wanna be dashing across Silver Peak at rush hour. You'll get yourself killed."

"W-whuh?" Isaac eked out. "What?"

"You all right?" Fred said, grease smudging his cheek. "You're white as a ghost and sweating like a pig. And your hand. It's bleeding. You don't look too good."

"What... no. I'm... I'm okay. I scraped it on my basket. I'm headed home."

"Hang on a minute. Let me get the first aid kit. Clean that wound. Come on inside. It'll just take a minute."

Isaac turned to face the gas station office, a one-story building connected to the service garage. The interior lights were on. He then looked at Fred, at the traffic whooshing by, and to the train trestle on the other side of Silver Peak Way. A tall, shadowy figure emerged.

"Oh shit," Isaac whispered, panic thundering between his ears. Maybe Fred was in on it, maybe not. Either way, Isaac dug his foot into the pedal, and with his bike still heavy from the crate of papers, he sped off, disappearing into the night.

Isaac rode around town, unsure what to do. But he figured that if Ms. Gagne's killer hadn't caught up to him by then, it was probably safe to go home.

Probably.

So in stealthy, spy-like fashion, he made his way, then slipped through the back door of his house. All the lights were off.

His mom was still at book club, the usual for Wednesday night, while his dad was passed out on the couch, a bottle of sleeping pills lying on the fuzzy brown carpet, just beyond his limp hand.

Pretty sure he was safe, Isaac quick-stepped around his dad, turned into the short hallway by the front door, and went upstairs.

The bathroom was at the top of the landing, Isaac's room to the right, his sister's room to the left.

Frankie's door remained closed.

That's what happens when your sister dies. Her body was long gone, but her spirit lingered. It was still her room. It always would be.

Isaac entered his own room, sat at his desk, and turned on the lamp. He drew both hands down his face, then took a breath, sighed, took another. It was then he realized his hand was throbbing.

The bleeding had stopped, but there was a deep, nasty scratch from the top knuckle on his middle finger across the back of his hand, nearly down to the wrist.

He ambled into the unlit hallway and locked himself in the bathroom. Trembling, he ran the wound under the faucet, moonlight leaking through the blinds.

Before his father lost his job, before he fell into a well of depression and despair, Isaac had someone to talk to. After that, his mother tried to be there for him, but she said that men were always trying to fix problems, when the bigger problem was them trying to fix the problem in the first place.

At least, that's what she used to say. Lately, she hadn't said much of anything.

Which probably made the most sense of all. Because Isaac didn't have the slightest idea about what to say or who to tell.

He'd witnessed a murder. He saw the blood.

Or had he?

Now that his wave of hysteria had burned off, he was starting to think that maybe he'd let his imagination get the best of him.

That after too many spy games, he'd taken things a bit too far, conjuring the notion of a crime, a reason to intervene, to feel like he had a purpose. A reason to keep going.

But a murder? On his route? Even he had a tough time believing it.

After all, for how long had he really looked inside Ms. Gagne's window? And how carefully?

He'd panicked so quickly, so intensely, he hadn't taken the time to confirm what he'd seen, or what he thought he'd seen.

It was just all too much.

Exhausted, Isaac finished cleaning his hand and wrapped it in a wad of white gauze he found in the linen closet. He then kicked off his sneakers and crawled into bed, fully clothed.

If he woke the next day and was still convinced Ms. Gagne was dead, he would tell someone. Maybe even the police.

But unless he knew for sure there was something to report, he thought it best to keep the whole thing to himself.

CHAPTER 4

THURSDAY CLASSES WENT BY IN A blur.

Isaac only picked at his lunch—beefaroni, green beans, a cup of pear cubes, and a single-serve carton of whole milk—and had no idea what answers he put down for his English test on *Lord of the Flies*.

On the blacktop behind the gymnasium, he was unhooking the rubber-coated coil lock from his front bicycle wheel when Dani Larsson came by. "Hey, Isaac. Got a sec?"

"No, not really," he said, feeling the tension mount in his gut. "I gotta grab my papers."

Isaac and the other carriers would ride from the back of the school over to the Baskin-Robbins, a half dozen blocks away, on Essex Avenue.

The Daily Ledger office, where they picked up their bundles of papers, was on the backside of the ice cream shop, facing the strip mall's parking lot.

"Okay, that's cool," Dani said, books against her chest. "Mind if I come?"

A few times a month Dani would work the route with him. She never asked for money, and wouldn't take it, even when Isaac offered. She just liked to be with him. But when she suggested the ride-along, she usually had something on her mind. She wanted to talk.

Isaac never told her so, but he got a thrill—his heart would speed up, his palms would sweat—whenever she joined him. Or, to be more precise, when she *asked* to come along.

"Sorry. Not today." He wrapped the coil lock around his handlebars, then fit the metal teeth from one end into the grooves on the other. He rotated the number pegs back and forth to ensure the lock was secure. "I gotta catch up from yesterday."

Dani's body slumped, almost disappearing within her oversized Duran Duran t-shirt. "Why? What happened?"

"Will you just leave me alone?"

There was a look of stunned hurt on Dani's face, the recipient of Isaac's anxiety, even though she was the one person he wanted to confide in most of all.

Only he couldn't get the words out.

What if he was wrong about Ms. Gagne? Or worse, what if he was right?

Feeling like a worthless piece of shit, the words *I'm sorry* crawled up his chest, into this throat, and finally to the tip of his tongue. But then the late bell rang in the courtyard as the last of the students dispersed.

"I-I don't understand," Dani said. "Are you okay? Can I just come with y—?"

"I said *no,* alright?" Isaac gripped the handlebars, extracting the front tire from between two metal slats on the bike rack. He climbed onto the seat, his Piranha much lighter with an empty milk crate. "It's not like you're my *girlfriend.*"

There was a heavy silence then, the aftershock of words spoken that could never be unsaid.

Isaac averted his gaze, as if breaking eye contact with Dani would somehow erase his sin, giving him the chance to make it right with her.

Too late.

She ran across the blacktop, through the football and soccer teams readying for practice.

Dressed in full gear, shin guards and all, his pal Ronnie came over tossing a black-and-white soccer ball in the air, then bounced it on his thigh.

"Nice going, stud. You really know how to treat a lady."

BASED ON THE configuration of his route, Ms. Gagne's house was one of the first stops.

But Isaac rode home to collect his undelivered papers from the day before and worked the route in reverse. Partly to make sure he made good on the papers he owed, but also to give him time.

If he was going to check on Ms. Gagne, he wanted his route completed and his milk crate empty by the time he got there, weighted for a quick getaway.

He wasn't going to make that mistake again.

By the time he arrived at Ms. Gagne's, at the end of his route instead of the beginning, it was gloomier than normal, the sun giving way to charcoal clouds before sinking below the horizon.

Isaac surveyed Sycamore for possible assailants, but other than Halloween jack-o-lanterns, scarecrows, and fake spiderwebs, there was no one around.

He curled the remaining paper into a cylinder and gripped it like a club. He patted it into his open hand a few times.

Sold on its clubbing power, he looked at the drab house before him. More than five hundred times he'd taken the short walk up the concrete path.

But this wasn't just any path. Not any longer.

For all he knew—and he *knew* what he saw—Isaac wasn't approaching Ms. Gagne's front door. He was encroaching on a murder scene. Violence had been perpetrated behind those walls.

He had seen her old, wrinkled face.

Her eyes open, but vacant, locked in a permanent gaze, staring into the great void. (Or the wall. It was hard to tell.)

He saw the pool of brick-red blood spill from beneath her head, like a toppled can of paint, and ripple across the hardwood floor.

With each step closer his heartbeat escalated—*step, thud-thud, step, THUD-THUD*—until finally his anxiety exploded like buckshot.

Isaac hesitated at the base of the first step, tightening his grip on the newspaper club.

He looked up at the white oak overhanging the side of the house, its branches old and skinny in the waning twilight, like whiskers on a witch's broom.

He never noticed them before. He wondered what else he had overlooked.

In a moment of panic, Isaac decided to toss the paper onto the stoop, using it like bait, to see who, or what, would come slithering out from the house and claim it while he hid at a safe distance.

No, he thought then, *I'm not gonna do that. Ms. Gagne deserves better. Somebody has to look. Somebody has to care.*

Isaac inhaled deeply, struck by the sweet fusion of decaying leaves, unwrapped candy bars, and evening chill.

Quiet as he could, he scooted toward the house then leapt to the top step in a single go.

No attacker.

But the real test would matter most.

Still gripping the newspaper club, he leaned on the rail like he'd done the night before, then reached up with his free hand onto the bottom pane.

He peered through the window, preparing himself for Ms. Gagne's corpse.

Unable to see clearly into the living room, Isaac leaned closer, his nose now pressed against the cool glass.

The front door abruptly opened then, causing Isaac to nearly pass out.

Blackness whooshed over his eyes.

He almost sprained his wrist to keep from falling into the bushes.

"Oh, hey there," a friendly voice said. "You must be Isaac."

His breaths constricted, Isaac stared at the man in the porch-light.

About fifty, he was taller than Isaac, solidly built, clean-shaven, with wavy, salt-and-pepper hair. He was standing on crutches, his left foot in a cast.

"Ms. Gagne left this for you." From the doorway, the stranger—her killer?— extended his hand, proffering a plain white envelope. It said *Paperboy*, in her handwriting. "She's sorry for being late. This should cover it."

"What?" Isaac said, shaking. "Who are you?"

The man held open the storm door. "Me? I'm her brother." He gestured with his head. "I live next door."

CHAPTER 5

REFLEXIVELY, ISAAC LOOKED AT THE BROTHER'S cast, at the ankle, checking for a bloody footprint. Nothing but white plaster.

"I, uh," Isaac mumbled, fighting through his mental haze. "I don't remember. Did we, um... what?"

"Wow. You really weren't expecting me, were you?" The brother laughed, offering the kind of bright smile and amiable confidence that made you want to be his friend.

"No." Isaac shook his head and chuckled nervously at himself. "I guess not."

"Not to worry, young man. I'm Gus Rotchford. I'm watching the house while my sister... Ms. Gagne... is on vacation. She'll be gone awhile."

"Vacation?" Isaac said. "She never said anything about that. Where'd she go?"

"Ha. Your guess is as good as mine!"

An answer without an answer.

Isaac stood there, his mouth hanging open, his mind like an old ball of yarn he couldn't untangle.

"What I mean is," Rotchford said, "she's on the road. Rented one of those big RVs with a friend of hers. They're going cross-country, stopping... I don't even know where! Wherever the wind blows."

"Oh, okay," Isaac said, doubting himself again. Not because he hadn't really seen Ms. Gagne, but because her brother, or whoever he was, was so nice and calm and pleasant it didn't seem possible a murder could have taken place just feet from where he was standing.

Could it?

"When is she coming back?" Isaac asked.

"I honestly don't know. Two months. Maybe more. Retirement, right? You can do whatever you want!"

Isaac smiled despite himself. "Yeah, I guess. Um, so... should I keep bringing the paper?"

"Why not? I usually grab one while I'm out. But thanks to this darn thing"—Gus stuck out his broken foot—"I'll be home more than usual. My sister said to keep 'em coming. If she wants to cancel, she'll do it later. Should I leave an envelope for you?"

Isaac felt the tension drain from his chest. But not all of it.

Like staring at a lava lamp, amoeba-like blotches morphed before his eyes. He breathed deep, exhaled slow. "Um, y-yeah, okay. That works. Every Thursday's good. Two seventy-five. You know. Plus tip. If you want."

"Two seventy-five. Plus tip, huh?" Gus gave Isaac a playful up-and-down glance, like he was studying him. Sizing him up. "Deal. I'll leave the envelope"—Gus raised the crutch, which nearly caught Isaac in the face, causing him to fall back a step. But then Gus brought the crutch high enough to tap the mailbox three times—"right here."

Isaac agreed, then asked, "Should I deliver it to your house instead?"

He wasn't sure what happened then, but he felt a twinge of energy, a shift in the dynamic.

Isaac was a step lower, beneath Gus, his subordinate foothold positioning him such that the porchlight nearly blinded him. A tactical disadvantage. He held up his hand.

"Mmm... nah," Gus said. "Leave the paper here. Let's stick to the routine."

"Okay," Isaac said, their transaction now complete, though hardly settled "I guess I'll see ya."

Gus looked up into the dimming sky. "Hmph," he grunted with a close-lipped smile. Then his eyes narrowed at Isaac. "Not unless I see you first."

THE BACK PORCHLIGHT did a poor job illuminating the yard, but the night suited Isaac just fine. He didn't want Dani to look him in the eyes.

Not just because he'd been wrong, but because he'd let his

anxiety fester like an unlanced boil.

"I snapped at you," he said as he buttoned his jeans jacket up to his neck, "but it wasn't you. It was… shit. It doesn't matter. I'm sorry, Dani." He looked toward the chain-link fence in the back of the yard, concealed by thorny bushes and the hanging branches of a weeping willow. "I'm…" He shrugged. "I'm a dick. I'm sorry."

Isaac picked up a fallen branch, nervous about how she took his apology, if she accepted it at all. Apologizing also helped defuse his angst, expressing gratitude for someone he valued more than he'd been willing to acknowledge or admit.

Head down but eyes up, he studied Dani, who, as she matured, in one moment could look like the twig-thin ten-year-old girl when they first met and instantly became his closest friend, and in the next a beautiful teen with a button nose, freckles, and adventure behind her eyes.

"You really hurt me," she said, wearing her dad's hooded university sweatshirt, her hair pulled back into a ponytail. The porch light grazing her cheek, Isaac wanted to brush his hand against it, feel the smooth arch of her skin. "You made me feel like I don't matter. That I'm not good enough for you. I was crying all day. Becky and Andrea were messing with me again. I just needed you to listen."

"I know," Isaac said. "I mean… about hurting you. I don't know why I did that. I… say mean things sometimes because"—his heart was all *thud-thud, thud-thud*—"I don't know how to say the things I really want to say, the way I want to say them. It doesn't matter. If anyone's not good enough, it's me. I'm the dumbass."

There was a lull between them then, Isaac searching his internal pathways for a way out of the tense and awkward maze he'd wandered into.

Dani hugged herself to keep warm. "You are kind of a dumbass. Not a huge one, but…"

"Still a dumbass?"

"A little bit," she said. "Medium sized. Maybe I'll write a song about it. Check it out. *Isaac Fuller is a dumb-aaass*," she improvised. "*He falls a-sleep in the crab-graaass. His leak-y brain needs a by-paaass.*"

Isaac chuckled. "Nice tune. But you cried? All day? Hmph. What a baby." Two squirrels scurried along the overhead branches. An acorn fell on his head. "Ow." He rubbed his noggin.

"Ow? From an acorn? Looks like *you're* the baby."

"Nuh-uh," Isaac said. "*You're* the baby."

"Yeah," Dani teased. "Whatever."

They shared a laugh, but it faded, the two young teens—a boy and a girl, nearly inseparable, but something deeper, more intimate—standing together in the frosty air.

Their hearts pounded, having crossed a threshold they couldn't define, but knew was there, uncertain how to advance.

"And I'm sorry they were being bitches to you again," Isaac said. "I can't stand them, Andrea especially. They're such... you know... bitches."

Dani's posture changed then. Her shoulders relaxed, the tension gone from her eyes, replaced with gentleness. Her breath formed a white mist in front of her mouth.

"You want to stay for dinner?" she said, dipping her head. "It's taco night."

Yes was right there on the tip of his tongue. But Isaac held back.

The thought of sitting at her dining room table in her nice house, with her nice and thoughtful parents asking him nice and thoughtful questions about how he was doing and how was school and how were his folks holding up and everything else he didn't want to talk about compelled him to dive off the top of Montague Falls onto the concrete basin below.

Which he knew was pathetic and lame and stupid because he really did want to be with Dani, but just the two of them.

Alone.

In private.

Then at least he could take his time, maybe work his way up to saying the kinds of things he really *did* want to say but knew he'd screw up if he went too fast or tried to be funny or cool or all the things he was pretty sure he wasn't but, for some reason, Dani maybe thought he was.

But then the spy in him kicked in.

James Bond wouldn't pass up an invitation from a lovely lady, especially Dani. She was the coolest, most authentic girl he knew.

And some part of him knew he'd never meet anyone as remarkable as her again, no matter where he went, what he did, or how long he lived.

She wasn't just some girl who went to his school, or even just a friend.

She was *Dani Larsson.*

"That depends," he said finally, a grin taking over his face. "Your mom have the taco sauce?"

"Pfft," Dani retorted. "Who do you think you're dealing with? Not just *the* taco sauce? *Extra chunky* taco sauce. In the *big* bottle."

"Oh, yeah?" Isaac pursed his lips, trying to hold back his giddiness. "How big?"

"Huge," Dani said. "Godzilla-size."

"Sold. But no stealing my taco shells!"

"Too late, Fuller. I didn't agree to that! Oh!" She slapped him on the arm. "Didja hear about Ms. Gagne? It was all over school. She took off in an RV! With another woman! Some kinda drug dealer!"

Isaac froze, the joy he'd been sharing with Dani instantly gone.

"What's wrong?" she said, still smiling. "She settle up? Pay what she owed?"

Isaac stepped on a swath of fallen leaves. They crunched beneath his white Puma sneakers.

"Doubt it," he said, unable to hold back any longer. "Let's go inside. There's something I need to tell you."

CROSS-LEGGED ON HER bed, Dani clutched her ruffled pillow against her chest, Isaac more on the edge, one foot curled beneath him, the other on the floor.

He'd been in her bedroom dozens of times before, the purple walls covered with magazine clippings, photos, and posters, including ones of Madonna, Journey, and The Go-Go's, and of her favorite movies, *The Blues Brothers, Superman,* and *This is Spinal Tap.*

But somehow sharing this time with Dani, inside her private

space, was an exhilarating, nerve-wracking transformational experience in a way it never had been before.

Isaac now saw Dani's bedroom as her inner sanctum, where she fantasized and wondered.

Where she worried and cried and laughed and sang and played her Yamaha acoustic guitar.

Where she slept and undressed and tried on makeup and outfits and even studied herself in the mirror, mounted on the back of the door.

Where she talked to him on the phone, about everything.

Where she looked up at night, studying moonbeams on the wall.

Such that Isaac felt exposed beneath the overhead light, as if it were shining only on him.

"You saw *what?*" she said, her eyes bulging. "A dead body? With blood oozing out? Why didn't you tell me?"

"I don't know. I freaked out, I guess. I mean… you know Ms. Gagne. With that pointy nose and those sunken eyes. Like she wanted to cook you in an oven. And that gray, greasy hair."

"And the mole on her lip," they said in unison, and shared another laugh.

Which ended with Dani's hand on his bare forearm. She left her fingers there—skin on skin—longer than Isaac had ever remembered.

She retracted her hand, a tinge of awkwardness between them, and then continued her line of questioning.

"You've been working that route for almost two years and you've never seen that guy? And then you see Ms. Gagne, dead on the floor, and suddenly he appears… in her *house?*"

Isaac realized then just how little he knew about Rotchford, or Ms. Gagne for that matter. But he was sure she was dead, no matter what Rotchford said.

"Yeah, that *is* weird. He was so… calm. Almost too calm. Like he was…"

"Rehearsed?"

"Yes! Exactly. Like he knew what to say. Nobody's that smooth," Isaac said, scrunching up his mouth, revealing his insecurity. And yet he also felt a surge, if not confidence then daring, calling upon his alter ego, who wouldn't let a little thing like diffidence interfere with his mojo. Isaac inched his hand back over to Dani's, his pointer finger wrapped around hers. He shuddered, then stared into her upturned eyes, brown as fresh toffee. "Are they?"

Without answering, Dani kissed him, her lips spongy and warm against his.

It was a short kiss—two seconds, maybe three—but to Isaac it was as long and glorious as the Universe itself. He saw stars.

First kisses are like that.

Their faces parted, he curled his lips, elated.

"Hold on," Dani said, grinning back at him. Her braces sparkled.

She bounced from the bed and into the hallway, her feet trundling down and then back up the stairs. She returned with the White Pages and sat next to him, the side of her right thigh flush against his left.

"Okay," she said, and flipped through the pages. "N, P... Q... R. Here we go. Rota, Rotam, Rotchford. Okay, let's see. Rotchford, A on Milligan Drive. Rotchford, B on Wacha Circle, and... here it is. Rotchford, G. Nineteen Sycamore Lane. That's him. We got it."

Isaac took the phonebook from her, intentionally bumping his hip against hers.

"Let me see that." He examined the name, compelled to authenticate it himself. "Maybe," he said. "The name is right. But who says the guy I saw is the guy listed here? If he's dangerous enough to murder Ms. Gagne and say he's her brother... maybe he killed the real Rotchford too and stole his identity. And now lives in his house."

Isaac and Dani sat there together in silence, for what seemed like a long time, Isaac staring at her, lost in the contours of her cheek, the tiny freckles beneath her left eye.

And the longer their eyes lingered, the bigger those freckles became, like beacons calling him to shore, a siren song only he could hear, a yearning that stoked the glowing embers in a part of his soul that until then had never come alive.

Isaac wanted to kiss her again—needed to—but wasn't sure if he should.

Until Dani locked her eyes with his. "So what's your next move, Fuller? Are you gonna... do something about it?"

Even Isaac understood the question posed wasn't merely a question, but a challenge. James Bond wouldn't hesitate.

"Yeah," he said, right before pressing his lips to hers once more. "I think I just might."

CHAPTER 6

DETECTIVE JONATHAN BUTLER WAS DUE AT the courthouse in ninety minutes. He didn't mind testifying, if he was prepared, and in this case in particular, he didn't want to leave anything to chance.

David Lincoln had beaten his wife to death with a blender in the middle of their kitchen. The medical examiner found several of Anita's teeth in the puddle of a chocolate blueberry shake she'd been mixing.

Detective Butler had begged Anita to get help, but no matter how many times Dave beat the pulp out of her, and the increasingly absurd and humiliating lies she regurgitated to explain away her injuries, she wouldn't leave.

I love him, she'd repeated over the four years Butler had been involved with their domestic violence. He'd seen cases like theirs far too often in far too many homes—hell, one was too many.

He hadn't been able to save Anita, but maybe he could send her dirtbag husband to Longrow Prison long enough for Lincoln to meet a fellow inmate who regarded him at least as well as Lincoln regarded his wife.

One could dream.

"Melissa," Butler shouted across the squad room to the day-shift secretary while pawing his chest pocket for a pack of smokes. "Where's Les?"

On the phone, Melissa held up a hand and patted the air, telling him to wait.

"Damn it, Mel. Have you seen—?"

"Don't give yourself a hemorrhage," Melissa said, cupping her hand over the receiver. "He's over there."

Broad-shouldered, black, and sporting a respectable middle-age gut, Butler looked across the squad room. "Where? I don't...

oh. Got it." Yet before he could make his way over to Detective Lester Narapoli, Narapoli came to him, accompanied by two teenagers who looked very much out of their element.

"JB," Narapoli said. "The kid here's got a story to tell. His friend's here for... moral support."

"Oh, yeah?" Butler said. "I like stories. But not today. I need a better tie. I'm due in court."

"Lincoln case?"

"Yep."

A former middleweight boxer with a vicious left jab, Narapoli snarled. "I hope they fry that goddamn motherfuh..." He reeled himself in, remembering the juveniles with him. "Hope they fry that piece 'a crap."

Butler tapped out his Camel Light in a black ashtray littered with other dead butts. "What's with the kid?"

"Says he won't leave until we hear him out. Says he knows about a murder."

Butler eyed Narapoli. Narapoli eyed Butler.

"Murder, huh? Okay. Sit." Butler pulled two chairs over to his desk. "Tell me what happened."

The kids, Isaac Fuller and Dani Larsson, sat down beside each other, clasping their fingers.

Isaac told his story.

"Whoa," Butler said, ignoring the escalating squad room chatter around him. "What'd you do then? You tell anyone? Your friends? Your parents?"

Isaac shook his head. "Only her. Just Dani."

Butler rolled his tongue along the inside of his gums. The lower left was sore. That damn infection again. He needed to go to the dentist, as loath as he was to do it.

"When was this? The murder, I mean."

"Wednesday."

"Wednesday? That was two days ago. And you're just coming here now?"

Isaac shrugged.

"And you didn't tell a soul? Nothing to nobody? Your parents? Teachers? Anybody?"

Isaac hunched, enough to signal to Butler that he might be

lying, or if not lying, then holding back. Butler sighed, taking a gulp of coffee that had gone stale sitting all day in a white Styrofoam cup. It was as cold as half his cases.

"What about you, sweetheart? What do you think?"

"He knows what he saw," Dani said, re-gripping Isaac's fingers. "He wouldn't make this up."

"Sure," Butler said. "But let's back up. Two days ago, Wednesday, you delivered your papers, like usual, after school. You put the paper in Ms."—Butler checked his skinny notepad—"Ms. Gagne's mailbox."

"Gone-yay," Isaac corrected. "Not Gag-knee. Gone-yay."

"Gagne, right," Butler continued. "So you peeked through the window and saw her body in a pool of blood. And then...?"

"I ran. I saw the man's feet. So I ran."

"Man?" Narapoli said. "What man?"

"When I saw the blood, it freaked me out. And then"—Isaac smacked his lips—"I saw these two feet. Brown loafers. They stepped over the body. I thought maybe he saw me, so I took off."

Butler raised an eyebrow. "You saw two brown loafers step over the body? You get a good look? You know who it was?"

"Yes, I mean no. I mean..."

"Isaac," Butler said, tipping his fingers downward. "It's a lot, I know. But try to slow down. Les. Get him some water, will ya?"

Narapoli came back with a filled paper cup, which Isaac drank from nervously.

Butler leaned forward. "Who did it, Isaac? Who'd you see?"

"I didn't see his face," Isaac said. "Only the feet."

"Then how do you know who it was?"

"Gus Rotchford," Dani said. "Her brother. He lives next door to Ms. Gagne. He's in the phonebook."

Butler wrote on his pad: *Rotchford, Gus. ND Neighbor. Brother.*

"Brother? You sure? We don't get sibling murders too often. How do you know?"

Isaac straightened up. "Because I talked to him."

"Whoa, Isaac. Hang on." Butler pulled his chair closer. "You talked to him *when?*"

"After I... you know... calmed down, I thought I made a mistake.

That I didn't really see it. So I did my route the next day and went back to the house. To Ms. Gagne."

Ever the boxer, Narapoli went for the body. He leaned over the desk. "You thought you saw a dead body inside the house... murdered... and you went back? Jesus, kid. Either you're brave as hell or dumb as shit. What then?"

"I delivered the paper, then the front door opened."

"You. Dani," Narapoli said. "You see this? Were you there?"

She shook her head.

"When I went up the stoop," Isaac continued, "I saw him— Rotchford—in the house. Then he came to the door. He talked to me."

"You mean his sister's house? Next door. Not his own house?"

"Yes."

Narapoli's expression turned curious. "What was he doing there?"

"He said Ms. Gagne was on vacation, and he was taking in the mail, the papers. Stuff like that."

"Housesitting," Butler said. "So this Rotchford guy, her brother, was in her house. He answered the door?"

"He didn't really answer the door. He was just... there."

"Just there," Butler repeated, watching Officer Tighe walk a handcuffed prisoner into the holding pen. "And you think he killed his own sister? You're sure it was him?"

"I-I... guess. Who else could it be?"

Butler and Narapoli exchanged glances. "So you're standing on the stoop," Butler said. "He's got the door open. Did you see Ms. Gagne?"

Isaac shook his head.

"What about the blood?"

Another headshake.

"No body, no blood," Butler said. "Anything you can tell me about this guy? The brother?"

"Not really. I mean... he's about your age. White. Kinda regular. Some gray hair."

"Regular," Butler said. "White. About my age."

"And he's got a broken foot," Dani interjected. "With crutches."

Narapoli jumped in again. "Hold on. You're saying that

Rotchford... the brother... he, what, kills his sister, which, by the way, is really hard to do. Then he cleans up the blood and gets rid of the body, which is even harder to do. And he does all this... *by himself*... in broad daylight... *with a broken foot*... and without anyone noticing? And then he hangs around afterward? That's what you're saying? And in the two days since, no one has reported her missing or asked any questions?"

Isaac blinked several times before answering. "I mean... I don't know. Yeah? I guess?"

Narapoli was about to stand up when Melissa came by with a manila folder. He opened it, scanned the paperwork. "Wait here," Narapoli said. "Give us a minute."

THE DETECTIVES HUDDLED by a row of dented lockers. "Come on, JB. This thing's all wrong. Story makes *no sense.*"

"I know," Butler said. "I know. But you ever remember, ever... even once... a teenage kid coming in, on his own, and reporting a murder? Much less a fake murder? That's a new one on me."

"I get that. But listen. I thought maybe I recognized the kid, maybe his name. Check it out." Narapoli re-opened the folder. "You remember this case? It was right before you transferred in. Summertime, a Saturday afternoon, summer of seventy-nine. This regular guy, a dad, is outside on his new deck he's building. He's with his two kids—a son, about nine, and a baby girl, about eighteen months. Dad's hammering some nails into the two-by-fours. He's on his knees facing the yard, so his back is to his kids. Son goes inside to take a whiz. While unsupervised, the baby girl finds a stray nail on the deck, puts it in her mouth."

Butler nodded in recognition. "I heard about that. Baby starts choking, right?"

"Yup. As she's gasping for air, little thing tumbles down the steps. Lands on her head, on the concrete. She died a month later. Fucking tragic."

"It was," Butler said. "And?"

"This kid? Isaac? It was his little sister. Frances Fuller. Frankie. I went to their house to investigate. You know, see if the dad was drunk at the time, or if there'd been a history of negligence or violence."

"Was there?"

"A kid's dead, JB. Of course there was. But what could we do? It's the same shit that happens every day to every parent in every house in every town in every part of the fucking world. Maybe if the dad had been facing the kid, he could've gotten to her in time. Maybe not. We pressed him pretty hard, but I didn't see any culpability. D.A. agreed, so we didn't charge him. It was just an accident. You don't have kids, but I tell ya, it only takes a second, a breath, a blink of an eye, for your life to change forever. And it doesn't mean you don't care or you're a shit-for-nothing parent. Or maybe it does. Who the fuck knows? The same kind of shit's happened to me and my kids."

"Only yours didn't choke to death."

"But they very easily could've. Many times. The line between your kids being safe and ruined for life is as thin as my paycheck. I don't know, JB. But I remember now, I interviewed the kid. Isaac. One minute his sister's happy as a clam, next she's brain-dead. He was supposed to watch her, but…"

"He was only nine."

Narapoli puffed out his cheeks, sighed. "So what do you want to do?"

Butler checked his silver Quartz watch again. 2:27 p.m. He needed to get to court.

"I don't know. Kid's probably carrying a lot of weight on his shoulders. And now he's saying a guy with a broken foot mur-dered his own sister and disposed of the body without anybody noticing? And then the guy chats the kid up like nothing ever happened?" The burly detective sighed, his breath warm and stinking of cigarettes and old coffee. "I don't know."

"You ask me," Narapoli said, "the kid's chasing shadows. He's got too much guilt with no place to put it. And now he's got the fresh hell of high school to deal with. He doesn't need a cop. He needs a shrink."

"Remind me never to go to couples counseling with you," Butler said. "But I hear you."

THEY RETURNED TO Butler's desk. "Isaac," he said. "Do you remem-ber Detective Narapoli here? From a few years back?"

Without looking, Isaac shook his head 'no'.

"I understand," Narapoli said. "You were pretty shaken up. It was after your sister fell." He laid out the scene, a truncated version of what he'd done for Butler. They wanted to see how Isaac reacted to them knowing his story. "That was a hard day. For all of us. But you most of all."

Butler could see the Fuller kid tense up, steely-eyed, his muscles contorting into a protective shell. Fuller gripped Dani's hand even tighter, even as she winced in pain, holding strong for him.

"You were supposed to watch her," Narapoli continued, "so your dad could work. But you went inside. You left her unprotected."

Butler saw Dani's mouth fall open slightly. A tiny pant slipped past her lips, her eyes fixed.

"Frankie choked on a nail," Narapoli said. "It's why she fell."

Dani gasped this time, re-clenching Isaac's fingers.

"Horrible, I know," Narapoli said. "It must be hard to live with. It wasn't your fault. Not really. But the guilt? The regret? Would be hard for me. Hard for anyone."

Fuller slouched then, the fire he'd come in with extinguished, revealing the sad, depressed kid he had every right to be.

In turn, Dani unclasped her fingers from Isaac's hand, and hugged herself.

Butler had worked enough cases to know her gestures, and the look on her face—sympathy, shock, anguish—meant she was hearing the details about Isaac's sister for the first time.

"That was tough, no doubt," Butler said. "Sometimes we try to make up for one mistake by fixing another. I get it, Isaac. I really do. We're cops. We live it every day."

"We appreciate you coming down," Narapoli said, "and we're not saying you didn't see something. But there's not enough here to investigate."

"Don't misunderstand," Butler said. "We take these reports seriously. We're gonna send a patrol car to Gagne's house. If he sees anything suspicious, anything out of order, Detective Narapoli and I will come by ourselves. We'll check it out personally. Otherwise… it's best if you let it go."

CHAPTER 7

NOT A WORD WAS SHARED BETWEEN them.

Isaac and Dani stopped at the corner, their feet on the pavement, palms on handlebars. Two cars entered the intersection from opposite sides of the 7-Eleven parking lot, each claiming the right of way, causing a bottleneck on Silver Peak Way. Horns honked.

"I didn't know about Frankie," Dani said. "You never talk about it. I knew she died from a fall, but that's it. I'm sorry I didn't know."

"I started a million times. You're the only one I wanted to tell. The only one I really lo... uh... uh..."

Isaac wanted to complete that word. It was right here.

But he if spoke it aloud—*love*—he would've collapsed into a blubbery mess, unequipped to cope with such a transformative declaration. Especially since *love* did not sufficiently articulate the depth and complexity of his feelings for her.

"But every time I tried to bring it up..." His eyes welled up. Some spy. "A brother's supposed to protect his little sister. Whether he really can or not."

"It wasn't your fault," Dani said, offering her hand. But he was too far away. Just out of reach. "You couldn't have known."

Isaac knew Dani meant well, that she was trying to comfort him. Being a friend.

But given his fragile state, his internal alchemy necromanced her compassion into a shrieking affirmation of his inadequacy— *She doesn't love you. Not really. You know why? Because she pities you. Your sister is dead. Your parents checked out. You're all alone. You're a loser.*

Consumed now with impotence and rage, Isaac laser focused

on the traffic light—red—as it dangled from a wire over the intersection. Anticipating the change to green, his signal to take off, he raised the pedal on his right side, shifted his weight, and planted his foot.

"I know," he said and dug deep for the icy-hearted spy in him. There was no room for emotion in the field. Sentiment gets you killed. "But there's no way to fill that hole in my heart. No way to make it right. It doesn't matter now anyway."

He advanced through the intersection. Alone.

Leaving Dani behind.

Because I'm never turning my back again. I've got a job to do. And god damn I'm gonna do it.

A FUNNY THING happened on his way home.

As if the bicycle pedals were somehow connected to Isaac's soul, each downstroke of one leg and upstroke of the other seemed to cleanse his very self, purging the albatross of ineptitude that for years had weighed him down.

His anger wasn't gone. Hell, no, it was alive and kicking. But he finally knew what to do with it. Carry on with what he did best, plying his trade as a skilled spy. A lone avenger.

Because who needed the cops? He sure didn't.

When he walked into his house, both his parents out somewhere, Isaac grabbed a Mountain Dew and some cold pepperoni pizza from the fridge. Time to refuel.

Gnawing on the slice, from across the dining room he saw the little red blinking light. He went to the answering machine, pressed play, and listened.

Hi, my babies. It's Grandma Marge. Just making sure you're coming for dinner next Sunday. Five o'clock. And bring the lemon meringue pie from Alberto's. Not Beckman's. Alberto's—"

Isaac skipped to the next message, from some guy selling custom windows who wanted to drop by for an appointment. Another skip. The next was a message from his pal Ronnie, asking if he wanted to go see *The Terminator* opening night.

The message after that, though, got his attention.

"Yes, hello. Mr. and Mrs. Fuller. This is Detective Jonathan Butler from the Montague Falls Police Department," the message

began, rousing Isaac's anxiety. *"As soon as you're able, please call me back. It's about your son, Isaac. I'm not sure if you've spoken to him over the last few days or if he explained the situation. I suspect it's nothing to worry about, but I think you should know... I'm about to leave for the day, but you can page me any time, day or night."*

Detective Butler left the number and hung up.

Isaac's heart continued to pound, the machine's blinking red light taunting him, daring him to do what needed to be done. Which is exactly what he did.

He deleted the detective's message.

And got back to work.

MONDAY NIGHT, DRESSED in all black—black jeans, black sneakers, black sweatshirt, black skull cap—for better speed and agility Isaac switched bikes to his ten-speed, which he'd also spray painted black, including the spokes.

He'd spent the last two nights staking out Rotchford's house, to track his patterns. Time to see where it led.

With Rotchford on the move, Isaac stayed back on the sidewalks, swerving around the gleam of porch lights and street lamps, making sure nothing shone right on him, revealing his presence.

But even though he was on his ten-speed, Rotchford was driving a car. So Isaac needed to learn something of value soon if he was to learn anything at all. Unless he caught a break.

Which, as it turned out, he did.

Rotchford stuck to the side streets, came to a complete halt at every stop sign, and waited at every red light, enabling Isaac to keep up, barely, but keep up nonetheless.

Sweat rolled down his temples and along his nose. His eyes stung, even as a cool mist began to fall. The moisture settled everywhere, especially in his knuckles where the scratch was still healing. They cramped up.

And despite the whirring pedals, rotating bicycle chain, and thin wheels *ka-thumping* over the uneven seams in the sidewalks, all Isaac could hear was his labored breaths, his heart pounding in his ears.

His attention, though, was on Rotchford's bumper, still a half-block ahead of him.

The mist continued to form, tiny droplets dancing in the pitch-black air, the car's red taillights like two piercing eyes mistrustful of the night.

Isaac wasn't sure where Rotchford was headed, or why. And then it occurred to him: *Does Rotchford know I'm here? Is he taking me on a wild goose chase? Testing my commitment? How deep I'm willing to go?*

The realization that Isaac might not have been the hunter, but the hunted, nearly knocked him off his bike. That and the low-hanging tree branch that would have taken his head clean off had he not ducked under it just in time.

"Oh shit," he said, then regained his balance—and composure.

Rotchford made a right onto Belmont and then up to Silver Peak Way, the light ahead of him already yellow. Which meant Isaac needed to catch up quick.

If Rotchford sped through the intersection, Isaac would've been stuck behind the forthcoming light change and the cross-cutting flow of traffic.

But he caught a break.

Rotchford turned on his left blinker and waited at the light—a notoriously long red. Rather than hunker back at a safe distance, Isaac took a calculated risk.

A block behind Rotchford's car, Isaac peeled a sharp left, then stood up on the pedals, racing away from Rotchford but parallel with Silver Peak Way. Finally at the corner he made a hard right, taking him even with Rotchford, only one block over.

And just in time. Because the light changed.

Isaac shot through the intersection, following dangerously in the middle of the road, alongside a Big Bob's Furniture delivery truck, weaving in and out of traffic to the other side of Silver Peak Way. He ducked behind a parked Ford pickup, and again to his good fortune, saw Rotchford approach, this time with his right blinker flashing. Which meant he would drive right by.

Isaac hid between the Ford and a Salvation Army drop box, and waited.

THE HEAVY MIST turned to a drizzle.

Cold raindrops falling on him, Isaac resumed the tail.

Rotchford turned left onto Ellington, then took the first right onto Mayfield, a short block with five houses on each side of the street.

Isaac studied the block, new to him, in a part of Montague Falls he'd only driven by with his parents.

Yet despite his unfamiliarity with this part of the grid, it was utterly familiar. Another section of the suburban landscape, filled with strangers, all with their own stories—comedies and tragedies—unaware of the very real dangers lurking in the shadows around them.

His lungs ripped raw, Isaac studied Rotchford as he slowly pulled his car into a driveway that curled behind a house covered in aqua blue aluminum siding and fitted with an ecosystem of white gutters. Isaac held back, considering his next move.

Until the decision was made for him.

Out of the darkness he saw Rotchford driving again, only this time in a different car, a maroon, two-door Plymouth. It pulled out of the driveway, turned in the opposite direction from how he'd arrived, and cruised down the block.

His knuckles throbbing and frozen, Isaac messily jotted down the license plate in his collection book, then hid his bike in a row of bushes.

He darted across the street, taking each step gingerly, as if landing too forcefully on the ground might trigger an alarm, the kind his alter ego might have planted on a secret mission.

Isaac shuffled down the driveway, toward the back of the house, and found what he thought he'd find—Rotchford's other car, the one he'd been following.

Not sure what to make of it, Isaac turned back to the house.

A short, concrete staircase led into the well.

He snuck down the stairs and, following the playbook that had gotten him into this cloak and dagger in the first place, peeped through the door's curtained window.

It was tough to make out, but he could see a washing machine and dryer and, beyond them, a kitchen. He realized it was a split-level home, leading to questions Isaac couldn't yet answer.

Does Rotchford live here, too? Is this a safehouse? Does he have a partner-in-crime? Is he living a double life? Is his name even Gus Rotchford? Is anything about him real?

Isaac turned to face the ranch-style house across the street. Two giant pumpkins, carved with jagged features, seemed to be staring at him.

And as thoughts of All Hallows Eve twirled like spirits in a graveyard, Isaac finally had an idea about what to do next.

CHAPTER 8

SPICY BROWN MUSTARD LEAKED OUT OF Detective Butler's ham and cheese sandwich. He had six open cases, and if things continued as they'd been the last few months, there would be another case right around the corner.

"JB," Narapoli said, crunching on a Bavarian pretzel. "You hear 'bout the Lincoln case?"

Bile shot up Butler's chest, burning his esophageal lining. It wasn't the mustard, but his instincts kicking in, a premonition eating him alive from the inside out. A chunk of sliced Virginia ham dangled from his mouth.

"What?"

"That wife-beating fuckhead got a reduced sentence. Three years. With good behavior, out in half."

"What? How?" Butler tossed away the extraneous ham. "He bashed his wife's face in."

"Remember that shit-ass apartment building that burned down last year in Kenmore? Killed nine people? Lincoln knew the torch, Corbin Mulroney, and he flipped on him. D.A. wanted that fire-starting prick bad enough to cut Lincoln a deal. Turns out it's the fourth building Mulroney torched in the last ten years. Fucker's got twenty-three bodies on him. Believe that? As far as the D.A.'s concerned, it's a net win. Huge."

A Vietnam vet who'd climbed through its steamy, soaking jungles for two tours, Butler knew even the most steady-pulsed soldier had to find a way to let out his rage, terror, and humiliation once in a while, lest he lose control when he most needed to keep his cool.

"Fuck it all to hell."

He slammed his notepad on the desk, sighing hard enough

to practically pass out, and leaned back in his rolling chair. It squeaked. He sat there, stewing, then looked to the notepad. It was open to a page he'd forgotten about.

He stood up with conviction and grabbed his navy-blue blazer from the back of his chair.

"Les," Butler said, slipping his burly arms through the sleeves. "Let's take a ride."

"Where to?"

"Check out the kid's story. The paperboy. He says the old lady's dead. Murdered in her own house." Butler removed his .38 revolver from his desk drawer and slipped it into his holster. "Maybe she was, maybe she wasn't. But I'll tell you what. I haven't been able to track down the RV. No sales or rentals under Gagne's name. Maybe I just haven't found it yet, maybe I never will. But either way... I don't like it."

"Yes?" the man said pleasantly, the sun shining on his face. "Can I help you?"

"Sorry to bother you," Butler said. "Are you Gus Rotchford?"

"The one and only."

"The one and only." Butler produced his badge. "I'm Detective Butler. This is Detective Narapoli. Mind if we come in?"

"Uh, sure," Rotchford said. "What about?"

"We'll explain."

With Rotchford's permission, they entered his home and sat on the green, deep-cushioned couch bookended with cedarwood night tables.

"What's with the foot?" Narapoli said, jutting his chin at Rotchford's cast. "Kick the wrong dog?"

"Ha, no. I was working on my sister's kitchen sink while she's on vacation. She lives next door. I got grease all over my shirt, so I pulled it over my head, to chuck it in the wash. But before I got it off, I tripped over my own feet." He laughed at himself. "Broke my ankle here"—he tapped the cast with one of the crutches—"and got a bloody nose."

Butler and Narapoli exchanged glances. In the space of thirty seconds, before they could frame up the interview in the sequence they wanted, Rotchford acknowledged that his sister lived next door, and was away on vacation, while explaining away the blood on the floor.

Either this guy knows how to tell a story, Butler thought, *or he knew we were coming.*

"Over your own feet," Narapoli said. "Really?"

"It's a gift," Rotchford said. "Fred Astaire's got nothing on me."

"You said you're watching your sister's place?" Butler said. "Is that"—he flipped through his notepad—"Beatrice Gagne?"

"Y-yes." Rotchford eyed them skeptically. "How did you know that? Is something wrong?"

"Her name is Gagne," Narapoli said.

"That's right."

"But yours is Rotchford. She's not married, is she?"

"My sister... Bea ... she's much older than me. She married a French-Canadian back in fifty-seven. Miro Gagne. They lived in Quebec for a while, then Montreal. He died in a car accident. She kept his name."

Butler jotted notes in his pad. *Quebec. Montreal. Widow. Miro. Car accident.*

"Your sister's on vacation?"

Rotchford shifted in his chair. "Yes. You asked that already."

"Right," Butler said. "Just double checking. Where'd she go?"

"I'm sorry. What's this about? Is she okay?"

Rotchford seems genuinely concerned, Butler thought, *but I've been burned before.*

Reading his partner's cues, Narapoli dove in. "What's your line of work?"

"My what?" Rotchford said. "What's that got to do with—?"

"Your employment," Narapoli pushed further. "How do you pay the bills?"

"I'm an insurance salesman with Helion Life. Been with them twenty-one years. Why?"

"Twenty-one years?" Narapoli nodded, his lips pursed. "You hear that, JB? Been on the job longer than we have. Shit, I hit my twenty and I'm thinking real hard about the pension."

"You get along with your sister?" Butler asked. "Any issues?"

"What? No... Like I said, she's sixteen years older than me, so we didn't grow up together. She's more like an aunt than a sister.

There's always been this awkward distance between us. So I bought this house about three years ago. Thought we could get to know each other better, now that we're both adults."

"How's that going?" Narapoli said. "Must've been tough, having a sister you hardly knew."

"It was. But we're doing okay."

"Just okay?" Butler said. "I thought you were close now."

"Wait. No, I meant... hang on. What's going on?"

Here we go, Butler thought. *It's coming together.*

"During the course of another investigation, it came to our attention that your sister had gone missing."

"Missing? Missing *how*? She just left."

Narapoli threw another jab. "And she may have been assaulted."

"Assaulted?" Rotchford leaned forward. "By who? When? What are you talking about?"

Butler turned to a clean page. "When was the last time you saw your sister?"

"I, uh," Rotchford stammered, "let me think. What day is today? Tuesday? She left a week ago. Last Wednesday. The twenty-fourth. Yeah. I saw her that morning, before she left."

Butler flipped back through his notepad. "Okay. Here it is. She left Sunday, the twenty-first," he said, fabricating dates, to throw Rotchford off balance.

Come on you sonuvabitch. Spill it. Confess. You know you want to. It's right there. I can feel it.

"Mmm, no. It was Wednesday," Rotchford said. "For sure. That's when I broke my ankle. Go figure."

Narapoli loved that moment, when he saw the opening, when the suspect slips up. "That's a helluva coincidence, don'tcha think, JB? Sister goes missing same day he busts his ankle... and bloodies the floor."

"Helluva coincidence," Butler said.

"One in a million," Narapoli said.

"A hundred million."

Eyes wide, Rotchford looked back and forth, studying them. "My sister isn't missing. She's on *vacation*. Like I told you. She's... wait. You think... oh, come on. You think I *did* something to her?"

"Hang on," Narapoli said. "We never said you did anything. I didn't say you did anything. JB, you say anything?"

"Not a word. Must be a guilty conscience."

"Guilty? I'm not guilty of anything!"

"We can clear this up right now," Narapoli said. "Get your sister on the phone. We'll have her stop into the nearest precinct, wherever she is, and if it all checks out, everybody goes home. Whadaya say, Gus? Give her a ring?"

Butler had conducted thousands of interviews. The guilty tend to stay calm at first, while the innocent get nervous. They can't understand why they're being questioned, what they might've done wrong, knowing the mere insinuation of guilt could devastate their reputations and disrupt their lives forever.

Rotchford was acting reasonably nervous. But if his sister was in fact alive and well, he'd been given the perfect out.

"Uh," Rotchford said, after an uncomfortable pause. "It's... not that simple."

"Really?" Narapoli eyed Butler, his glance saying *here it is, we got him.* "And how's that, exactly?"

"Like I told you, she's on the road. In an RV. Grand Canyon, Yosemite. Places like that. With a friend of hers."

"A friend," Butler said. "Which friend is that?"

Rotchford sunk into the couch, not a lot, but enough.

Narapoli picked up on it, too. "What kind of friend? You mean a friend... or a *friend* friend? A boyfriend?"

"No. Just a friend. Theresa Dunlap. She has a PhD in... I forget. She works for a drug company. Well... worked. Crescent Labs, I think."

"Okay," Narapoli said. "So whadaya say we call your sister and see how things are going?"

"She doesn't have a phone," Rotchford said. "She said after teaching for thirty-three years she didn't want anyone to find her... unless she wanted to be found."

If Rotchford was trying to help himself, he was going about it the wrong way.

"That's awfully convenient, isn't it JB?"

"Real convenient," Butler said.

"Way convenient," Narapoli said.

"No, what I mean is," Rotchford fumbled, trying to course correct, "she has an answering service. She said she'd check it along the way. We can call her right now. But I can't say when she'll hear the message or when she'll call back. It could be two minutes, two days, or two weeks. I have no idea. But she'll call back for sure. She's very responsible."

"Two weeks, huh?" Narapoli rose from the couch. "Dial her up. Let's do it."

Crutches under his armpits, Rotchford hobbled to the kitchen, the detectives following him. The rotary phone was mounted on the wall next to the refrigerator. He handed Narapoli the receiver and a small square of paper with Gagne's answering service number.

The detective dialed. The recorded message kicked in after the second ring.

"Hi. Ms. Gagne? This is Detective Lester Narapoli with the Montague Falls Police Department. Today is Tuesday, October thirtieth. It's"—he checked his gold Rolex knock-off—"about one-forty p.m. local time. I'm here with your brother, Gus Rotchford, at his house. We don't want to alarm you, but it's urgent you give me a call. We have some questions for you and time is critical. Please call and ask either for me—again, I'm Detective Lester Narapoli—or my partner, Detective Jonathan Butler." Narapoli left the number. "I understand you're on the road and not always checking messages, but if it's at all possible, please call back today. October thirtieth." He repeated the number again. "Thank you."

"Maybe we'll get lucky," Butler said. "Mind if we see your sister's place, while we wait?"

He wanted to get into Gagne's house. She lived right next door and yet she felt a million miles away.

"Uh... s-sure," Rotchford said. "Like I said, she might not call back for a while. I just never know."

"That's okay," Butler said. "It won't take long."

That was the moment. Butler quick-glanced to Narapoli, who quick-glanced back. The two detectives geared back on Rotchford, who removed a ring of keys hanging from a silver hook secured to the wall.

"We can go now," he said.

Butler and Narapoli followed Rotchford as he tottered on his crutches down the walkway from his house, onto the sidewalk, then up his sister's walkway next door.

The two detectives scanned the front lawns, separated by a five-foot-wide grass alley and a white wooden fence, waist-high.

Out on the curb were two white oaks, one in front of each house, a telephone pole equidistant between them. Detached garages flanked both residences on opposite sides.

"Most siblings don't live next door to each other," Butler said. "A little too close for comfort. Cause any issues?"

"Sometimes," Rotchford said. "Just regular brother-sister bickering. But I travel a lot, so we're not together that much."

Up on his sister's front stoop, he used the spare key to let the detectives inside.

The first thing Butler noticed was the smell. "Clean in here. Lemony."

"My sister's a clean freak," Rotchford said. "Gets it from my mom. Real on-hands-and-knees-with-a-soapy-sponge type. Bea made me promise to keep the place immaculate. 'Guuuus,' she said. 'You must scrub scrub scrub.' So I did. I do. Though I'm not as vigilant as I should be. Especially with my foot."

Butler eyed the floor, looking for blood. Nothing obvious. Without the lab guys, there'd be no way to know for sure.

"Right," Narapoli said. "Your foot. This is where you fell? You were stumbling from the kitchen... back there. And then you pulled the shirt over your head and tripped over your own feet? Explain to me again how—" He looked to his hip, checking his beeper. "It's the station. Can I use the phone?"

"Over there. By the couch."

Narapoli called in. "Hey, it's Les. You paged." In short order the vigor drained from his face. "You got her. Really? That fast?" He nodded. "Patch her through."

Butler asked if there was another phone. Rotchford led him into the kitchen, to the wall-mount next to the fridge.

With the receiver cradled at his neck, Butler eyed Gagne's bunny rabbit motif—oven mitt, pot holder, clock—then looked down the hallway to the living room, making eye contact with

Narapoli. There were two clicks on the line.

"Helloooo." Female. French accent. High-pitched. It matched the tone Rotchford had used when mimicking his sister.

"Yes, hello... Ms. Gagne? This is Detective Narapoli and Detective Butler with the Montague Falls PD. Thank you for calling so quick."

"Of course, of course," she said. "Is everything all right? With the house? Is Gus there?"

"Yes," Narapoli said. "He's here. Uh... so... you enjoying your trip?"

"*Oui, oui,*" she said. "We saw the Grand Canyon. Is very big, yes?"

"Ha, yes. I guess it is. And if you don't mind my asking... who are you with?"

"Ooh. You are with many questions. And you a stranger to me. Is very rude. But if you must know, I am with Theresa Dunlap. She is using the ladies' room. May I speak with Gus, *si vous plait?*"

As if it materialized from the ether, Butler saw the slip of paper on the fridge, mounted behind a Bugs Bunny magnet and next to a calendar featuring droopy-eyed rabbits in classic French royalty outfits.

On the paper was a name: *Theresa Dunlap*, along with her address and phone number. He jotted it down.

In the living room, Narapoli handed the phone to Rotchford.

"Yes," Rotchford said to his sister after exchanging pleasantries. "My ankle's fine..." He listened again, growing visibly fidgety. "I know, I know. I'll be more careful... The sink's okay for now, but we'll have to replace that pipe before"—Rotchford stopped, presumably steamrolled by his sister. "Okay, yes. We'll talk about it when you get back."

Rotchford said goodbye and handed the phone back to Narapoli, who shrugged dejectedly at Butler.

"*Oui, oui,*" Ms. Gagne said. "Are we finished, yes? No more trouble?"

Narapoli sighed. "No, no trouble, ma'am. Thank you for your cooperation. Enjoy your trip."

His shoulder muscles tensing up, Butler felt like a fool, like a rookie, chasing a ghost on the cusp of Halloween.

He led Narapoli toward the front door, Rotchford right behind them.

"We apologize for the intrusion," Butler said. "Sorry to bother you."

"It's all right," Rotchford said as the detectives left the house looking exactly like what they were—two middle-aged cops investigating a crime that had never taken place. "Anyone can make a mistake."

CHAPTER 9

ISAAC USED TO LOVE DRESSING UP on Halloween, walking the trick-or-treat route with his dad, as he told stories about his time as an engineer, working on bridges and tunnels, connecting land, connecting lives. Being of service.

But that was a different time, a different dad.

A different son.

Isaac hadn't been able to stomach the ritual the last few years. How could he enjoy the most devilishly sacred night of childhood when little Frankie wasn't dressing up in her little ghost costume to play dead, because she *was* dead.

Yet now with his face covered in a white base, black paint around his eyes and mouth, he felt distant, detached, as if watching the scene unfold from the River Styx, waiting to take the last ferry to the other side.

At fourteen Isaac was too old for trick-or-treating, but there had never been a better time, for a better reason. At least, that's what he told himself.

He was Isaac-the-undead, Isaac-the-apparition.

And while camouflaged as a ghoul, he was a living, breathing soul on the hunt for an actual ghoul who needed to be sent to Hell where he belonged.

With afternoon giving way to night, the sky a blend of black and purple, Isaac ambled up to a house with a cardboard, glow-in-the-dark skeleton hanging from the white door.

Isaac rang the bell. The door opened.

"Trick or treat," he said from behind his makeup.

"Hey, there." An old, white-haired man in baggy pants, maroon sweater, and black-framed glasses tossed a handful of Hershey's Kisses into Isaac's Halloween bag. "Another zombie, huh?"

"Yeah, I've been feeling a bit zombie-ish these days," he answered the old man, who stood in the doorway of his aluminum-sided house.

Isaac then put his plan into action. "Hey, is Terry around?"

The old man looked at him as if he'd spoken in Klingon.

A small pack of trick-or-treaters stumbled up to the stoop, including a Stormtrooper, Raggedy Ann, Cinderella, Wonder Woman, and two *Ghostbusters*, proton packs and all.

"Terry? I don't...," the old man started. "Who you lookin' for, son?"

"Terry Gates? We played soccer together." A truth buried in a lie. Terry was actually an all-star halfback, but moved to Brackwood years ago. "Isn't this his house?"

"*Trick or treat*," said the other kids. The old man tossed the silver-wrapped chocolates into their bags. The trick-or-treaters then scurried next door.

"Sorry, son. Think you got your houses confused. Ain't no Terry here."

"Really. You sure? I wrote it down." Isaac reached into his back jeans pocket for a crumpled, handwritten note. "Nineteen sixty-eight Mayfield Circle."

"This is Mayfield *Lane*, son. Mayfield Circle's over by the reservoir. Mailman gets that wrong all the time. It's one'a those... whadaya call 'em... cul-de-sacs. Near the highway."

"Oh, sorry," Isaac said. "Must've written it down wrong."

Across the street he saw another bunch of kids, dressed in homemade post-apocalyptic warrior costumes, pointing plastic ray guns at each other and shouting "you're busted you're busted you're totally dusted!" Which sent Isaac's heart into spasms.

For years he'd been playing spy. Pretending. Scheming. Always in control, always the hero, able to fight, talk, sneak, or gadget his way out of trouble.

Because none of it was real.

But disguise or not, he was on his own, investigating a real murder—and a real murderer—who knew his name and might very well be on to him.

Rotchford had killed at least once already. And Isaac was snooping around in his business, almost daring Rotchford to try again.

Just hours earlier, when Isaac had delivered his papers, there it was, the headline, staring him in the face:

INDIRA GANDHI ASSASSINATED

Murder was in the air.

"I thought I saw someone living around back," Isaac continued.

"Back there?" the old man said. "Oh, no. That's Dougie. He rents the back a the house."

"Huh. Don't know how I did that," Isaac said. "My mistake. You like that, though? Having a tenant? My folks are thinking about it. You know, to make ends meet."

"Heck yes, son. Dougie's great. Pays his rent on time, always in cash. Maybe you're too young to un'erstand, but that always helps."

"I hear ya'," Isaac said. "How long's he been with you?"

"Dougie? Oh, lemme see. Gotta be seven, goin' on eight years. He ain't around much. He's a liquor salesman, so he works late hours. Travels a lot. Restaurants, bars. Places like that. I hardly see 'im."

"Well, thanks," Isaac said, uneasy that he'd been there too long, drawing attention to himself. But he hadn't gotten everything he needed. "Hey... is that your car back there? Behind the house?"

"Me? Nah. My drivin' days are done. Can't see shit more'n ten feet away, even with my glasses. That's Dougie's car. He uses one for work, another for gettin' around. Guess he can write it off on his taxes. Damn shame, though. He just gave notice. Says he's movin' out west, sometime next week. Tired of the seasons here. He's headin' out to L.A., the lucky dog. I wouldn't mind sayin' a howya do to one'a them Laker girls. Am I right?"

"He's moving?" Isaac inquired more desperately than he intended, immediately consumed with the pressure imposed by a ticking clock. "With a broken foot?"

Immediately realizing his mistake, Isaac went flush, his heart beating like a timpani drum.

BOWM buhm BOWM buhm BOWM buhm.

Sweat drizzled down from his temples, the salty fluid eating through his white make-up like a river of acid.

The old man looked at Isaac. "Busted foot? How'd you know that?"

"Uh, I mean... you, um"—*think Isaac thinkthinkthink comeoncomeoncomeon*—"you said... he was on crutches... so I just figured, a broken foot. Yeah. Seemed to make sense."

c"Did I say that?" the old man said. "Shoot. I don't remember that at all. Memory's goin' ta' shit, I'm tellin' ya. I'm lucky I can remember my own name half the time. Anyway, I'm runnin' outta candy and there's more kids to treat. Thanks for comin' by, son. Happy Halloween."

Isaac did all he could to keep from shaking uncontrollably, knowing he might have just dodged an actual bullet.

"Yeah," he said. "Happy Halloween."

CHAPTER 10

THE BEST DETECTIVES REFUSE TO LET go of a case until it's been worked as hard as it can be. Every lead followed. Every witness interviewed. Every suspect interrogated.

They are relentless, fanatical even.

Jonathan Butler was a good detective. Not the best, but damn good when he put his mind to it, and if he kept his mouth shut for a few more years, he had a chance to be the squad's first black Captain. He already had a pile of open cases on his desk, but there was one he couldn't let go of, one that kept him awake at night, more so than usual.

The only problem was, the case wasn't even a case.

The kid, Isaac Fuller, was a terrible witness. An unreliable witness. Maybe not even an actual witness. Yet he was damn convincing.

And the suspect? Gus Rotchford? Maybe he didn't kill his sister—Butler and Narapoli had spoken to her directly—yet Rotchford still lingered on the edges of Butler's mind, like a planet that had not yet committed to an orbit.

Credibly anxious when facing two detectives in his house, and yet... almost too cooperative. Willing to answer questions without entirely knowing why. Rotchford also said his sister checked her messages infrequently, days or even weeks apart. Yet she called back within an hour. A stroke of luck or... something else?

Those elements unto themselves were proof of nothing. But as Butler thought it through, he realized he hadn't actually spoken to the friend, Theresa Dunlap. He just assumed they were on the road together.

There was probably nothing to learn, another dead end. But that's what Butler really wanted—certainty. There wasn't a whole lot of it in the detective business. Even less in life.

Which is why, with yet another court appearance he had to prepare for, Butler instead drove out to North Bryarsville.

It was nearly five thirty p.m. when he parked in front of Theresa Dunlap's house, a yellow, two-story Cape Cod with a glassed-in sunroom off the den and a tiered deck in back.

Butler trundled up the walk, a little sad that a canopy of patchy clouds blocked the stars. After a long shift, he took comfort in those twinkling lights, to remind him that he wasn't out their alone.

Standing beneath the porch light, he rang the bell twice and knocked a few times. He didn't expect anyone to answer. No one did.

In the radiance of the neighbor's kitchen window light, he checked around the side of Dunlap's house. No car in the driveway. The windowless garage was closed, so he couldn't check inside.

He breathed in, to slow himself down, feeling for the vibrations in the air.

It seemed foolish, checking the wind, but when you work enough cases you learn to trust the elements in ways you didn't when you were first starting out. The elements know things, whisper things, if you're willing to listen.

But when he gathered himself, all Butler saw was an empty house on a quiet street.

Maybe he really was wasting his time.

Convinced there was nothing left to investigate, he slow-walked back to his car. He put the key in the door lock, turned it until the inside button popped up, then reached for the handle.

"Excuse me," a woman said, from directly across the street. "Hello?"

Approaching was a portly, middle-aged suburbanite wrapped in a brown, wool-knit sweater, waddling on black heels unequipped to properly support her build. She entered the halo of the nearby street lamp, hugging herself.

"Hi, there," she said, her cherubic face highlighted with fake eyelashes, sparkling silver eye shadow, and a nest of tight, black curls coiffed with what must have been an entire can of hair spray. "Are you looking for Theresa?"

Exhaustion rolled over him like a wave at high tide. "Yes. I was just... following up on a case."

"You're the police? My goodness. Is everything all right?"

"Yes. Sorry. I'm Detective Butler." He was used to suspicion, a burly black man knocking on doors, at night, in a mostly white neighborhood. He produced his badge. "I hope I didn't startle you."

"No, no, it's fine," she said. "I'm Rebecca Treamont. I've been Theresa's neighbor for... oh, wow... must be twenty years at least. She's away, you know? On vacation. In one of those RVs." She half giggled, half huffed. "It's so unlike her. Then again, Theresa's not who I thought she was."

"Really?" Butler stood more upright, squaring his shoulders. "How so?"

"Oh, I really shouldn't gossip." She looked around, making sure no one was within earshot. "It's not my place."

"I'm the police, ma'am. You can tell me."

Relieved, maybe even excited to have been given permission to churn the rumor mill, Treamont inched closer, touching Butler's arm.

Police or not, it wasn't lost on him that a white woman was putting her hand on a black man. Without moving otherwise, he glanced around them. He knew to be careful.

"Theresa," Treamont said. "She was married once to a nice man, about ten years ago. But they got divorced. She said it was because the... oh... it's so embarrassing."

"It's okay. Go on."

"She said their sex life was very dull. No passion. No spark."

Butler raised his eyes. "That's it?"

"Well..." Treamont inched closer. "Turns out Theresa... and don't get me wrong, she's a dear friend, a lovely woman... she's a... oh, maybe I shouldn't."

Butler opened his mouth to encourage her further, then stopped himself before actually saying anything. But that gesture was enough to lubricate her gears.

"Turns out she's a..."—she whispered—"a lesbian." Treamont blushed and fanned herself. "I never knew a lesbian before. And we're so close. We've gone shopping! For personals." She pawed at Butler's arm. "You know. Undergarments. You figure I would've noticed. The signs."

"What signs?"

"Well… I don't know. She never said anything about other women or anything like that. And she's not a man-hater. Although it's easy to be one sometimes. No offense."

An image of Anita Lincoln's pulverized face flashed in his mind. "None taken."

"I guess you just really never know about someone."

"No," Butler said as half-bare trees rustled in the breeze. "You really don't."

"Do you want to come in for coffee?" she asked. "It's getting a bit nippy out here."

"Oh, no, thank you, ma'am. I need to be heading home."

"If I can ask," Treamont said, "why did you want Theresa? Do you need to get in touch?"

Butler sighed, his urgency deflated. "No, it's okay. It was part of a routine investigation. It's nothing. I actually spoke with Beatrice Gagne yesterday. She called from the road."

There was an immediate shift in the air, those signs from the elements. A nearby street lamp flickered, then returned to casting a faint glow on the side of Treamont's face.

"Something wrong, ma'am?" Butler said. "Is there something you want to tell me?"

Treamont simmered a moment. Then she spoke.

"It's one thing to betray me like that. To get *divorced*. Free from a do-nothing husband in a do-nothing life. Seems like it's happening every day around here. Third one on this block alone. And then to admit she's a lesbian. I mean… a lesbian! But then to say she's in love with"—Treamont's face coiled up like a nauseous badger—"*her?*" One arm rested on her midsection. "Nasty little wench, if you ask me."

"Yes, I'd heard that," Butler said, wondering if the lesbian angle played into this circle of confusion, although he couldn't see how. "She did come off a bit brusque, especially with that accent of hers. But she seemed all right."

It took a moment to register, but Treamont looked at him,

befuddled. "What accent? Gag knee? Gag me? Whatever her name is. She doesn't have an accent."

Butler's heart pounded. "What do you mean? She had a French accent. Very *oui oui* and *s'il vous plait* and all that."

Treamont looked at him again. "I know she was a French *teacher*. We met a few times because of Theresa. But she's definitely not French. Not at all. She sounds as American as you and me."

Butler's thoughts swirled him back to the beginning. "The kid was right," he said aloud. "I gotta go."

"What kid? Theresa doesn't have a kid. You're not going to tell her what I said, are you? About… you know? That's private!"

"Don't worry," Butler said as he hurried to his car. He got in, patted the gun holster beneath his jacket, then looked in the glove box to check for an extra round of ammunition. "Your secret's safe with me."

CHAPTER 11

Isaac took the call. He didn't want to, but couldn't stop himself.

"No," Dani told him. "Don't do it. You can't. That's... that's *crazy*."

"Uh-huh," he said, remote, needing to keep his mind sharp.

"Let the police do it," she said. "That's their job. You're gonna get hurt, or trapped, or..." Dani's voice hung in the ether. "Or killed."

"Police don't care. Nobody cares."

Isaac was going to break into Ms. Gagne's house. Find the evidence. Prove himself.

To Dani.

To the cops.

To himself.

Because *he* cared.

"Please, Isaac. Don't. You can't do this. You're not a real spy, and you're not a cop. You're just a regular kid. Just a... a fucking *paperboy!*"

Of all the insults he endured throughout his life, that one hurt worst of all.

He wanted to say something awful in return, something cruel, but all that came out was an angry whimper. He was used to being insulted, ignored. Sometimes even belittled.

But never by her.

"Oh... Isaac, I'm sorry," Dani said, choking on tears. "I didn't mean it like that. I'm just worried that—"

Isaac hung up.

Whatever fantasies he'd indulged about being a spy were gone. If he landed in trouble, he had no guns, gadgets, or fighting skills to call upon. No backup or airstrike teams to bail him out. He was just a high school freshman. A paperboy, as Dani made so clear.

Maybe he wasn't the trained assassin he'd pretended to be, but he was ready to do what no one else would—go out on his own, into a killer's lair.

Decked out in black, Isaac geared up.

Screwdriver? *Check.*

Flashlight keychain? *Check.*

Instead of pedaling straight over to Ms. Gagne's, Isaac took the long way around—up Coral Turnpike, to Bergen, to Washington, then back to Greenfield Street—to throw Rotchford off his scent.

He pressed one hand on the edge of the milk crate to keep it from rattling. Self-made whisper mode.

Isaac did his best to avoid the street lamps breaking up the darkness until he came upon Sycamore Lane from the far end.

He stopped near the corner, then stashed his bike on the side of Mr. Utrecht's place, a one-story house whose lights were all off. The house provided effective camouflage, and easy access for a quick getaway.

Now on foot, Isaac ducked behind a station wagon when Mr. Jankowski rounded the corner in his yellow Ford. Isaac waited until he parked in the driveway and lumbered tiredly into his house.

The coast clear, Isaac resumed his mission, coming up on the edge of Rotchford's property.

Interior lights glowed behind drawn shades. One in the dining room, one upstairs. Rotchford's porchlight illuminated his front lawn.

It was only then, upon his approach, did Isaac realize how Rotchford had slipped in and out of Ms. Gagne's house so easily—and undetected.

Lining Rotchford's garage was a tall hedgerow of dwarf hollies, seven feet high with dense clusters of prickly evergreen leaves peppered with red berries. Perfect cover.

It was a tight fit for sure, but on the side farthest from the house, Isaac maneuvered himself between the hedges and Rotchford's garage.

Isaac took some leaves in the face, but he kept going until he reached the fence at the back of Rotchford's yard.

In a ninety-degree angle to the left, the hedgerow wrapped around the back of the garage and along the chain-link fence, which ran the length of Rotchford's yard, a barrier between his property and the house behind it.

Following that path, Isaac then came to the short white fence separating Rotchford's and Ms. Gagne's properties. He climbed the divider easily, then continued into Ms. Gagne's yard, all the way to her garage.

That's how he did it. In and out, even in the daylight, without anyone knowing. It's why I never saw him.

Isaac emerged from the hedges, hunched so he was nearly squatting. He duck-walked to the back of Ms. Gagne's house, flush against the outer wall, right below the kitchen window. Lower down he found his way inside.

As a kid, Isaac spent countless hours on training missions, climbing beneath his own house, accessible through a small window above the foundation. Shimmying face down, he could maneuver though the crawlspace under his dining room all the way into the basement, and from the basement all the way out to the backyard.

He found those same crawlspace windows along the foundation of Ms. Gagne's house.

The trick, then, was to slide the window—a rectangular pane set within a white wood frame—back on its hinges, without breaking the glass, staying as silent as a cemetery.

He surveyed the yard for Rotchford again.

All clear.

Isaac took short breaths to steady his nerves, then knelt down in the patch of moist soil in front of the crawlspace window.

He popped the flashlight in his mouth then laid down on his belly, his shoulders even with the window frame. He reached into his back pocket for the screwdriver.

With his hand securely on the grip, he manipulated the flat silver head into the frame's upper right corner, such that the windowpane began to lift. The bottom side tilted up, toward the inside of the house.

Isaac slipped the screwdriver back into his pocket, then, like a waiter with a serving tray, placed his palms flat on the glass. Near the corner edges built into the frame, the windowpane moved. He eased it off the pegs, holding the pane free and clear.

He exhaled as if he had diffused a bomb, knowing it could have detonated had he made even one wrong move.

Carefully, he placed the boxed pane against the side of the house, then plucked the flashlight from his mouth, turned it off, and took one last scan of his surroundings.

Confident he was alone, Isaac switched the flashlight on again, popped it back into his mouth, then reached one arm through the open window frame. He felt for the ground beneath the house. He patted it twice.

Head first, Isaac writhed his shoulders through the frame, sliding his torso beneath the house, his nose inches from the cool dust.

With a fireman's crawl he bent his left knee to propel himself while reaching his right hand forward, pulling his body ahead. He sucked in his gut, lifting it just enough to get over the frame's bottom lip.

He was almost all the way under the house.

And then he felt it.

A knob pressed down, hard, in the middle of his back. The pressure on his spine forced his solar plexus against the bottom lip of the frame.

Saliva dripping from his mouth, Isaac dropped the flashlight from his teeth.

He couldn't move.

He couldn't breathe.

He was trapped.

"Ease your way back," Rotchford said. "And stay quiet. I'd rather not kill you here, but I will if I have to. Understand?"

Blood rushed to Isaac's head.

"I said," Rotchford repeated, pushing harder into Isaac's back, "*do* you understand?"

"Yes," Isaac hissed through gritted teeth.

"Good. Now back out. Slowly." Isaac heard a metal clack,

which he assumed was the gun's hammer. "But let me take this." Isaac felt Rotchford pull the screwdriver out of his back pocket. "Let's go."

Isaac extracted himself from beneath the house, his left hand on the grass. He squeezed his other hand into the moist soil beneath him, making a fist. An adrenaline reflex.

Aware of his nerves, he stood up, slowly, as instructed.

But he wasn't going down without a fight.

I can do it, he thought. *I can spin around and knock the gun away. I'm younger than him. I'm faster. I can do it. I can—*

Leaning on his crutches, Rotchford stuck the gun in Isaac's back. "Through the door."

Isaac climbed the short steps, opened the back door, and entered the house. Rotchford closed the door behind them.

It wasn't until the bolt slipped into the latch plate—*click*—that Isaac realized he might never walk out of that house again.

He clamped his eyes shut, his heart slamming against his chest.

Isaac saw little Frankie in his mind. With dull, faraway eyes, she looked up at him, and smiled in the way only a toddler can at her big brother. But then her expression turned cold. Calculating. Directing him to take action.

To escape.

Rotchford switched on the kitchen light, Isaac laser-focused on the moment.

In one swift motion, he unclenched his fist and, over his shoulder, tossed the dirt he was still holding. Right into Rotchford's eyes.

Rotchford flinched, pawed at his face with his gun hand.

Isaac spun around and drove into the blinded Rotchford, pinning his attacker's hip and left arm against the stove. Shoulder-to-shoulder, Isaac then grabbed Rotchford's right wrist, and reached behind his back to pull away the crutch.

Feeling the momentum shift in his favor, Isaac twisted Rotchford so that he was nearly facing the stove, smashing Rotchford's gun hand down against the stovetop.

Isaac repeated the action, raising Rotchford's wrist just enough to slam it even harder in order to knock the gun loose.

But being an inexperienced fighter, Isaac had made a tactical mistake. With his attention solely on Rotchford's gun hand, Isaac forgot about the other one.

With his free hand, Rotchford plunged the screwdriver into Isaac's unprotected gut.

White starbursts danced across Isaac's eyes.

Shock overriding his pain receptors, Isaac grabbed Rotchford's gun hand once more as the two combatants tangled up with each other.

The taller, much stronger man jerked them both to the side.

Then the gun went off.

CHAPTER 12

Isaac opened his eyes, his drool-smeared cheek resting flush against the bloody linoleum. He found himself splayed on the kitchen floor, on his side, a screwdriver wedged in his gut.

It hurt like hell.

The lemon-scented cleanser soaked into the floor acted like smelling salts, piercing his brain.

He managed to right himself, pressing his back against the refrigerator. The telephone was mounted on the wall above him. The cord dangled, too high to reach.

"Hey." Rotchford's voice was weak. "You're alive."

With only five feet separating them, Rotchford sat on the floor, his back propped against the white stove. His legs were outstretched in a V, a bullet hole in his left thigh, blood seeping out of it, pooling on the floor. The cast on his right leg was also smeared with his blood.

Isaac couldn't see his own face, but it was equally draining of life.

"You really... got me good," Rotchford said, his skin layered in a grimy layer of sweat. "Dirt in the eyes. Didn't see it coming. I should've. But then I didn't see"—he coughed, wincing as he did—"a lot of things."

There Isaac was, on the floor, wounded, in Ms. Gagne's kitchen. He'd known her for years—rather, he'd *seen her around*, when delivering papers to her door.

And now that Isaac was in Ms. Gagne's house for the first time... he didn't care.

He didn't care who she was, what she loved or hated, or how she'd become the person he'd barely known.

Her killer, though—Isaac wanted to know him, to understand why Rotchford had killed his sister.

Because as the two of them slowly bled to death, there didn't seem to be anything else worth knowing.

Barely conscious, Isaac grazed his finger near the wound, flinched, then surveyed the terrain.

The entrance to the living room was to his immediate right, Rotchford to his left. A bunny rabbit clock ticked away above the table on the other side of the kitchen. The refrigerator hummed.

"Guess I got you, too," Rotchford said. "I'm bleeding out. Can't move. You're not much better. Can you reach the phone?"

Isaac tried to lift his arm above his waist, but his hand fell back to his side. "I can't," he said, panting.

"Isaac. Listen to me."

Even with its white linoleum floor, white appliances, and white overhead light, Isaac saw the kitchen fading to black.

Rotchford pushed his crutch against the wall. It made a slight thud. "Wake up!"

Isaac's eyes snapped opened. "I'm here. I'm awake."

"I can get us medical attention in ten minutes," Rotchford said. "But you have to reach the phone."

Isaac ignored Rotchford. If he didn't ask then, he would never get the chance. "Why"—Isaac grimaced—"why'd you kill her? Ms. Gagne."

Silence.

Maybe Rotchford was saving his final breaths. Maybe he didn't want to answer.

Whatever the reason, Rotchford stared at Isaac, his puffy-eyed gaze laser-locked, yet distant somehow. Markers of the big sleep.

The two of them scarcely breathing, surely dying, Isaac followed those eyes.

And then he realized Rotchford hadn't been staring at *him*, but at the object in the puddle of blood leaking from his gut.

Rotchford's gun—a Browning Double Action .9 mm pistol, fitted with a silencer.

Isaac didn't know a damn thing about guns. Not actual ones, anyway. They terrified him.

But not now.

He crab-walked his fingers along the bloody linoleum, slipped his pointer finger through the trigger guard, and hoisted the gun into his lap.

"I've never," Isaac said, his breaths labored, "I've never held a gun before. Never even seen one. It's heavy."

"The weight makes it real." Rotchford squeezed his thigh, trying to stanch the wound. "Let's you know it has power. That it can kill."

"Think we're... gonna make it?"

Rotchford sighed. "No. Probably not."

Isaac curled his finger around the trigger. "Yeah. Probably not. But why'd you do it?" His gut roared again. Panicking, he shuffled his feet along the floor, fighting back the pain, fending off death's tightening grip. The thrashing only made it worse. "She's...," he hissed through gritted teeth, "your sister."

Rotchford's stare revealed nothing, but he seemed to be thinking, deciding what to say, if he was going to say anything. The bunny rabbit clock ticked, one second at a time.

"My dad got druhh... drafted in World War Two," Rotchford said finally, his voice weak as a sleepy child. "He was almost forty years old. They took everyone back then. They sent him to the South Pacific, and then kamikazes sank his ship. The Deloitte. He survived... but he was never the same. His head wasn't right. He"—Rotchford winced—"he wandered the country, like a hobo. He'd come back, talking gibberish, then leave again. Until one day... he was gone for good. I was just a kid. Maybe four. I guess it's why I went into insurance. I thought if I traveled enough, went to enough cities, maybe..."

"You'd find him."

Rotchford's eyes drifted. "Something like that."

Isaac understood, more than he wanted to. "But you never did."

"No. I didn't."

"Must be hard to live with," Isaac said.

"It is."

"I'm nervous all the time," Isaac confessed. "Even if I forget, even for just a minute, my guilt is always there. It hovers over me, like a vulture. Like it's waiting for me to die, so it can pick apart my soul."

Rotchford hmm'd. "It was the same for me. Until I got a second job."

"Second?" Isaac said. "You mean... the liquor thing?"

Rotchford coughed. "No, not the liquor thing. Just like insurance, that's a cover."

"I don't... understand," Isaac said, the pain flaring up again. "A cover for what?"

Rotchford gripped his blood-sopped thigh. "I'm with the CIA," he said. "I'm a spy."

As he sat in a pool of his own blood, Rotchford doing the same, Isaac fought to keep the threads of his sanity in place. He'd fantasized about being on missions, about secret codes and Russian spies, and now he was face to face with an actual spy, holding his own gun on him.

"No way," Isaac said, pushing back. "How could you—?"

"Your name is Isaac Paul Fuller. Address, Twenty-three fifty-nine Fenwick Drive. Born June twenty-six, nineteen seventy. Parents, Howard Alan Fuller and Deborah Stacey Fuller. Younger sister, Frances Mary Fuller, deceased, aged two, nineteen eighty. Your father was, ahh"—Rotchford seized, panting, until the pain faded—"an electrical... engineer. Now he's a toll booth operator. Your mother works puh... part time as a receptionist in a doctor's office... in Linwood. Your aptitude scores indicate above average intelligence but you've had below average grades since your sister's death. You broke your left arm when you were six. You've had a paper route for the past nineteen months. And lately... you've been watching me. But as I think you've figured out"— Rotchford expelled a shallow breath—"I've been watching you."

Without realizing it, Isaac gripped the gun tighter. He nearly pulled the trigger.

"It's a lot to swallow, Isaac, I know. But here's a status report: we are both gravely injured, and fading in and out of consciousness. Without immediate medical attention, we're both going to die."

There was little doubt Isaac's life was draining from his body, and he very much wanted to live. Only...

"Is Ms. Gagne really your sister? Why'd you kill her?"

"You need to focus, Isaac. We have to work together, and

we have to do it now." Rotchford, or whoever he was, shoved the brace end of his crutch so the nub end inched closer toward Isaac. "Can you"—Rotchford's eyes rolled back, then settled again—"can you reach this? Grab the end. Use it to pull yourself up. Make a call."

"Ms. Gagne," Isaac repeated, committed to getting answers. "Why—?"

"Because she's Russian," Rotchford said. "An agent hiding on U.S. soil. But she knows the Cold War is almost over, and they're gonna lose. She wanted to defect. And I was about to make it happen."

Isaac chortled, each huff another punch to his gut. He'd spent so many years plotting fantasy spy games, stalking imagined enemies, protecting America, he never considered those adversaries might be real.

"A Russian spy," he said, wheezing. "Right under my nose."

Rotchford smiled, as much as a dying man could. *"Malenkih vorishek veshayut, a bolshie vory ubegayut."*

Isaac shrugged.

"Little thieves are hanged," Rotchford said, translating the Russian proverb, *"but big thieves run away."* He squinted, still holding his bloody thigh. "The question is… which one are you?"

Isaac's half-smile drew back, consumed by the enormity of his predicament. He couldn't have moved more than an inch, but as Isaac shifted on the blood-smeared linoleum, the screwdriver moved, too. More white starbursts shot across his eyes. He howled.

"Take the crutch," Rotchford said. "Pull yourself up. Get the phone. Call for help."

"I… I can't."

"You can."

"No, I—"

"Isaac! We're going… to fucking… die. Do it!"

Isaac leaned to his side. On the verge of retching, he stretched his bloody fingers as far as he could. They nabbed the rubber tip, inching the crutch toward him.

But then Rotchford shoved the crutch forward, knocking the gun from Isaac's hands.

Like it was a briquette of hot coal, Isaac fumbled the pistol. It fell to the floor, close enough for Rotchford to reclaim. He pointed it at Isaac.

"I knew"—Isaac hunched over in agony—"I knew you weren't CIA."

"No," Rotchford said. "I'm not. And Bea wasn't a Russian spy." With his free hand, Rotchford clutched at a newspaper on the floor next to him—one Isaac had delivered—smearing it with blood, as if the headlines had been scrawled in red ink. "I am."

Isaac didn't know what to do with that.

For years he'd been playing spy games, concocting an elaborate backstory and infrastructure of supporting characters, clever enemies, and all manner of preposterous scenarios that only the most daring agents could rectify.

It all made perfect sense to him, a thrilling fantasy world where he knew the rules, understood the players, and could push the boundaries as far as he wanted.

Yet now that Rotchford was confessing himself to be the very kind of villain Isaac had been hunting in his mind, it was somehow humiliating.

"I was always on the road," Rotchford said, "with access to financial records. It's amazing what people will share—what Americans will share—with a total stranger. You know why? Because they hate responsibility. They'd rather pay someone else to be in charge of their lives... in case something goes wrong. Because then they have someone to blame." Rotchford coughed, wiped blood from his mouth. "I'd been on the road a couple of years, then one night in Dayton, Ohio, I met a guy in a bar. We started talking. You know, the usual. Marriage, sex, money, sports, and, when you get enough liquor in you... politics. I told him about my dad. How I was chasing the memory of a man I never really knew... and never would. You know what he said to me? He said: *'Kazhdiy chelovek – kuznets svoyey sud'by.'* It means: *'Every person is the blacksmith of their destiny.'*"

Rotchford clenched his jaw, breathing long and slow to manage the pain. "It was before your time, but in World War Two we *had* to fight the Germans. The Japs, too. And then fighting for *our* freedom—for the whole world—my dad took some friendly fire.

A shell fragment, in the head. The Navy, our own government... they took my dad from me. Sent him back with a broken mind... a lost soul. I never thought I hated this country. Never thought I could. Until I realized I did. I knew then I had to do something. I had to take control. To be my own blacksmith. But what I don't want, Isaac—and I don't think you want either—is to die on this floor. Not here. Not tonight. So grab the crutch, pick yourself up, and get to that fuh... fucking phone. Because if you don't make the call"—Rotchford cocked the gun's trigger, pointing the weapon at Isaac's heart—"I'm going to kill you right now."

CHAPTER 13

ALL ISAAC COULD SEE WAS THE gun. The barrel was only four inches long, the silencer another three, but to him it was the size of a Burmese python.

Fighting through the fear and agony and threat of his imminent death, he pressed his left hand against his side. He then rolled his hips so that his torso followed, onto his knees, facing the crutch.

The thought fleeting but vivid, Isaac sneered at his captor, imagining himself do to Rotchford what Rotchford had done to him—use the crutch to get the gun back.

As if reading his mind, Rotchford fired.

The bullet whizzed past Isaac's head and into the wall just behind him. Had Isaac still been seated where he had been only a minute before, on the floor against the fridge, the bullet would have split his face open like an overripe cantaloupe, splattering his brains across the wall.

Heart pounding, Isaac inhaled through his nose and, using the crutch, pried himself off the floor. In doing so his elbow accidentally jostled the screwdriver, the pain so acute he nearly blacked out again. Pressing his bloody hands against the refrigerator, he battled through.

"That's it," Rotchford said. "Now get the phone."

Trembling, Isaac savored each intake of air, then exhaled. If these were to be his final breaths, he wanted them to count.

"I was supposed to keep an eye on Frankie." Isaac stumbled toward the wall-mounted phone. "But I"—his heart raced, his throat as dry as a pumice stone—"I didn't want to watch her. I wanted to watch my show. *Voltron* was starting. So I went inside, to the bathroom, while my dad was working on the deck..."

"And you never came back," Rotchford said.

"No. I didn't. I knew it was wrong. It was my job to watch her. But it wasn't fair. So I sat in front of the TV, ignoring her. Then as soon as my show started, she fell. I didn't push her myself... but she's dead just the same."

Though smothered in tears, relief washed over him. Isaac had been holding in his confession for far too long. It needed to come out.

At least someone heard it.

But there was still one more confession to go.

"What really happened with Ms. Gagne? Did she know you're a spy? Is she even your sister?"

Rotchford chuckled, coughed. "You're relentless, kid, I'll give you that." He spit up blood. "But yes. She really was my sister. And no, she didn't know about me."

"Then why'd you kill her?"

Rotchford's eyes fell and remained closed, before he twitched himself awake. "She found my bag."

"What bag?"

"My go..." Rotchford began, then coughed up more blood, which he wiped on his arm. "My go-bag. My sister was packing for her trip, digging through old suitcases. She found my go-bag. Fake passports, pistol, cash. If the Feds ever tracked me down, I didn't want them to find it. So I kept it here. I never know... when I'll need to skip town. When I'll need to run."

"Now," Isaac said, "seems like a pretty good time."

Captor and captive laughed weakly.

"She confronted me about the bag," Rotchford said. "I told her it was nothing, not to worry. But she grabbed it from me. So I grabbed it back and pushed her away. Only, harder than I meant. She went down, hit her head on the table. She cracked her skull. I should've called an ambulance. She's old, people fall. It happens all the time. Just an accident. But"—he pulled his lips together, sighed—"I panicked."

Isaac offered a single nod. "That's when I saw you, through the window?"

"I thought I saw you, too, but I wasn't sure. And then you came the next day, and the cops after that."

"Why didn't you run?"

"I wanted to, believe me. I almost did. But my handlers told me to stay put. They have a lot invested in me. They were gonna squash the case, like it never happened. They had another asset speak to the cops, pretending to be my sister. I was gonna hide out, at my other place in town, but you found that, too. Your surveillance was good. Damn good."

"But what did you"—Isaac struggled to maintain consciousness—"do with Ms. Gagne?"

Rotchford went silent then. It seemed like half a lifetime before he resumed speaking.

"She's in a junkyard," he said, shaking. "I thought I could just wah... walk away from it. Put it behind me. But... you don't come back from that... do you?"

That one hit Isaac close to home.

"I thought I could handle it," Rotchford said. "Don't think about it, just get it done. I had no choice, right? But I puked right there in the junkyard. Stumbled into an engine block. Got this for my trouble." Rotchford tapped his cast. "And a whole lot more, thanks to you."

He spoke again in Russian. *"Smert ne sprosit, pridet da skosit... The Reaper won't ask your opinion when it comes to collect your soul."*

Their business concluded, Isaac resigned himself to the inevitable. "Who do I call?"

Rotchford told him the number. Repeated it. Leaning against the nook where the fridge met the wall, Isaac reached for the rotary phone. Picked up the receiver. He inserted his pointer finger into the first number slot, about to dial, when he looked toward the front door.

He couldn't be sure, but he thought he saw shadows outside the window.

And then the shadows jumped to life.

Detectives Butler and Narapoli barged in, their guns drawn, bulletproof vests over their shirts and ties. Butler reached for the nearest toggle switch on the wall, turned on the foyer light.

"Isaac," Butler said, spotting the pale, sweaty kid in the kitchen, his belly drenched with blood. "You okay?"

Narapoli eyed the wound. "He's hurt—"

"Gun!" Butler shouted. "Behind him!"

Holding his breath, Isaac stepped aside into the nook, enough for the detectives to get a better line on Rotchford.

"He's... Russian," Isaac blurted. "A spy."

"Jesus," Narapoli said, regripping his pistol. "He's a what?"

"I t-told you he did it," Isaac said, struggling to maintain lucid thoughts. "He... killed Ms. Gagne. I was right."

"You were," Butler said. "I'm sorry we didn't believe you."

"And we found Beatrice Gagne," Narapoli said. "In the trunk of a car." He snapped at Rotchford. "You happy, you a piece a' shit? You proud?"

"Isaac," Rotchford said, ignoring Narapoli. "The envelopes my sister left? When you collect? You know why she never wrote your name? Only *Paperboy*? Because she didn't think much of you. All she saw was disappointment. Wasted space. A shell of a kid, not worthy of his own name."

Isaac bristled, the pain grazing his heart, because someone had finally told him the truth. Yet during a night of surprises, Rotchford surprised him once more.

"She was wrong. You could've been a good one... a spy or a cop. You got good instincts."

Isaac smiled, Rotchford's words meaning more to him than they should have. In his mind, Isaac saw little Frankie again. She gurgled, cute and perfect, knowing her big brother was there.

From behind the detectives, in the living room, came a gasp. Dani Larsson's hands went up to her mouth. "Isaac."

"Oh, Christ," Narapoli barked. "Get outta here, kid. Go!"

Though close to death, Isaac never felt more alive. "Dani," he said, smiling weakly at her. "You look so pretty. So sweet."

"Oh," Dani whimpered. "You're..."

Isaac's eyes rolled back. He slid down the wall, phone receiver still clutched in his bloody hand.

"Yeah. You would've made a good one," Rotchford said. "Maybe next time."

Shots rang out, but all Isaac heard were faint crackles, like popcorn on a stove.

NARAPOLI TOOK A bullet to the neck.

As his partner went down, Butler fired at Rotchford. Three shots hit the wall, one in the floor. Another went through Rotchford's already bloody thigh, and one more in his chest. The kill shot.

Four uniformed officers charged into the house. Red and blue flashing lights shone through the windows.

Butler stood there, weapon still aimed at Rotchford. One of the uniforms checked Narapoli for a pulse. He shook his head.

When Isaac opened his eyes again, he realized he'd been fitted with an oxygen mask and an IV, laying face up on a gurney. The medics wheeled him out into the night, the house surrounded by police officers, squad cars, ambulances, and a crowd of neighbors.

Isaac recognized some of his customers.

Mrs. McGuire, who Isaac had nearly fake assassinated just days before, stared in disbelief.

Dani stood over him, unable to fight back a stream of tears. "See?" she whispered. "You're a spy after all."

"Yeah," Isaac whispered back, police chatter crackling through the radios. "Double Oh Seven's got nothing on me."

Butler staggered out of the house, his partner lying dead on the living room floor in almost the same spot Ms. Gagne had met her own maker. It took all Butler had to remain on his feet.

Weary, he turned to the medic. "Kid gonna make it?"

"Don't know. He's lost a lot of blood."

"We gotta call the kid's parents," Butler said. "Get 'em to the hospital. If they lose another one… Just fuck it all to Hell."

Live? Die? That was the life of a spy. Isaac knew the risks, knew the cost.

As he was hoisted into the ambulance, he stared at a pumpkin on the neighbor's stoop, left over from Halloween. The jack-o-lantern's orange hue endured, its grin crooked and off-center.

From its perch, the pumpkin had been watching all along, keeping its slitted eyes on Isaac—the paperboy, who, despite his best efforts, was leaving his route unattended and unguarded, when there was still so much left to protect.

THE DEVIL'S DELINQUENTS

BY SAWNEY HATTON

PART I: THE INFERNAL ONES

Hail Satan, ruler of the damned,
Rise up from the pit of Hell
Come to us, Lord Lucifer
Take our souls we got to sell.
Come to us, prince of darkness
Let us be your demonic slaves
We're here for you, ready to do
Whatever evil you crave.

"SEE ANYTHING?" CAL ASKS, SQUINTING HIS eyes at the lopsided pentagram Derry drew in white chalk on the blacktop.

"Nope," Derry answers, whisking a strand of his long, straight, raven hair out of his face. His square, almost superhero-worthy jaw looks incongruous with his otherwise chubby features. His eyelids exhibit the telltale droop of a seasoned stoner.

The two teenagers sit cross-legged at the far end of Martin Van Buren High School's parking lot, by the brick maintenance shed. It's a starless night, and there are no lights here. The black candle they'd lit and set in the center of the five-pointed star burns bright as a beacon.

"Guess it didn't work," Cal says, scratching one of the swollen pimples on his cheek. His copper-red hair is thin enough to discern, even in the faint candlelight, the constellation of acne also afflicting his scalp.

"Guess not." Derry takes another hit off the joint they're sharing. Ash from the tip falls in one of the folds of his XXL Grimstone "The Hell We Are" tour T-shirt that hugs his rotund frame. He shoves the handwritten loose-leaf paper he'd been reading from into his jeans pocket. "But it'll make a kickass song."

Cal grins. "Hell yeah. I liked the demonic slaves part. That's dope."

Derry nods and passes him the joint.

"So what do ya wanna do now?"

AN HOUR LATER, Derry drives his dinged, dented and duct-taped blue '87 Plymouth Sundance through the suburban streets of Montague Falls, Frankenpriest's death metal anthem "Raise the Blaze" blasting from the stereo cassette player. All the huddled-together homes they pass look structurally similar, a few already decorated for Halloween with ghosts and witches, skeletons and scarecrows.

Cal sits in the passenger seat, peering hawk-like out his window. He points his scrawny arm at something ahead of them. "There's a good one!" he shouts over the music.

"Got it!"

Derry swerves the car and plows into a plastic trash can set out on the curb. Pizza boxes, soda cans, and junk mail fly into the air and over the hood of the car.

Derry continues to speed down the block, sharply rounding the corner.

"Yee hah!" he exclaims. "How many fingers was that?!"

Cal holds up a latex severed hand, the kind bought from a novelty store, with pale skin and ragged fingernails, a shard of bone poking out of its bloody stump. He bends down the index finger and thumb, leaving three fingers extended.

"Three!"

"Bullshit! That was a fuckin' four, at least!"

"The hand of judgment says three!"

"Fuck the hand!"

Cal bends down all of the grisly prop's fingers except the middle one, flipping Derry the bird. Derry lashes out, grabs the offending digit, and twists it. Cal jerks it away from him.

"Stop, dickhead! You'll rip it!"

Something outside catches Cal's attention. "Hey! Go down that way!"

Derry stops the car short, then turns onto the dimly illuminated street. He accelerates, aims, and sideswipes a cluster of garbage cans. Discarded foods and soiled paper towels erupt from them, scattering across the adjacent lawn, almost up to the house's porch. A cylindrical container still filled with something thick and white—likely cottage cheese or yogurt—twirls through the air and explodes against the front door, coating it in soggy chunks.

"That was wicked!" Derry whoops as they race away.

"Five fingers, dude!"

"Hell yeah!" Derry high-fives the rubber hand.

DERRY AWAKENS IN the morning to a loud thump against his car.

His vision blurred from the bright daylight assaulting him, he first focuses on the Jesus Christ statue looming over them, arms splayed, in the St. Matthew's Catholic Church parking lot. Derry's eyes then drift down to the lifeless squirrel on the car's hood.

He nudges the still-sleeping Cal with his elbow.

"Yo, Cal. Check it out. A dead squirrel."

"Wuh?" Cal responds groggily, adjusting his lanky frame in the creaky seat.

"Dead squirrel. There."

Cal looks where Derry is gesturing. The gray squirrel lies on its spine, paws curled, mouth agape.

"Cool," Cal finally says.

"Must've fallen out of that tree. Had a heart attack maybe."

Cal rolls down his window and stares up at the lofty birch tree, its green leaves beginning to mingle with yellow ones. "Maybe another squirrel pushed it."

Derry chortles. "Squirrel murder. I like it." He digs into an opened bag of Ruffles bar-b-q potato chips in the center console and claws out a handful. He offers some to Cal, who shakes his head no.

"What time is it?" Cal asks.

Munching on the chips, Derry keys the ignition. The car's digital dashboard clock flashes on—8:14 AM.

"Ah, shit. We're late," he grumps. "Gotta roll."

Derry starts the engine, shifts into reverse, and motors backward a few feet, causing the squirrel to tumble off the hood onto the asphalt. Kicking into drive, he barrels forward, squashing the carcass as he steers out of the lot.

THE OUTSIDE OF Van Buren High is quiet, void of any people. With the lot almost full, Derry has to park near the football field, beneath a banner depicting a fang-baring cobra alongside the words "GO VIPERS!"

The brisk breeze ruffling their hair and clothes, the boys hustle through a whirlwind of fallen leaves and junk food litter into the rear entrance of the school.

The inside of the two-story building is even quieter. Derry and Cal sneak through the mustard yellow hall, lined with rows of student lockers interspersed between closed classroom doors, until they reach a wide staircase.

"Catch you at lunch," Derry says as he heads for the stairs.

Cal nods.

"Mister Rhodes and Mister Virgil!"

The gruff voice booms from Mr. Richards, Van Buren's vice principal. Bald, burly, and wearing a snug-fitting burnt umber suit that seems a half size too small for him, he towers over the boys. He firmly clasps his hands on their shoulders.

"My watch reads a quarter past nine," he says. "Which means classes are in session. And you gents are not in class."

"We don't got watches," Cal says.

"That's too bad. But I'm sure the both of you will plan on being on time for detention with me this afternoon at three on the dot." He glowers at them, squeezing their shoulder a little tighter. "Am I correct?"

"Yessir," Cal answers.

"Yeah," Derry groans.

"Good." Mr. Richards releases his grips on them. "I'll pencil you in. Now get to where you belong."

He turns around and marches up the hall. For such a large man, the footfalls of his brown loafers hardly make a sound on the linoleum tiled floor.

With the vice principal's back to them, Derry gives him the finger. Cal mimics the gesture as they shamble off in the opposite direction.

"For that, you can add another detention tomorrow, gents," Mr. Richards bellows from the end of the hallway without facing them.

The boys retract their offending fingers.

"How the hell does he do that?" Derry grumbles.

Cal shrugs. "He don't got no eyes in the back of his head."

"Maybe they're in his ass," Derry says, and the two boys go their separate ways.

THE SCHOOL CAFETERIA teems with students, the space humming with their chatter and laughter. Painted along the entire upper wall is a huge cobra, with team-spirit slogans written on it like "Vipers #1" and "We Got Bite!" and "Score More in '94!" A group of pretty girls—a few of them in cheerleader outfits—sits at a table with a bunch of jock guys in matching Van Buren Vipers football jerseys.

Amanda, one of the cheerleaders seated in the center of the pack, sports a long, blonde ponytail that whips around every time she turns her head. Beside her, her buff boyfriend Kyle occasionally grabs the flailing tress, yanks her head back, and kisses her on the mouth. This makes her smile. Sometimes in response she rakes her fingernails across his buzzed scalp. This makes him grit his teeth.

Derry sits alone at a table in the rear of the lunchroom, wolfing down a hamburger. Ketchup oozes from between the buns each time he takes a bite.

Kyle and two of his buddies rise from their chairs. His eyes zero in on Derry across the room. With a mischievous grin, Kyle scoops a handful of lime Jell-O from Amanda's tray and hurls it at Derry. It hits him square in the face, leaving tiny green globs on his cheeks and nose. Derry cleans himself with a napkin without giving Kyle so much as an annoyed glance. The jocks laugh and swagger out of the cafeteria.

Cal enters from the cashier's line with his meal tray, on which is a slice of pizza, a bottle of apple juice, and a package of chocolate chip cookies.

"Hey!" Amanda calls out to him as he passes by her table. "Is that pepperoni or sausage?"

Cal stops. "It's, uh, just regular. Plain."

"I meant on your face."

Her friends giggle.

"Mmmm." Amanda licks her lips sensuously. "You look so yummy."

"Oh, leave him alone, Amanda," one of her friends says, tittering. "You're so cruel."

Cal lowers his head, angling his spotty face away from them, and continues walking to Derry's table. He slumps into the chair opposite his friend and stares at his food, not touching it.

"You want this?" Cal asks.

"You're not gonna have it?" Derry answers.

"Nah. I'm not hungry."

Derry's eyes widen. "Sure, I'll take it."

Still grasping his hamburger in his other hand, Derry snatches the slice of pizza from Cal's tray and chomps a big bite out of it, grease drizzling down his chin.

THE WALLS OF Derry and Cal's English classroom are adorned with rumpled posters of William Shakespeare, Edgar Allan Poe, and Emily Dickinson, a dried white spitball still clinging to the poetess's nose.

The period dismissal bell rings like a dying seagull. Students rise from their desks and file pass the teacher's tabletop lectern on their way out, picking up their term papers from the gray-haired, gray-suited Mr. Crapshaw.

"Very good, Miss Berman," the educator says to a mousy girl with braided brunette hair as he hands her her report. "Keep it up." She sees her grade and smiles.

Cal and Derry, last in line after the mousy girl, step up to Mr. Crapshaw.

"Ah, Mr. Virgil. Nice of you to join us today for your afternoon nap. Since you chose not to hand in a paper, you will summarily receive a failing grade."

Cal does not react, waiting for the teacher to elaborate.

"That would be an 'F'."

Cal nods.

"And Mr. Rhodes, your single page essay, written in verse, on..."—Crapshaw consults the sheet of loose-leaf—"*The Devil Does Metal*, I found to be grossly inadequate and chock full of grammatical errors. Nevertheless, I'm giving you a 'D' for the little effort you put into it." The teacher hands Derry his paper.

"Alright," Derry says. He flaunts his work in front of Cal's face. "Got a 'D'!"

"'D' for Dick," mocks Cal.

"At least it's not 'F' for, uh... for Fail."

"'F' for my folks are gonna be royally pissed."

"I will be offering some extra credit assignments before the winter break," Mr. Crapshaw informs them. "I encourage you both to take advantage of those if you want to raise your averages in this class."

"Okay," Cal replies tepidly.

"I'm good, Mr. C," Derry says, proudly holding up his essay with a circled red "*D*" in its top margin.

DERRY AND CAL arrive at the detention hall two minutes early, according to the clock high up on the powder blue wall. The space is larger than the typical classroom, featuring a gunmetal gray teacher's desk facing two rows of long Formica tables and a paned window overlooking the school parking lot.

Seated at the tables are other rule-breakers serving their sentences—one of the jocks from the cafeteria on the left, another boy with a tie-dyed shirt and tousled hair farther back in the same row, and a girl midway between them on the right. Derry notices her immediately.

She sports jet black hair like him, but cut short and spiked with gel, and a goth ensemble consisting of a lace halter top (her purple bra can be seen through it), shiny vinyl pants, Doc Marten combat boots, and, most arresting, a black pirate's patch over her right eye. She wears thick dark eyeliner on her left one, and a deep red lipstick that starkly contrasts with her pasty complexion. She's writing something in a composition book.

Derry nudges Cal, pointing the girl out to him. Cal, already looking at her, nods. Derry leading, the boys take seats directly behind her. Caught up in her writing, she pays them no mind. They can now see she is sketching a brawny demon creature with coiled horns, bat-like wings, and six breasts.

Mr. Richards enters the room—at three on the dot—and sets

his leather attaché case on the desk. He pulls a spiral register and a stack of papers from it and places them in front of him.

The disciplinarian scans the detainees.

"Mr. Rhodes, move two seats back."

Derry rises from his chair and plops into another in a different row.

"We have a fresh face among us." Mr. Richards views his roster. "Miss Natalie Glantz—"

Natalie raises her eye upon hearing her name.

"Let me welcome you to my detention center."

She returns her attention to her drawing.

"For the edification of our newest guest, and for those who may have forgotten, here are the house rules. There is to be no talking or any other form of communication, no getting up without my permission, and no clowning around whatsoever. You may read, study, or do your homework, as long as you do it quietly. Understood?"

Nobody responds.

"I'll take that as an affirmative." Mr. Richards checks his watch. "Enjoy your stay, gentlemen. And lady." He settles in at the desk, plucks a red pen out of his shirt pocket, and begins marking his paperwork.

Cal raises his hand. "Mr. Richards, can I go to the bathroom?"

"No," Mr. Richard answers without looking up.

"But I gotta pee."

"Then you should have gone before coming here, Mr. Virgil."

"I didn't wanna be late."

"That's commendable. But you're on my time for the next fifty-seven minutes and relieving yourself is not permitted. So hold it."

"I can't."

"You can, Mr. Virgil. I believe in you."

Cal frowns and fidgets in his chair.

Silence pervades the room for several seconds. Then Derry loudly passes gas.

Mr. Richards glares at him.

"Sorry, Mr. Richards," Derry says. "They had baked beans for lunch."

Cal shoots his hand up again. "Can I move, Mr. Richards? His farts stink."

"Tough it out, Mr. Virgil."

Another moment of silence, then Cal starts to cough violently, sounding like a dog choking on a bone. Mr. Richards shoots him an admonishing stare.

"I'm fine," Cal croaks, clearing his throat.

Derry wriggles in his chair, making it creak. Mr. Richards looks at him, irritated, his anger swelling. Derry slows, but does not stop, his squirming.

"My butt itches."

"Move over a seat."

"That ain't fair!" Cal blurts. "He gets to move just 'cause his ass is making the chair squeak?"

"Shut up!" the vice principal barks. "I don't want another peep in here! Or else—"

On that cue, Natalie begins screaming in unbridled terror. She collapses out of her chair and writhes on the floor, her hands wrenching her clothes torturously.

Mr. Richards springs from his seat. "What the hell's wrong with you?"

"The spiders!" she wails. "The spiders... they're all over me!"

"What?" The vice principal regards her with a crooked mouth and furrowed brow.

"They're crawlin' all over inside of me!"

"What are you talking about? Are you on drugs?"

"Aw, man," Derry chimes in, quaking his upraised hands. "She's freaking me out!"

"They're biting me!" Natalie continues. "They're drinking my blood!"

"Quit this nonsense!"

"I bet she's possessed, Mr. Richards," Derry whimpers. "She's gonna start puking up spiders!"

The pitch of Natalie's screaming heightens, commingling with hysterical laughter as she contorts her body more dramatically, her limbs skewing in all different directions.

Watching the performance, Mr. Richards's face becomes beet red. A plump blue vein in his forehead pulses. He clenches his fists.

Cal raises his hand again. "Can I go pee now?"

Snapping his head toward him, Mr. Richards yells through gritted teeth, "SHUT THE FUCK UP!"

A hush instantly falls across the room. Everyone stops their antics, their jaws dropping, their stunned eyes directed at the vice principal.

A moment later, all the students break out snickering.

Mr. Richards composes himself, breathing in deeply through his nose and exhaling out his taut lips. He walks back to his desk and sits down.

Natalie returns to her seat.

Mr. Richards eyes the students with disdain.

"You can fool around all you want in life. Fail all you want. Brats like you, before you reach twenty, you'll either wind up dead, or in jail, or worse." He flashes them an ice-cold smirk. "You kids have no future."

After detention, Derry and Cal go outside, loitering in the recessed area by the school's rear entrance. They struggle to light up cigarettes with their Bics, helping each other shield the flame from the gusting breeze.

"Can I bum a cancer stick?"

The boys turn their heads in unison to see Natalie Glantz standing by them, her eye flitting back and forth between them.

"Sure," Derry answers.

He offers her his pack of Marlboro reds. She slips a cigarette from it and sticks it between her lips. After lighting it with her own lighter—a silver Zippo engraved with a Ferrari logo—she takes a refreshing drag.

"Thanks," she says as she blows out a cloud of smoke.

Derry smiles stiffly. "Anytime... Your name's Natalie, right?"

"Yeah. Call me Nat."

"I'm Derry. This is Cal."

"You a freshman?" Cal asks her.

"Junior. Just transferred here from South Harvest this week."

Derry tilts his head toward his shoulder, taking another puff off his cigarette. "Ain't that a special school?"

"Must be. I'm special." Her slight smirk evaporates. "My mother thought I had mental problems. Like, I'm disturbed."

"Are ya?"

"Are you?"

"Hell yeah." Derry grins fiendishly. "We're fuckin' ravin' psychos."

Natalie chuckles, chewing on her bottom lip.

"We're both in eleventh grade too," Cal says.

"But I'm a year older than him," Derry adds haughtily. "'Cause I got left back in junior high."

Natalie nods.

"So... what happened to your eye?" Derry asks.

Without hesitation, Natalie flips up her eyepatch, revealing a milky white pupil, the socket surrounded by mottled, scarred skin.

"A roman candle blew up in my face when I was a kid."

"It looks pretty cool," Derry says.

"Yeah," Cal agrees. "Real cool."

Natalie re-covers her damaged eye.

"What did you get detention for?" Cal asks.

"I cut this off Amanda Wilkens." From the interior pocket of her black blazer, she fishes out an inch-long lock of blonde hair.

"Holy shit," squawks Derry. "Why'd you do that for?"

"Gonna give that stuck-up bitch one nonstop period for the rest of her life."

"You can do that with hair?"

"If you know the right spell."

The boys nod, gawking at the golden strands. She returns it to her pocket.

"You know her boyfriend's Kyle Banningham?" Derry says.

Natalie rolls her eye.

"He's not gonna be happy you did that to her."

"What's he going to do? Rape me?"

The boys do not have a response for this.

"So you're, like, into magic?" Cal asks her.

Natalie sucks on her cigarette before answering. "I conjure dark forces," she says, smoke spilling from her mouth.

"Y'mean, like demons and shit?" Derry says.

"Yeah."

"Cooool," Cal purrs. "Me and Derry once heard this big-ass crow say 'Satan Rules' as it flew over us. And it said it twice, so we weren't just imagining it."

"It was like, 'SAY-TAN RULES, SAY-TAN RULES,'" caws Derry, imitating the bird. "It was sick."

Natalie nods aloofly.

"You ever talk to the Devil?" Derry asks.

"Not yet." Natalie flicks her cigarette to the ground and crushes it beneath her boot. "I've only been able to summon his minions."

"What do they do?"

"They give me information. Teach me the ways of their Master."

"No shit?"

Natalie shakes her head. "And they carved this into my flesh to mark my loyalty to him." She raises her shirt to display the ragged scars of a pentagram etched into her belly around her navel.

The boys' eyes widen and their jaws gape. They utter "whoa," "wicked," "fuckin' wild" and other awed phrases. She lets them touch it.

A shiny yellow Ford Mustang, a cobra airbrushed on its hood, roars across the parking lot toward the three teens. It skids to a stop on the pavement alongside them. Amanda leaps from the car, followed by Kyle.

"You fucking freak!" Amanda shrieks. She barrels toward Natalie until their noses nearly connect.

Natalie doesn't shrink from her. "Oh. You mean me?"

"You cut my hair!"

"It was an accident."

"How the hell do you cut someone else's hair by accident?"

Natalie shrugs. "When it's in my way. I was trimming my nails."

"You're full of shit. You so deserve a beating. But I don't want to get myself dirty. My boyfriend, though." Kyle approaches them. "He doesn't mind making a mess."

Kyle steps toward Natalie, scowling at her.

"Really?" Natalie says to him, unflustered. "You gonna beat up a girl?"

A long moment elapses as they stare each other down.

"C'mon Kyle," Derry implores. "Leave her alone."

"Shut up, you fat piece of shit." Kyle keeps his fierce eyes fixed on Natalie a few seconds more, then spits a frothy loogie in her face.

Natalie whips her head away, her lips pursed in disgust.

"You upset my girlfriend again, next time I'll make you eat my shit."

Amanda smirks. Kyle turns around, takes his girlfriend's hand, and leads her back to his car. She plants a jubilant kiss on his mouth as he peels off, the Mustang's tires kicking up gravel at the three teens.

"You alright?" Cal asks Natalie.

She nods, threads of Kyle's saliva still clinging to her chin and cheek.

"Here." He offers her a white handkerchief from his jeans pocket.

Natalie accepts it and wipes her face.

"They're such assholes," Derry says.

Natalie's snarl transforms into a smile.

"They're nothing. Their fate is already written in the Book of Lambs. More fodder for the slaughter."

Derry and Cal nod dumbly.

"Hey," Derry says. "You need a lift home?"

NATALIE USHERS DERRY and Cal into her house. Dingy curtains make it murky inside despite the many windows. The teens pass through the living room, the dining room, and into the den. Beatific portraits of Jesus Christ, the Virgin Mary, and assorted apostles hang on the wood-paneled walls. Natalie's petite mother, dressed in a floral housecoat, sits in an armchair in the lamplit far corner.

She reads aloud from a Bible in her lap. *"Because they have not hearkened to my words, saith the Lord, which I sent unto them by my servants the prophets..."*

Across from her is Natalie's catatonic father, shoulders slumped in a wheelchair, an argyle quilt draping him up to his chest.

"...rising up early and sending them; but ye would not hear—"

"Hey mother, did you hear the good news?" Natalie interrupts.

"Jesus is dead as a cross nail. Turns out he got crucified. Really fucked him up."

Her mother twitches an eye and flares her nostrils. "Don't you blaspheme in this house." Her tone sounds like the mom from *The Brady Bunch* show if she were a fire-and-brimstone preacher.

"Oh, please." Her daughter laughs at her. "This ain't a god-damn church."

Her mother stares sharply at her.

"May the Lord have mercy on your rotten soul, Natalie Maria Glantz."

"Why don't you just pray for me, mother? You do for everything else."

Natalie exits the room. Derry and Cal follow her.

"Hi," Cal says to her mother, meekly waving at her.

The teens walk down a dim, narrow hallway decorated with antique rifles, family photographs, and more religious iconography.

"Hey, was that guy your dad?" Derry asks, gesturing his thumb toward the den.

"Yes," Natalie confirms.

"What's wrong with him?"

"He got in a car accident a few years ago. Smashed up his brains and turned him into a zombie."

"He's living dead?" Cal asks, a little too excitedly.

"Something like that. My mom thinks reading the Bible to him will snap him out of it. I think it just annoys the hell out of him and the poor bastard can't do shit about it."

Natalie removes a picture from the wall—the Glantz family dwarfed by a panorama of the Grand Canyon—and retrieves a silver key stuck in its frame.

The boys scan the gallery of snapshots. Derry focuses on one showing a much younger Natalie, wearing the eyepatch, standing with two older girls, the tallest of them in a graduation gown, in front of their house.

Derry points to the other girls. "Are these your sisters?"

"Yep," Natalie says.

"They look a lot older than you," Cal says.

"They are. The super blonde one is now in the Navy and the

other's living in Jersey, married to some rich guy in banking, or accounting, whatever."

"They're pretty," Cal says. Natalie doesn't respond.

Derry studies another framed photograph. Natalie's overjoyed father poses in a red jumpsuit and black helmet with a broad white stripe running down the middle. He holds a large gold trophy cup.

"Did your dad win something?"

"He was a champion race car driver. That's the Thunder Run Three Hundred Trophy. I saw him win it."

"That's cool."

"He used to say it was safer racing around a track at a hundred eighty miles an hour than driving on the highway doing sixty. He was right. He had his worst accident on the I-95. Was the last one he ever had."

Natalie inserts the hidden key into the knob of the hallway's lone door.

"You got a lock for your room?" Cal asks.

"Keeps Mother Superior out of my stuff," Natalie answers as she replaces the key in the frame and resets the picture on the wall.

NATALIE SHUTS HER bedroom door behind them and relocks it.

Derry and Cal appraise her room with a combination of surprise and wonder. The walls and ceiling are entirely festooned in burgundy and black velvet fabrics. A grotesque array of ceramic demon faces adorns the canopy over her bed, and a gold-painted pentagram is carved into the knotty pine headboard. A black racing helmet with a white stripe sits on the far side of the bed beside a pink teddy bear with a sequin heart on its chest.

"Wow," says Derry. "Cool crib." He notices the helmet on the bed and picks it up. "Hey, is this the same one your dad was wearing in the photo?"

"Put that down!" Natalie barks at him.

Derry obeys.

"Everything in here is tuned to my personal energy," Natalie declares. "So don't touch *anything*."

Cal scrutinizes an adult human skull on top of the bureau,

melted candles clustered around it and a tapered red candle stuck onto its crown.

"Hey, is this real?"

"Yeah," Natalie answers. "That's the skull of a ninth level grand warlock. I dug it up from a graveyard in Connecticut when I lived there."

"And it had a candle in it?"

She regards Cal dubiously. "No. I put that there."

"What are those?" Derry asks, gesturing toward a row of tatty, leather-bound books tucked on a shelf over her bed, next to newer copies of *The Satanic Bible* and *To Kill a Mockingbird*.

"My black magic spellbooks."

"Can I look at one?"

"No. You'll taint it."

Derry nods blankly.

Natalie cants her head, her eye ping-ponging between Derry and Cal.

"But I will show you something," she says, lowering her voice. "If you swear not to ever tell anybody about it, no matter what."

Derry and Cal agree.

"Nobody," she insists. "Not even if they scrape off your skin, pour boiling oil on you, and chop off your dicks."

"Okay," they both say.

Natalie enters her closet and rummages inside. Moments later, she reemerges with an object wrapped in a black cloth bag, sealed with a drawstring. She beckons the boys nearer. She then unties the sash and slips the bag off a Mason jar filled with a yellowish liquid. Preserved in it is some unrecognizable animal, resembling nothing from this world. Or perhaps an extremely deformed monkey fetus.

"I had this," Natalie explains, "after I had sex with an incubus."

"A what bus?"

"An incubus. A male demon that fucks women in their sleep."

"So..." Cal puts it together, "that's your kid?"

Natalie nods.

"Holy shit," says Derry. He and Cal examine the creature closer. "Is it dead?"

"He's dormant," she answers. "In a deep sleep." She beams

at her progeny like an adoring mother. "He'll awaken to fight for Satan's army when Armageddon comes down."

Derry knocks on the glass.

"Stop that!" Natalie yells. "What did I tell you? Don't touch anything."

"Sorry," he says.

THE BOYS LEAVE Natalie's shortly after six p.m. Derry drops Cal off at his house, a ranch-style property with a well-landscaped yard boasting a mature sugar maple tree whose leaves are just turning their autumn colors.

"Catch ya later," Cal says as he steps out of Derry's car.

"Not if I'm faster!" Derry punches the gas and pulls away. Cal manages a playful kick to his rear fender. Derry responds by honking his horn obnoxiously until rounding the corner.

"Hi, Calvin!"

Cal looks across the street where Mr. Harrison, wearing hospital scrubs, teaches his nineteen-year-old son Tony how to ride a shamrock-green BMX bicycle. With his striped shirt and woolen cap, the younger man bears enough of a likeness to "Where's Waldo?" to make Cal snicker. With his father gently clasping his waist to help him keep balance, Tony pedals down the paved driveway to the sidewalk.

Cal waves to them. "Hi Tony. Hi Mr. Harrison."

"How are you doing, Calvin?" Mr. Harrison asks, scratching his grizzled beard.

"I'm good."

"Wanna see me ride my bike?" Tony shouts at Cal.

"Maybe later. I'm kinda in a hurry."

Cal rushes up the walkway to his front door.

"Bye, Calvin! I'm gonna go eat din—" Tony's shrill voice pierces the air like a siren, following Cal inside his house until he slams the door shut behind him.

Cal enters his kitchen where his mother, donned in a ruffled pink apron, seasons a whole chicken at the counter. His father, in navy blue mechanic's coveralls, lounges at the small bistro table, sorting through the day's mail.

"Aww, look who decided to come home," his father moans

in feigned disappointment. He downs the last swig of a can of Budweiser. "Now we can't rent out your room."

"Funny, Dad."

Cal heads for the refrigerator and fetches himself a beer.

"Grab me one of those too, would ya?" his father says.

Cal produces another can out of the fridge and hands it to his father. They both pop the tabs in unison and take a sip.

"Did you sleep over Derry's house again?" his mother asks.

"Yeah," Cal burps.

"Excuse you."

Cal's father belches even louder.

"Excuse both of you." She shakes her head. "Next time call us so we know where you are."

"I did," Cal replies. "The phone was busy."

"Well, you know I stop my telemarketing calls after seven. You could've tried then."

"We were out driving around."

"Your mother worries, Calvin."

"You don't, Dad?"

"I've always worried about you," his father jests.

"Ha ha," Cal groans as he exits the kitchen.

"Supper will be ready in half an hour!" his mother announces.

Cal shambles into his quirkily cluttered bedroom. Plastering its walls are full-color magazine clippings of modern horror movies—the chest-burster from *Alien*, the machete-in-head zombie from *Dawn of the Dead*, the werewolf transformation from *The Howling*, and a host of other grisly images. A shelf unit displays a collection of resin creature figures, from Frankenstein's monster to *Friday the 13th*'s Jason Vorhees, some of them placed in combat poses. Nightmarish masks and fake body parts complete the décor.

Cal places his beer on the dresser and crosses over to the media console, pressing play on the stereo cassette player. As Metallica's "Creeping Death" blares from the twin speakers, he inserts a VHS tape into the TV/VCR combo. A scene of a young blonde girl being chased by a chainsaw-wielding maniac flashes onto the thirteen-inch screen.

Cal picks up a pair of wood drumsticks from his desk and

sits cross-legged on his bed, watching the violent video while whomping his pillow to the blistering beat of the music.

DERRY ARRIVES HOME to find his stepfather Rick hunched forward in the La-Z-Boy in a white T-shirt and blue boxers, arranging and assembling a jumble of electrical ware scattered on the glass-top coffee table before him. He has a wiry, weathered physique, the ink of the Marine tattoos on his forearms so faded they look more like birthmarks.

Derry's mother lies on the ivy-print couch, idly nibbling on the split ends of her strawberry blonde hair. His twelve-year-old brother Bobby is sprawled on the shag carpeted floor, watching *The X-Files* on TV. Wearing *Star Wars* pajamas, he's short and pudgy, the formative version of his older sibling.

"Where the hell have you been?" Rick growls at Derry.

"I stayed over at Cal's."

"Again? You guys gone queer for each other?"

"No," Derry answers brusquely.

"I'm kidding, big boy." Rick completes piecing together a lamp socket. "I need you at the store Sunday for inventory."

Derry huffs. "Why can't Bobby do it?"

Rick glares at him. "'Cause I'm tellin' you to do it."

Bobby sticks out his tongue at his brother.

"I'm busy Sunday."

"Yeah right," Rick scoffs. "Doing what? Gonna hang out with that Cal kid all day long doing jack squat. Some real work will do ya good."

"Do I get paid at least?"

"Sure. You'll get to keep livin' under this roof for free, and your mother will keep doin' your laundry and cookin' your meals."

"Am I getting paid or not?" Derry responds impatiently.

Rick mulls it over. "I'll give ya thirty bucks, long as ya don't slack off or goof around."

Derry nods and tromps out of the living room. He heads into the pantry, through which he accesses the attached garage, packed with lawn implements, power tools, bicycles, toys, and, strapped to the rafters, two kayaks.

In one corner is Derry's glossy black Stratocaster, plugged

into a small Marshall amp set on a red milk crate. He takes the guitar from its stand, puts the nylon strap over his head, and switches on the amp. He strums each of the six strings, plays a fuzzy-sounding chord, then launches into a distorted series of notes that might sound like a song if the listener were stoned or hardly hanging on to their sanity.

Pausing to tune one of the strings, he hears his mother and stepfather yelling at one another inside the house. Derry raises the volume on his amp and continues jamming, the noise overwhelming the clamor of their quarreling.

Moments later, a flung can hits Derry in the forehead, splashing beer on him.

Derry winces from pain.

Rick's sinewy silhouette fills the doorway. "Turn that shit down!" he thunders, then slams the door.

Derry rubs his temple, mumbling "asshole." He blots his face with his shirt, then uses a rag to mop up the spilt beer on his equipment.

His mood to practice soured, Derry replaces the guitar on its stand and retreats to his room. He passes his mother in the master bedroom, sitting on the edge of the king-sized bed, dabbing her reddened cheeks with a tissue.

Derry stops and takes a couple of tentative steps toward her. "You okay, mom?"

"Hmm mmm." She nods feebly, turning her teary eyes away from her son. "Just been a rough day."

Rick appears at the threshold of the room.

"I'm going out."

Derry narrows his eyes at him.

"You got a problem, big boy?" Rick asks, his voice teeming with venom.

Almost shamefully, Derry gazes again at his mother.

"I changed the oil in your car," Rick tells her.

"Thank you," she answers, barely audible.

Rick leaves them. Derry hears the thud of the front door closing.

His mother sniffles. "Could you clean up the broken glass in the kitchen, Derry?"

Derry grits his teeth. "Sure," he sighs and gives his mother her privacy.

NATALIE KNEELS NAKED in the middle of her room, a soot-smudged saucer and the skull from her bureau placed on the hardwood floor in front of her. With her Zippo, she lights the red candle on the skull's crown. Bearing witness to the ritual is her demon-spawn suspended in the Mason jar.

She presses the lock of Amanda Wilkens's blonde hair to her lips and whispers something into it. She then dips it into the candle flame. She puts the smoldering hair on the saucer, where it sizzles and shrivels up into a charred clump.

Natalie shuts her eye and concentrates her mind...

AMANDA WILKENS ROUSES to the dawn sunlight falling upon her face, birds chirping outside her bedroom window. The cheerleader, attired in a hot pink teddy, drowsily lifts her arm and rubs her eyes with her palm... notices her hand is coated in thick, moist blood.

"What the fuck?"

She bolts upright and inspects herself, discovers her crotch drenched in gore. It has soaked most of her bed as well, dripping off the gold sateen sheets and spreading into a puddle on the floor. Within moments it is gushing from her, filling the room, submerging everything. Amanda tries to scream, but her own menses muffles her. Drowns her—

NATALIE IS JOLTED from her reverie by an urgent rapping.

"Is something burning in there?" her mother asks through the door.

"No," Natalie answers, aggravated. "Everything's fine. I just lit a candle."

"It smells funny."

"It's a scented candle... It's myrrh."

"Is it? Interesting. Well, be sure to put it out when you go to bed."

"I will."

"Okay... goodnight, Natalie."

"'Night, mother."

The following morning, Natalie awakens to an overcast sky, fog condensing on her window. Today she chooses to dress like a Japanese schoolgirl, in a pleated checkered skirt with thigh-high socks and a charcoal gray necktie. For breakfast, she makes herself microwavable blueberry waffles. By the time she leaves her house, the sun is poking through the clouds. She walks to school via Essex Avenue, ignoring the car horns honking at her.

Upon entering Van Buren High's parking lot, Natalie spots Kyle and Amanda with a group of their friends, gathered like a pack of wolves by Kyle's Mustang.

Natalie approaches them, confidently marching up to Kyle.

"What the fuck do you want?" he sneers at her.

"I want you..." she answers in a deep, diabolical voice, "in the palm of my hand."

Natalie thrusts her fist forward, penetrating Kyle's chest. With a twist of her wrist, she yanks her hand back out, gripping his still beating heart.

Kyle gawks at his eviscerated vital organ in disbelief before flailing his arms and collapsing to the ground.

His friends gasp. Amanda screams.

Natalie calmly examines Kyle's blood-spurting heart, then proffers it to his girlfriend.

"Here," she says to Amanda. "I think he'd want you to have this."

"Hey Nat!"

Derry's voice snapping her out of her daydream, Natalie finds herself staring out the detention room window at Kyle's clique flocked together in the parking lot. She pivots around in her seat. Derry sits three rows behind her, Cal in front of the room on the opposite side. Mr. Richards is nowhere to be seen, though his attaché case rests on the desk.

"And we've made contact!" Derry jokes.

"Where's Mr. Richards?" Natalie asks.

"He stepped out like five minutes ago. Said he'd only be gone a minute."

"I think he's sick or something," Cal says. "He keeps messin' with his nose."

"It's almost four," says Derry. "Should we just leave?"

They mull this over an instant before rising in unison. They head to the door and peek out, then slip into the hall.

Derry offers to take Cal and Natalie home. Both accept, but since neither wants to go home yet, Derry drives them around for the next two hours. With Natalie up front and Cal in the backseat, they cruise up and down Jefferson Turnpike, past the Montague Falls Fall Carnival, through the regal Holy Crown Cemetery, and to the Gagne house over on Pearsall Place, where two people had violently died years before and has been vacant ever since. Natalie remarks it looks like the *Roseanne* TV show house.

"What d'ya wanna do now?" Derry asks.

"You got any weed?" Cal replies.

Derry shakes his head. "Got any cash on ya?"

"Just a couple of bucks. How 'bout you?"

Derry roots through the pockets of his denim jacket and scoops out some coins. He glances at the meager change in his palm and again shakes his head.

"I have money," Natalie says.

Derry swivels his body toward her. Cal pokes his head in-between them.

"Do you?" Cal says at the same time Derry asks, "How much?"

"I mean, I can get money," Natalie amends herself. "How much do you need?"

THEY STOP BY Natalie's house. While Derry and Cal wait in the car, Natalie sneaks through the rear patio door into the kitchen. Her father is propped in his wheelchair by the dishwasher, a portable radio beside him on the countertop playing pipe organ music.

Natalie glides past him and into the dining room. Bumping her hip into the farmhouse table, she freezes. When nobody reacts to the noise, she peeks around a corner.

She spies her mother in the den, her auburn hair sculpted into a prim bouffant, along with the pastor of her mother's church, a dapper younger gentleman attired in a formal black suit. They sit close to one another on the sofa, each with a Bible open in their laps, chatting too softly for Natalie to hear. The pastor's hand caresses her mother's knee. Her mother doesn't object.

Natalie slinks into the adjoining hallway, avoiding detection. She ducks into her parents' bedroom, brightly colored with floral accents on the bed linens, window curtains, and lamp shades. A fancy curio cabinet stands against the wall opposite the bed. Displayed on its shelves are a collection of her father's racing trophies and plaques.

Natalie unlatches the cabinet door and takes out a silver cup. She lifts its laurel-ringed lid, revealing a roll of money hidden inside. She swipes a couple of twenty-dollar bills, then replaces the bundle into the cup and the trophy onto the shelf.

Before exiting the room, Natalie pauses by the Shaker dresser. She gingerly slides out its bottom drawer and moves aside a stack of folded men's sweaters, exposing a cedar box underneath. She opens the box and picks up the nickel-plated .22 pistol nestled within. Natalie admires the weapon, appreciating its heft in her hand, her finger stroking the trigger. She poses with it in the dresser mirror, aiming it at her own reflection while wearing an imperious grin.

Natalie creeps out of her parents' bedroom and returns to the kitchen, heading for the rear door.

"Natalie," she hears a voice murmur behind her.

She whirls around to face her wheelchair-bound father. She approaches him and crouches down, touching his hand and looking deeply, hopefully into his glazed eyes.

"Daddy?"

He remains motionless, mindless.

Natalie withdraws her hand from his. She stands and studies him for a moment, watching his chest rise and fall with his breaths, until compelling herself to exit the house, unconcerned with the clank of the screen door banging shut behind her.

DERRY AND CAL escort Natalie to a pavilion gazebo tucked within a copse of fir trees in Greeley Park. The dry-rotting structure is emblazoned with so many layers of graffiti that it's difficult to discern what most of the words and designs are, except for numerous crude phalluses, a few skulls, and one "Fuck You Roy" or possibly "Ray."

A willowy, olive-skinned man in a black wife-beater and

beige chinos hangs out there, leaning against one of the columns.

"Hey Marco," Derry says.

"What's up?" Marco answers, running a comb through his slicked-back hair.

Derry presents Natalie's cash. "We'll trade ya our green stuff for your green stuff."

"How much you want?"

"An eighth."

"'Kay." Marco's numeric pager, clipped to his belt, emits a series of beeps. He turns it off and glances down at the digital message window.

"Who's she?" he asks, jutting his chin toward Natalie.

"She's a friend of ours. She's cool."

"She looks like she fucks dead people," Marco says with a chuckle.

"She's a legit Satanist, man," Cal says.

"Yeah? I knew a guy who was into that shit. And he fucked dead people."

"She fucked a demon once."

"Yeah?" Marco eyes Natalie. "Did you?"

She nods.

Marco appraises her, swirling his tongue inside his cheek. "You know, I can give y'all a discount if your chick friend shows me a good time."

Natalie sighs through her nose. Derry and Cal stand speechless for a moment. They look at the otherwise unfazed Natalie, then back at Marco.

"Nah, dude," Derry says. "We'll just pay for it."

Marco agrees to the arrangement. He trades them a baggy of bud for their money.

"Hey, I'm throwing a bash at my crib Saturday night. You guys are invited, if you wanna drop by."

"Cool," Derry says, enthused. "We'll try to come."

"You can come too, babe," Marco tells Natalie, a lascivious gleam in his eye.

"Maybe," she replies with snubbing nonchalance and starts walking away. Derry and Cal follow her, gleefully making tracks with their feet through the bed of pine needles on the ground.

DERRY DRIVES THEM to the reservoir, a man-made lake surrounded by concrete, much of it cracked and sprouting weeds. Cal rolls them a joint. Derry lights it and takes the first toke. The three teens lie next to one another on the hood of the car, Natalie sandwiched between the two boys, getting high while watching the sun set across the brackish water and listening to the whooshing of the dam-fed falls nearby.

"This pot rocks, man," Derry says, passing the joint to Natalie.

"Yeah," Cal agrees. "Man, they should just legalize this shit already. Then we could plant our own."

"And we can open our own reefer store. Call it..." Derry ponders.

"The Grim Reefer!" Cal trumpets.

Derry chortles. Natalie takes a hit off the joint and starts coughing harsh enough to hawk up a lung.

"Don't die on us, babe!" Cal says.

Her hacking peters out. She passes the joint to Cal.

"Hey Nat," Derry says. "You like Grimstone?"

"What's that?" she croaks, her throat raw.

"Hold on." Derry hops off the hood, circles around his car, and stoops into the open driver's window. He keys the ignition, then fumbles through the cassette tapes scattered around the center console. He finds the one he wants and inserts it into the stereo. Thrash metal music pounds from the speakers, so loud it rattles the car's windows.

"This is Grimstone. Best fucking band in the universe."

"Oh," Natalie says, unimpressed. "I don't listen to music."

Incredulous, Derry flares out his nostrils. "You don't?"

"It's too distracting."

"But Grimstone sings about the Devil. And about bringing the dead back alive, and killin' yourself to death, and space sharks. Kickass shit like that."

"And they did the soundtrack for the movie *Gutmunchers III*," Cal chimes in.

"Never saw it," Natalie says.

"Someday I'm gonna have my own band," Derry boasts, drawing the last toke off the joint and flicking it into the reservoir shallows. "I play guitar, and I write songs and sing. Cal's learning to play drums. Then we just need somebody on bass. And we gotta have an awesome name. Something real fuckin' badass and evil."

"Guess that's pretty cool," Natalie says. "My dad likes Elvis... He used to."

"Hey, can Satan get me a million-dollar record deal and hundreds of thousands of people worshipping me?"

"Satan can get you anything you want," Natalie replies. "You can be rich and famous. You can have total control over anybody and have them do your bidding. And you can get rid of your enemies. Everything in this mortal world can be yours, if you pledge your allegiance to him."

Both Cal and Derry gawk at her, enthralled.

"And you can be immortal. Never get hurt, never grow old, never die. So you don't have to take shit from anyone anymore."

"I want the power to read minds," Cal says.

"Satan will give you the power to do anything, if you give yourself to him. He made me realize I was superior to other people. Taught me that Hell isn't for the damned, but for the chosen, and if I was deserving of him, I could be one of his disciples."

Natalie slides herself from the hood, brushes off her skirt, and climbs into the front passenger's side of the car. She turns off the stereo and reclines her seat all the way, staring at the sagging fabric headliner above her.

Moments later, Derry and Cal join her in the car.

"So do you go to meetings with other Devil guys and do ritual stuff?" Derry asks her.

"You mean black masses?"

"Yeah."

"I don't attend any organized ceremonies anymore. It's all the same bullshit. I now practice my own rites of worship. And I get better results."

"Maybe we can help you out sometime," Derry suggests.

"Yeah," Cal adds. "That'd be cool."

"Maybe," Natalie responds.

There is a long lull in their conversation as the darkness falls over them. A nearby bullfrog produces a husky *rumm rumm rumm* call. Cal farts and blames it on the frog.

"You guys hungry?" an antsy Derry asks. "I'm hungry."

Cal and Natalie share his hankering.

"Then let's go get us some munchies," Derry says. He wrestles the car into gear, resumes blasting his heavy metal music, and ventures toward someplace to eat.

PART II: LOVE + HATE

THE TEENS STOP AT THE 7-ELEVEN on Essex Avenue for snacks, Slurpees, and smokes, Natalie's treat. Upon returning to Derry's car parked across the lot by a dumpster, they tear into their bags of chips, chocolate cakes, and beef jerky.

"We should do something to fuck with Mr. Richards," Derry proposes while chomping on a mouthful of Fritos.

"Like what?" Cal asks.

"I dunno. Torch his house?"

"That would be sweet."

"That would be first degree arson," Natalie says. "Or worse, if anybody gets killed."

"Yeah." Derry nods. "Hardcore, right?"

"Hard to get away with." She sucks on the straw of her cherry Slurpee. "If you want to torment somebody, you have to be smart about it. Can't leave anything that can be traced back to us."

"Like what?" Cal asks again.

"Your hair, skin, or spit. Fingerprints, shoe prints. Or there could be a witness."

"So we'd just have to be really careful," Derry says.

"He's not worth it."

"Mr. Richards ain't?"

Natalie nods. "There are those far more deserving."

As if on cue, Kyle's Mustang careens into the strip mall's lot, passing Derry's car and pulling into a handicapped spot in front of the 7-Eleven.

"Speak of the dickhole," Cal says.

They watch Kyle and Amanda get out of their car and head into the store.

"We should burn down *his* house," Cal says.

"I have a better idea," Natalie replies and exits the car.

"Where ya going?" Derry asks.

"Be right back. Honk if you see them coming out before I'm done."

"Done with w—" Derry hasn't time enough to finish his question before Natalie is dashing toward Kyle's vehicle. "Is she nuts?"

They observe her reaching the Mustang. She leans into the open driver's side window and rummages around the front seat.

"She's got balls," Cal says.

"What the hell is she... Oh shit!" Derry gasps. "They're coming out."

"Honk the horn!" Cal blurts.

Derry does. Natalie pops her head up and locks eyes with Kyle, chewing on a hotdog and snarling at the same time.

"What the fuck are you doing, freak?"

Natalie withdraws her upper torso from the Mustang. "I accidentally left something in your car."

"Left what?"

"My bra."

Amanda looks askance at her boyfriend. Kyle squinches up his face. "How the hell would that get in my ride?"

"From last afternoon. When we were together."

"I have no idea what she's talking about," Kyle says to Amanda.

"Did you forget already?" Natalie asks him kittenishly. "You said I have the best boobs you've ever felt."

Kyle faces his girlfriend, arms outstretched. "She's full of shit, babe. I would never do that to you. Especially not with *her*."

Amanda glares at Natalie. "I don't believe you."

"Relax, princess," Natalie replies, easing away from Kyle's car. "I'm sure it was a one-time thing."

"You're such a liar," Amanda says.

"Hey, it's all good. You're the kind of girl he's going to marry. I'm just a side piece for when he wants to get... freaky."

Amanda charges at Natalie, one hand grabbing a bunch of her close-cropped hair, the other slashing at her face, her pink-polished fingernails clawing Natalie's cheek.

Natalie clutches onto Amanda's forearms and kicks her in the shin with her combat boot. The cheerleader yelps in pain but doesn't let go of Natalie's hair.

"Fuck her up, Manda!" Kyle goads.

With her full body, Amanda shoves Natalie into Kyle's car, pinning her against the trunk. Her own hands occupied, Natalie clamps her teeth down onto Amanda's shoulder.

"Ow!" Amanda jerks Natalie's head back by her hair. "You wanna bite, bitch? I'll fucking blind you!"

Amanda uses all her strength to force her thumb onto the socket of Natalie's good eye. Trying futilely to push her hand away, Natalie grits her teeth as the other girl applies more and more pressure to her eyeball.

Something hits Amanda in her ear, bouncing off and landing on the ground.

"What the hell..." says Kyle. "Is that a hand?"

Amanda ceases her attack, looks down at her feet, and sees a severed hand, palm up, lying right beside her Steve Madden shoe.

"Holy shit!" she shrieks. "Is that real?"

"Get in, Nat!" Cal shouts at Natalie from Derry's Plymouth that has coasted up alongside the catfight.

Natalie releases the distracted Amanda's arms and races into the car. They peel out of the lot, leaving their stupefied adversaries behind.

Kyle nudges the bloody extremity with his high-top sneaker, lightly pressing down on it with his toe. "It's like... spongy."

"That's so gross," Amanda says.

Kyle picks it up, squishes it in his fist. "It's just fuckin' rubber." He peers at the road. "Which way did they go?"

"THANKS," NATALIE SAYS to the boys while blotting the scratches on her cheek with a 7-Eleven napkin. "I think that skank made me bleed."

Derry glances at her. "It doesn't look that bad."

Natalie's frown transforms into a mischievous grin. "Whatever. I got what I wanted."

She holds up a small black comb.

"What's that for?" Cal asks from the backseat.

"It's Kyle's. I needed something personal of his for the ritual."

"For what ritual?"

"I'm going to summon a demon to eliminate him, to make him suffer for eternity. Shred his cock with a Hell-made deli meat slicer."

"Cool," Derry and Cal utter in unison.

"Can we help?" Cal asks.

"Yes," she answers.

Bright high-beam headlights blaze on behind them, and a horn beeps manically at them.

Cal squints out the rear window. "Shit. It's Kyle."

"Aww, he's mad," Derry says. The Mustang speeds up and kisses his bumper. "We're not gonna outrun him."

"Gonna kill us before we kill him!" Cal squawks.

"Pull over in here," Natalie says.

"Why?" Derry asks skeptically.

"Just do it."

Derry cranks the steering wheel to the left, sharply veering into the Montague Falls train station. He brakes underneath the nearest trestle, startling a group of pigeons into flying away. Kyle's car stops diagonally behind Derry's, blocking them in.

The jock leaps from his vehicle and storms toward the other car. Fists balled, he loops around to the passenger side.

"You're so dead, mutherfu—"

Kyle halts before Natalie's rolled-down window. "Holy crap."

Natalie trembles in her seat, eye fluttering, her mouth oozing crimson foam.

"Something's seriously wrong with her, man!" Cal shouts out his window. "I think she's having a seizure or something."

"I gotta take her to the hospital!" Derry says.

Amanda inches up beside Kyle, her jaw agape. "What's up with her?"

"Maybe she's... seizuring," Kyle answers.

"C'mon, dude," Derry says. "She needs help. We gotta go."

Kyle and Amanda glance at one another, hesitating.

"If she dies while you're keepin' us here," Cal warns them, "it's on you guys."

"C'mon Manda," Kyle says. "I'm not getting caught up in this."

Kyle stalks back to his car. Amanda crouches at Natalie's

window. She watches her gasp and gurgle, her one undamaged pupil floating up into her head.

"I hope you choke," Amanda hisses at her, then rejoins Kyle in the Mustang. He reverses out of the station lot, revs his engine, and rumbles up the turnpike.

Derry and Cal regard Natalie, impressed.

"Great acting," Cal raves.

"Yeah," Derry says. "Gargling the cherry Slurpee was a nice touch."

"I was in the drama program at my old school," she tells them while wiping her sticky mouth with a napkin. "I played Juliet once."

THE TEENS SWING by Natalie's house to pick up her ritual kit which she keeps in a jam-packed Adidas duffel bag. They then drive to the forested area behind the Top Shop grocery store, parking the car on the berm.

"Want me to carry the bag?" Cal asks Natalie after getting out.

"Sure," Natalie says, passing the kit to him. He slings the strap over his left shoulder and grimaces, its weight making him lean sideways a bit.

"You got it?" Derry asks him.

"Yeah, yeah," he answers assuredly. "I'm good."

With Derry's flashlight from the glovebox illuminating their way, they hike into the dark woods, their footsteps crunching the brittle fallen leaves. After journeying about a quarter mile, they stop at a small clearing, the almost full moon visible through the broken canopy of tree branches.

Cal rests the duffel bag on a moss-covered log and Natalie unzips it, producing the tools for the ritual. She unfolds a 5'x5' black satin blanket, embroidered with a goat's head inside a white pentagram, and spreads it on the ground. She places her skull with the red candle on the goat's forehead in the center of the star, and tealights at each of its five points. Lastly, she sets down her grimy ceremonial saucer.

"Okay," Natalie says, satisfied with the arrangement. "Now disrobe."

"What?" the boys ask simultaneously.

"We need to take off our clothes for the ritual."

"Uh... why?" Cal asks.

"Clothes are human objects. If we don't shed them, demons will shun us."

Derry and Cal nod. Natalie begins to strip, first removing her blouse, then her skirt. The boys raptly watch her in the pale moonlight. Seeing they are not undressing, she gives them a peeved look.

"C'mon. Don't be wusses."

With unstifled enthusiasm, Derry kicks off his sneakers, shucks off his jeans, and removes his shirt. When Natalie slips out of her bra and panties, he follows by dropping his white briefs.

They both look at Cal, still fully garbed.

"C'mon," Derry says to him. "Don't be a pussy."

Cal pulls off his *Killer Klowns from Outer Space* T-shirt, revealing all the acne blotches on his chest and upper arms. He finishes baring himself as quickly as possible, as if doing so faster will somehow assuage his embarrassment. His eyes zero in on Natalie's nude body a moment before abashedly bouncing over to Derry's.

"Dude," Cal says, "you got a boner."

Derry glances down at himself. "Oh... I can't help it."

"It's alright," Natalie says. "We're animals. It's a natural animal reaction."

Cal peeks down at himself, then stammers, "It's k-k-kinda cold out."

Natalie kneels upon the satanic blanket. She gestures for the boys to do likewise at opposing points of the pentagram. As they settle into position, she places a small leather pouch next to her.

"Now we light the candles."

"I'll do it," Derry says, reaching over to his crumpled jeans to fish his Bic from its pocket. He ignites each of the wicks, saving the red candle on the skull for last.

Natalie inspects the altar. Satisfied, she instructs the boys to be quiet. She reaches toward her piled clothing and finds Kyle's comb. She holds it over the red candle. When the comb catches fire, she lays it on the saucer. The black plastic warps and bubbles.

"Man, that stinks," Derry says.

"Hush," Natalie commands.

She shuts her eye. For several seconds she passes her palms over the pentagram in slow, fluid motions, then extends her arms out deferentially.

"Master of the infernal realm, lord of the netherworld, grant me thy immortal strength so that I may do thy bidding."

She next dips her hand into the leather pouch, scooping out a pinch of gray dust. She sprinkles it over the red candle, thrice reciting the refrain, "The power of Satan impels me!" The flame flickers and crackles.

Natalie rotates her head about her shoulders in figure eights while chanting guttural, ancient-sounding words. Her body begins to shudder, gradually becoming more and more intense, as if an increasing surge of electricity were shooting through her.

Derry and Cal observe her, not blinking.

Within moments, Natalie's convulsions cease and her body sags, her chin drooping to her chest. She stays that way, breathing deeply.

"Are you okay?" Cal asks.

"I felt him," she mutters and lifts her head. Her lips have widened into a gratified, post-orgasmic smile. "He reached out to my soul and took me down into his dominion. I felt his utter, infinite power. I was helpless. And then he laid his hands on me. All over me. I experienced pleasures beyond pain. Burning ecstasy. I never wanted it to end. I wanted to serve him forever."

"Cool," Derry says.

Natalie shakes her head. "But I was cast out. I was unworthy of him."

"That sucks," Derry says.

"What about shredding Kyle's pecker?" Cal asks.

"Oh... that didn't come up."

They remain kneeling and naked, Natalie mesmerized by the red candle's dancing flame. Derry and Cal ogle her for a while, then look at one another.

"Now what?" Cal asks.

Natalie doesn't respond.

"I'm pretty hungry," Derry says. "Wanna hit White Castle?"

Natalie mumbles something.

"What did ya say, Nat?" Cal asks.

"He wants an offering," she repeats louder. "To earn our immortality and reign beside Satan in his kingdom, we must pay tribute to him."

"I can write a new song for him," Derry suggests.

"The Master demands a blood sacrifice," she clarifies.

A somber moment of silence lingers between them.

"Can we eat first?" Derry asks.

THE THREE TEENS sit at a booth in an uncrowded White Castle, each enjoying their own sack of burgers and cups of soda. They share a tray of french fries smothered in ketchup.

"What were those weird words you were sayin' during the ritual?" Cal asks Natalie, seated across from him and next to Derry.

"Yeah, I was wonderin' that too," Derry adds. "Was it some foreign language?"

Natalie sips her Sprite before answering. "I was speaking in the Devil's tongue."

"You mean that's how they talk in Hell?"

"It's how those in Hell communicate with Satan's followers on earth."

"Like a secret code?" Cal replies.

Natalie nods as she takes a bite out of a cheeseburger. She notices two college-aged couples enter the restaurant, dressed in nice sweaters, slacks, and shoes. One guy wears an NYU sweatshirt. They look in the teens' direction. The NYU guy gives his friends an "eek" expression, which makes the others snicker. They then turn their attentions to the menu board above the counter.

"So, what were you saying?" Derry asks.

"That's private. Between me and the Master." She sees the preppy quartet have sat down with their ordered food at a table on the other side of the dining area.

"Well, what was it about in general? Can you tell us that?"

"We discussed his plans for me." Natalie smiles. "He told me I'm doing well, and that he's proud of me."

"What about us?" Derry inquires. "We helped."

"He said... you two had potential."

"Cool," Derry responds.

"Awesome," Cal says.

While they continue eating, Natalie imagines one of the fries she picks up is the snooty NYU guy, miniaturized. She delightedly chomps down on his head, savoring his ketchup-flavored blood.

LATER THAT NIGHT, they drop off Natalie at her house. Cal offers to carry the ritual kit in for her, but she declines, taking it in herself. He hops into her vacated front seat. The boys wait for her to go inside before driving away.

Cal squirms in his seat and reaches under his butt.

"Your ass itch, dude?"

"I'm sitting on some—" Cal wrenches out Natalie's leather pouch. "Check it out. Nat left her bag of magic powder here. Should we go back and give it to her?"

"Nah. We can just give it to her tomorrow."

Cal opens the pouch and sniffs its contents. "What d'ya think it is?"

"Dunno."

Cal dips his index finger into the powder, pulls it out and licks the ashy residue off of it.

"Dumbass," Derry says. "That shit could be poison."

"It don't taste like nothin'."

"It don't gotta have a taste to kill ya."

Cal dumps a generous amount of the powder into the palm of his hand.

"Hey, don't spill any of that crap in my car."

Cal stirs his finger through the substance.

"Quit fucking around with it. Nat doesn't like anyone touchin' her stuff."

"She ain't here," Cal says. "How's she gonna know?"

"I'll know."

"So what? You gonna rat on me?"

"Just leave it alone, asshole."

"Okay, okay." Cal pours the powder back into the pouch. "Don't have to be a dick about it."

They don't speak another word to each other the rest of the way to Cal's house.

THE NEXT DAY, a Saturday, Derry cruises up to the curb in front of Cal's house and honks his horn. Beside him, Natalie rolls down her window to light a cigarette.

Cal exits his home and heads for the car.

"Hi, Calvin!"

Cal spots Tony waving at him from across the street.

"Hey, Tony," Cal says.

"My daddy's gonna take me to the carnival if it don't rain."

"That's nice, Tony."

"I can get you cotton candy."

Cal glimpses Natalie smirking at him.

"No thanks," Cal replies to Tony.

"Who's that guy?" Natalie asks Cal.

"That's Tony. He's, like, retarded I guess."

"Hey, Tony!" Derry yells out his window. "Ain't you gonna get us cotton candy?"

Tony nods. "Uh huh."

"Well, we don't want none, so when you get it for us, don't give us any, okay Tony?"

"Okay," Tony answers with a befuddled expression.

"Check this out," Derry says to Natalie. "Cal, do the ball thing."

Cal nods, then shouts "Yo Tony!"

The young man gawps at Cal, slack-jawed.

"Catch!" Cal tosses Tony an imaginary ball.

Tony tries to catch it in his open palms, becoming confused when he cannot see anything coming at him.

"It landed behind you," Cal says.

Tony eagerly combs the lawn behind him.

"Look in the bushes!" directs Derry.

Tony hunches down, then crawls into the shrubbery bordering his house.

Natalie and Derry snicker.

"He'll be looking all over the place for the next hour," Cal says to them.

"Hope you didn't lose our ball, Tony!" Derry carols. "Don't wanna have to tell your daddy!"

"I'll find it!" Tony assures him.

Cal slides into the backseat of Derry's car, and the threesome drive off laughing while Tony continues to frantically search the bushes, not noticing they have gone.

NATALIE IDENTIFIES A perfect opportunity later that afternoon.

The small white dog—Cal thinks it's some kind of terrier—plays with a rubber fire hydrant toy in the picket fenced yard of a Cape Cod-style house located a few towns away from theirs. The pet romps around unattended, the yard veiled in shadow from tall oak trees that surround it.

"Here, pooch," a voice whispers. The dog raises its head and pricks its ears.

Derry crouches at the ajar entry gate, his hand shaking a raw frankfurter. "C'mon. Come 'n' get it."

The dog yips and runs up to him. It sniffs the frank, then chomps its teeth into it.

"Good boy," Derry coos. He hooks his finger onto its bedazzled collar and scoops the dog into his arms. The animal contentedly licks its chops.

Derry stands and shuts the gate, gingerly re-latching it. After scanning the area for possible witnesses, he slinks off with the dog.

The three teens return to the forest clearing after nightfall. Once again they kneel naked on the black blanket, lit candles studding its pentagram design. In the center of them, on top of the goat's head stitching, lies the small dog, its tongue lolling from its maw. Natalie holds it down with one hand on its fluffy belly. Her other hand clutches a wood-handled steak knife.

"Lord Satan," she recites. "Accept this, our sacrifice to you. Let its spilt blood summon you from your kingly throne in Hell. Come forth and honor us with your presence, and bestow upon us your almighty power. Let us join your unholy legions, O Satan!"

Natalie raises the knife above the dog, its tip directed at its heart.

"Ready?" she asks Derry and Cal.

The boys nod. Derry cups his hands over Natalie's grip on the knife's handle. Cal does the same over Derry's knuckles. They exhale in unison, preparing to plunge the serrated blade down together.

Natalie draws a deep breath, shuts her eye, and chants "The power of Satan—"

Cal retracts his hands from the knife. "I can't!"

"What?" Natalie asks.

"I can't do this."

Natalie and Derry relax their arms.

"Why not?" Natalie asks in a more testy tone.

"Well... look at it."

She glances down at their docile sacrifice. The dog blinks at her.

"What are you talking about?"

"It's too... cute."

"Too cute?" Derry says. "Who the fuck cares?"

Cal shrugs. "I just can't."

"If you wanted Derry to get an ugly mutt," Natalie chides, "you should've said so."

"Sorry. I didn't think of it."

"Alright, we'll do it," Natalie huffs. "You don't even have to watch. Just recite the invocation."

"Invocation?" Cal asks, puzzled.

"Say the words I say."

Cal nods.

"Okay. Let's start from where we left off—"

The dog licks Natalie's hand still on its belly.

"Stop that!" she snaps. The dog obeys.

Natalie holds the knife aloft again and Derry clasps his hands around hers. Cal turns away from them.

Natalie resumes her chant: "The power of Satan impels us!"

A zealous Derry and halfhearted Cal join her for the following refrains.

"The power of Satan impels us! The power of Satan impels us! The power of Satan impels us!"

The dog whines. Natalie peers down at it, into its rheumy brown eyes.

"Just say when, Nat," Derry says. Cal cowers in anticipation.

The dog waves its furry paw at her and whimpers.

"Aw, screw this!" She springs to her feet and chucks the knife into the woods, narrowly missing Derry's head.

Cal twists his body around and smiles when he sees the dog is still alive and unscathed. He reaches over to pet its brow. It pants happily.

"Godfuckingdamnit!" Natalie stomps barefoot back and forth, her fists clenched, growling "fuckfuckfuckityfucker." She finally halts between Cal and Derry, collecting herself, then starts to get dressed.

"Are we done?" Cal asks.

"Looks like it," Natalie sardonically replies as she fastens her bra.

"What do we do now?" asks Derry.

Natalie shakes her head. "We're bullshitting ourselves. Satan would never answer to an animal offering."

Cal picks up the dog and cradles it in his lap. "Then what do we offer him?"

His question hangs in the cool autumn air.

AFTER RETURNING THE dog to its home pen, Derry, Natalie, and Cal continue driving around aimlessly. Noticing the *Confetti & Cakes* special event supply store on Jefferson Turnpike, Derry remembers Marco is throwing a party at his place. Lacking anything better to do, they decide to go.

The three teens arrive at the dope dealer's house, a recessed ranch with peeling paint, a patchy lawn, and an outdoor lantern fitted with a green bulb. Jimi Hendrix's "Purple Haze" blares within the residence, rattling the windows. Dozens of guests, most of them years older than the teens, mill about outside, drinking and smoking. One guy in a wool poncho pukes in the birdbath.

"Guess this is it," Derry says.

"Gotta be," Cal confirms.

The teens dawdle there at the curb, surveying the scene.

"So..." Natalie says. "Are we going in?"

Derry and Cal nod, but don't budge. Natalie takes the initiative, marching up the front walkway to the entrance. The boys follow her a couple of paces behind.

They enter Marco's home, packed with people in all stages of insobriety, the din of their raised chatter mixed with the almost deafening music. The teens tarry awkwardly in the foyer until Marco struts up to them with a bottle of Red Stripe.

"Hey, amigos! Glad you could make it."

The teens greet their merry host with headbobs and handshakes.

"There's brews in the fridge and booze in the dining room." Marco points his thumb toward each of the referenced rooms. "And if you wanna get baked, just ask yours truly." He clucks his tongue twice. "I know y'all don't know anybody, but everyone's here for basically the same thing—to get fucked up and have fun. So go wreck some brain cells, man!"

Marco chortles and slaps Derry on the shoulder, then moseys away from them.

"I'm gettin' a beer," Cal says. "You guys want?"

Derry and Natalie both tell him "yeah." Cal makes his way through the huddled masses of partygoers toward the kitchen.

"Hey, goth girl!" Marco calls out across the room. "C'mere a sec!"

Natalie gives Derry a quizzical look. He shrugs.

"Wait here for Cal," she says to him. "I'll be right back."

Natalie navigates the crowd toward Marco, now hobnobbing with a priggish-looking man in his twenties, wearing thick eyeglasses, sandals with socks, and an orange Nehru jacket.

"Heyyy..." Marco says. "Sorry, I forgot your name."

"Natalie."

"Right. Natalie, this is my old pal Reece from upstate. He's a pagan. Reece, Natalie here's into Satanism. I figured you two would be into talking or arguing or whatever you culty nuts do for kicks."

Marco winks at them, then leaves Natalie and Reece to each other's company.

Reece breaks the ice. "So, what made you want to become a Satanist?"

"Satan is my lord and master," Natalie responds. "He protects me, guides me, gives me the power to vanquish all who defy me."

"Ahh... sounds almost Christian-like."

"The Christian god abandoned mankind long ago, so Satan adopted us, and he takes care of us if we honor him."

"Praise the lord!" Reece whoops facetiously.

"So," Natalie says, straight-faced. "What made you want to be a pagan?"

"My eyes, man. I can see how great and terrible the forces of Nature are. Tornadoes and tidal waves. Volcanoes. Earthquakes. We are at Nature's mercy, and we must respect her or she'll destroy us."

"Ah. Sounds almost... stupid."

CAL, HOLDING THREE uncapped bottles of beer, finds his passage into the living room blocked by a throng of people engaged in animated dialogue. He turns around and detours through the dining room on his way back to his friends.

Mixing cocktails at the dining table, a freckled male partygoer sporting a prodigious afro gets Cal's attention.

"Hey! You."

Cal stops. "Huh?"

"Try this." The partygoer offers him a highball glass filled with a bright blue liquid.

Cal sets down the beer bottles on the table and accepts the glass.

"What is it?"

"It's my own recipe. Try it."

Cal sniffs it, then takes a sip. The sting of its potency makes him scrunch up his face.

"Wow," he says, his voice cracking. "That's strong."

"I call it Cobra Juice," the partygoer says, "'cause it's got a helluva bite."

"What's it made out of?"

The partygoer strains to remember the recipe. "Scotch, vodka, tequila, Irish cream, and gin. Oh, and peppermint schnapps. I think that's all."

"Why is it blue?"

"No idea. Strange, huh?"

STILL WAITING ON his own in the living room, Derry plops down into the unoccupied gray loveseat near him. As he twiddles his fingers, a buxom girl, looking not much older than Derry, prances up to him. Her appearance—caked-on mascara, blood red lipstick, and frosted blonde hair—screams heavy metal fan. She wears only a buttoned brown vinyl vest on top, accentuating her ample cleavage.

"Hey, you like Grimstone?" she asks him.

At first, Derry is thrown off by her addressing him, sputtering "uh" and "hm," then perks up when he realizes she is referring to his Grimstone T-shirt.

"Oh... yeah. I do. They're my favorite band."

"Me too!" she replies a little drunkenly. "I love them. Their new album is so fuckin' awesome."

"Yeah, it's cool, but it's not as good as *The Devil Made Me Do Her.*"

"Yeah, of course not." She sits down on the loveseat beside him. "That's *the* best Grimstone album, but *Hell's Bells-Zee-Bop* still rocks."

"'Ballad of the Black Mass' is a kickass song."

"Oooo." The girl's eyes sparkle. "That gives me chills when I listen to it. Valmont's voice is so fuckin' deep. It's like he's possessed or something."

Derry nods excitedly. "And that's no effect. That's really him."

"I know! He gets me soooo hot." She lets out an orgasmic breath. "I'm Jennie, by the way."

"Hi... I'm Derry."

She beams at him. "That's so cool you're into Grimstone. You ever see them in concert?"

"Five times."

"Nice. Did you see 'em at Corbett Stadium last summer?"

"I was in the second row."

"Oh my God! Were you really? That was a fuckin' incredible show. Did Valmont spit goat's blood on you?"

Derry nods. "Uh huh. Haven't washed the shirt I was wearing since then. Even though it reeks now, so I can't really wear it."

Jennie gasps. "I would do anything to smell it."

ACROSS THE ROOM, Natalie and Reece continue to debate their theologies.

"All that Satan represents is the flesh," Reece argues. "And the flesh is weak. It scars and wrinkles and rots."

"Satan champions temptation," Natalie rebuts, "and desire is the strongest feeling there is."

"Desire is temporary. It's fleeting."

"So is a fucking tree."

MEANWHILE, CAL SITS alone at the dining room table, a stock of wine, liquor, and soda bottles before him. Randomly choosing different beverages, he mixes himself another cocktail in a red Solo cup.

A hand clasps his shoulder. "Hey sweetie."

A redheaded older woman sashays up behind Cal, holding an empty cup in her other hand. She is tall and sexy, her generously tattooed body covered with the skimpiest of clothing—candy-striped halter top flaunting her flat belly and denim mini-skirt showing off her sleek legs.

"Can you pour me another rum and Coke?"

The woman circles around in front of Cal. He gazes up at her. Her flirtatious smile instantly dissolves when she sees his acne-riddled face.

"Umm... Sorry." She forces another smile. "Can you make me a rum and Coke, please?"

"Sure," Cal says.

Cal grins sheepishly at her. She averts her eyes from him, randomly studying other people at the party. His grin withering, he prepares her drink.

DERRY AND JENNIE, still sitting together, experience a lull in their conversation. As he glances idly around him, she slouches on the loveseat, staring at her ample chest. She squeezes her breasts together to further emphasize her cleavage.

"Do you think my boobs are too big?"

"Uh... uh..." Derry stammers. "N-no."

"My sister has small, super-firm boobs, but she's all into exercising and aerobics, shit like that. She hasn't an ounce of fat on her." Jennie cups her hands on her breasts, fondling them. "Guys like my tits. I think they're too soft. They're like water balloons. Touch 'em."

Derry's eyes widen a bit. He doesn't comply with her request.

"Go ahead," she says. "It's okay."

Derry extends his index finger and gently prods her left breast.

"I didn't say poke 'em, dude."

Derry blushes. "Sorry."

Jennie snickers. "Gimme your hand."

He lets her take his wrist. She places his hand on her breast, pressing down on his knuckles so he can get a satisfactory feel.

"What do you think?" she asks.

Derry swallows. "Y-yeah... They're nice."

CAL LURCHES INTO the bathroom, shutting the door.

Bracing his hands on the sink, he sullenly studies his reflection in the medicine cabinet mirror. He pinches the whiteheads of a couple of the larger pimples on his forehead and chin, then blots the swollen, bleeding wounds with toilet paper. They look even worse now, rawer, redder. His eyes well up.

Somebody raps on the door.

"Be out in a sec," he says, wiping his tears onto his sleeves. He steps away from the mirror and flicks off the light switch, cloaking himself in darkness.

CAL STAGGERS INTO the living room, swigging a half-emptied bottle of vodka he swiped from the dining table. He finds Natalie still in a heated discussion with Reece and sidles up beside them. They don't notice him.

"I'm telling you," Reece tells Natalie. "God *and* Satan are just myths. God was created by men to explain anything that didn't make sense to them, and the devil and hell and all that eternal damnation rubbish were invented by priests and monks to scare people into going to church."

"That's not true," she responds.

"You don't believe it 'cause you're brainwashed too. If your ass was on fire, you'd probably think it was Satan buttfucking you."

Natalie's temper flares. "You're an asshole!"

"And you're delus—" Reece censors himself. "Okay, you're right," he says placatingly. "I can get very dogmatic, defensive, when

I talk about this stuff. I'm sorry if I came across... assholey."

His apology seems to appease her. "Well, I've been known to play the queen bitch for the same reason."

"It's all good," Reece continues. "I like that you're passionate. It's hot."

Natalie doesn't react to his comment.

"Let's start over. How about we go to my place where it's less noisy and more comfortable." Reece leers at her. "Where we can be far more... civil to one another."

"No thanks, stud," Natalie says. "You're not my type."

"You're not mine either. But I figure a girl like you, with this whole punk pirate getup, you can't be too choosy. Take it where you can get it, babe."

Natalie narrows her eye and gnashes her teeth, then glimpses Derry in her peripheral vision, heavy petting a girl on the love-seat. She purses her lips and flounces over to them.

"You're a dick," Cal says to Reece.

Reece frowns at him. "Who the hell are you?"

"Am Nat's friend," Cal slurs, swaying on his feet. "'N you owe 'er apopalogy."

"Fuck off."

Natalie hovers over Derry. "I want to go home now."

Derry stops kissing Jennie. "Uh... why?"

"We have to prepare for tomorrow."

"We do?... Oh. Okay."

"Is this your girlfriend?" Jennie asks Derry scornfully.

"No... she's just a friend."

"And he's my ride," Natalie adds.

"In that case," Jennie says, "why don't you call a taxi? Can't you see he's having fun here? With me."

"She's dirty," Natalie says to Derry. "You don't want to catch anything from her."

"Oh, please. How pathetic." Jennie smirks. "Go boss around some other guy. This one obviously digs me more than you."

"Don't make me angry." Natalie stares daggers at Derry. "You know what I can do for you. And to you."

He regards Natalie, uncertain, uneasy.

"So you're threatening him?" Jennie jeers. "Nice friend you are."

"Let's go, Derry," Natalie demands. "Now."

"I-I-I b-better..." Derry stutters to Jennie.

"Go on, dude," Jennie says dismissively. "I like my men with bigger balls anyway. You're too much of a pussy for me."

They hear a hollow thunk and a grunt from across the room, followed by stunned gasps and exclaimed expletives from the partygoers. Natalie turns her head toward it.

Reece hunches forward, his hand cupping his bleeding scalp. Cal faces him, scowling, choking the neck of the vodka bottle.

Responding to the commotion, Marco rushes up between them, spreading his arms out to keep the two separated. "What the fuck happened?"

"This... this mutherfucker... hit me... with a bottle."

Marco goggles at Cal. "What the hell, man?"

"He was tryin' rape Nat," Cal says.

"That's bullshit!" Reece barks. "I want this dude arrested."

"It's true," Natalie interjects. "Pagan guy here grabbed my breasts."

"What?" Reece snaps. "You're lying."

"No she's not," Cal says. "You're a goddamn scumbag o' scum."

"This ain't cool, man," Marco says, snatching the vodka bottle away from Cal. "All you guys gotta go."

"I didn't do anything," Reece whines, a trickle of blood dribbling from his sideburn. "He attacked me."

"I don't care. I'm not putting up with this shit. Get out."

"I'm calling the cops."

"Fine. Sure they'll love hearing about how you groped a girl."

"An underaged girl," Natalie adds, arching her eyebrows at Reece.

Seething, Reece almost says something else to Natalie, but thinks better of it and instead storms from the house. Natalie and Derry each grasp one of Cal's shoulders and lead him out the front door, a few of the partygoers cheering for him.

THE THREE TEENS spot the swirling, flashing lights on Essex Avenue from more than a mile away. A congregation of emergency vehicles blocks traffic in both directions.

"Must be an accident," Derry says.

He pulls his car over to the shoulder of the road, as close to the activity as possible. They get out and move nearer, seeking the best position to observe. They halt at the curb beneath an elm tree. The space between a fire truck and a police car provides them with an unobstructed view.

The driver's side of a yellow Ford Mustang is buckled around a telephone pole. Tire skid marks arc from the opposite side of the intersection up to the pole, as though the driver had taken the turn too sharply and lost control.

"Holy shit," says Derry. "That's Kyle Banningham's car."

Natalie, Derry, and Cal watch as Kyle's girlfriend Amanda is wheeled away from the vehicle on a gurney, her eyes dazed, her face spattered with blood. Paramedics lift the gurney into the ambulance and shut the double doors. Through the window, the teens can see a paramedic strapping an oxygen mask over Amanda's mouth.

A fireman begins to employ hydraulically powered shears— Cal says they're called "jaws of life"—to cut through the roof of the wreckage.

"No way Kyle survived that," Derry comments.

"Yeah," Cal agrees. "No way."

"It's an omen," Natalie says.

"Like the movie?" Cal asks.

Natalie ignores the question. "The Master did this. It's a message from Him, telling us that He favors us. That our desires will be fulfilled, if we prove ourselves."

Its roof now peeled back, more first responders huddle around Kyle's car. They no longer appear to be in any hurry.

"Yeah," Derry says. "Kyle definitely bit it."

"It's an omen," Natalie repeats, her expression cold and calculating.

MINUTES LATER, DERRY drives them to the reservoir. There they smoke a joint from what was left of the weed in the glovebox. They don't speak for a while, zoning out on the moon's shimmery reflection in the water.

"Tomorrow night is the Autumn Equinox," Natalie says authoritatively. "When the barrier between this world and Hell is at its thinnest, and when Satan is most receptive to a mortal's voice."

The boys nod. Derry says, "That's cool."

"I need to do more, go farther than I ever have before. I need to perform a sacrifice worthy of our Master. Tomorrow. And I want you guys to be my apprentices."

"Awesome," Derry says.

"Yeah," Cal agrees.

Natalie explains her plan.

"What if we get caught?" Cal asks when she finishes.

"We won't," she answers.

"It sounds messy."

"That doesn't matter. He will protect us."

"But what if it don't work?"

"It *will* work. I know it will. And you guys have to believe it will too."

"I do," Derry says.

"Okay," Cal says, less resolute.

Natalie studies both boys, as if attempting to read their minds. She scooches across the seat toward Derry. She kisses him on the lips, mingling their tongues. She then unzips the fly of his jeans and pleasures him with her hand.

Derry's gravelly moans fill the car. Natalie focuses on him, anticipating his climax.

Cal watches them in silence, his eyes widening, his mouth twisting.

Natalie's hand quickens. Derry's moaning intensifies.

Cal slumps down in the backseat, burying his head in his arms and shutting his eyes, until he conks out.

CAL IS JOSTLED awake when the moving car hits a pothole in the street. Upon opening his eyes, he sees Derry and Natalie holding hands between the front seats.

Cal peeks out the window. "Where're we?"

"Drivin' ya home," Derry answers. He and Natalie separate their hands.

"We should all get some rest," Natalie says. She glances at Cal behind her. "And make sure you gather those items we need."

"Oh, ok..." he says, remembering. "We still doing that tomorrow?"

"There's no better time than the Equinox," Natalie reiterates.

"Right. I get that... but maybe we should plan it out more. Do it next one."

"Why?" Natalie scoffs. "There's not a heck of a lot we have to plan. We just have to be willing."

Cal rubs his temple. "I'm probably gonna be majorly hungover tomorrow."

"Since when has that ever stopped us from doing shit?" Derry says.

"I know. But... this is different, right? Serious shit."

"If you're not up to it," Derry says, "Nat and me can do it without ya."

"But you'll reap none of the rewards," Natalie reminds him.

"Yeah. Satan can fix your face so you won't scare off chicks anymore."

Natalie regards Cal sympathetically. "That, and anything else you want."

Cal doesn't respond. He notices Derry glaring at him in the rearview mirror. "Don't wuss out on us, Cal."

"I'm not."

"Sounds like it."

"No, it's ok... I'm in."

"You sure?" Natalie asks.

"Yeah," Cal replies, his voice quavering slightly.

"Good." Natalie smiles at him. He smiles back at her.

She looks at the road ahead. "After tomorrow, our lives will forever be changed."

"Hell yeah," says Derry, wringing his hands on the steering wheel.

Cal reads the dashboard clock—2:33 AM.

Tomorrow is already here.

PART III: THE BLACKEST MASS

SUNDAY MORNING BEGINS BRIGHT AND BREEZY. Crows circle the cloudless sky in search of anything edible. A church bell tolls in the distance, though Derry can't hear it.

In the garage, the teen plays his electric guitar loud and hard, rocking his head up and down in sync with the strafe of power chords. He freezes from strumming, letting the last note feedback from the speaker while triumphantly raising his fist into the air, index and pinky fingers extended.

He envisions himself bathed in brilliant stage lights, a huge red neon pentagram behind him, an audience of ravenous fans before him. He basks in their applause and adoration.

"Hail Satan!" he shouts.

His fans scream in affirmation as he flicks his tongue at them.

Derry resumes ripping up the strings of his guitar, creating an infernal cacophony of noise that defies music.

Then he feels a shocking wet cold sliding down his ass crack.

"What the—?!"

Derry wriggles his hips and sticks his hand down the back of his jeans. Shaking out his right leg, an ice cube drops from the cuff onto the concrete floor.

He spins around to see his younger brother Bobby peeping around the garage's interior entryway, holding a glass of cola and snickering at him.

"You little fuckwad!" snaps Derry.

"Lardass!" Bobby replies, then flees into the house.

With his guitar still strapped to him, Derry lunges after his brother, causing him to tug his amp when he stretches the cord too tight. He halts and scoots backward. The speaker teeters on its milk crate but doesn't fall. He mouths profanities as he inspects the connectors.

"Derry—"

He turns to see his mother now standing in the doorway.

"Don't forget to help out Rick today at the store."

"I'd rather forget it," Derry replies.

"Just do it. You already said you would."

"I just said that to shut him up."

"Please, Derry," she pleads. "Don't upset him."

"I don't c—" Derry stops himself from protesting further, his attitude softening as he regards his mother wearing a fretful expression.

"I won't, mom... I'll go in a few minutes."

"Thank you, Derry."

They exchange stiff-lipped, heavy-hearted smiles. Abashed, his mother averts her eyes from his and walks away. Derry grinds his teeth and flexes his jaw.

THE DEMON VISITS Cal in the middle of the night.

"Cal," it whispers.

His eyelids flutter.

Above him, surrounded by a pitch-black void, levitates the otherworldly creature, bewitching Cal with its luminous red eyes and lithe hourglass body. As his vision clears, he recognizes it— her, Natalie—wearing sexy devil lingerie, complete with feathered gargoyle wings and cute strap-on horns.

She floats over Cal, then sensuously mounts him on his bed, straddling his crotch.

"I've wanted you sooo bad."

She undulates her body atop his, moaning with burgeoning ecstasy, her black-lacquered fingernails digging into his bare chest.

"Ohhh, Calvin..."

"Natalie..."

He thrusts his pelvis into hers, professing his love as their bodies merge.

"Calvin!"

Cal opens his eyes, wincing from the sunshine flooding his

room through the window whose curtains his mother has just parted.

He sits up in his bed. Suddenly conscious of his hand down his underwear touching himself, he jerks it away. He bunches up his sheets over his lap to conceal his arousal.

"Jeez, Mom! Can't you knock?"

"I did," she replies. "You didn't answer me."

"Duh," he says, blushing. "I was sleeping."

"You managed to sleep half the day away."

"So?"

"So, I made lunch."

"I'm not hungry."

"It's mac and cheese."

Cal reconsiders. "I'll be out in a minute."

"Don't forget your father and I will be gone tonight."

"I know."

"That means you're on your own for dinner."

"I *know*. Can you leave me alone now?"

His mother smirks at him and exits his room, closing the door behind her.

Cal sighs, rubbing his eyes with the heels of his hands. Swinging his legs off the edge of the bed, he notices brownish red specks stippling his pillow. Exploring his face with his fingertips, he feels the caked blood of pimples that had popped in his sleep. He rises from the bed, shuffles over to the window, and re-shuts the curtains.

With her Jesus-freak mother at church, Natalie readies for the upcoming ritual. She inventories her kit, adding a few new precautionary items to it. She selects her outfit, her jewelry, her makeup. From the hall wall, she takes down the photograph of her father in his racing uniform, removes the cardboard backing from its frame, and peels out his picture—

And she remembers. Her father driving their red Ford Thunderbird, eight-year-old Natalie beside him in the passenger seat. He wears a plaid flannel shirt, she a sunflower yellow dress. She gets angry at him about something, something meaningless now, and she throws her Burger King cup at him. It hits him in his cheek, surprising him. She then remembers rolling, over and over, her small body thrashing against the seat belt. She hears glass crunching, metal crushing. A searing-hot scrap of it strikes her right eye. Then all goes black.

Natalie folds the photo and tucks it into her bra.

She retrieves the jar containing her demon child from the closet. She gazes at it reverentially for a moment, peering into its unformed eyes, then unscrews the lid. Reaching her hand into the jar, she extracts the creature and gently sets it into a Doc Marten shoebox lined with black satin. She slides the uncovered box beneath her bed.

Natalie exits her room with the ritual kit, locking the door behind her.

Her father, swathed in a cornucopia-pattern quilt, sits in his wheelchair in the den, positioned near enough the window so that he can be in the daylight. Maybe he enjoys it, but one cannot tell for certain since his face registers no enjoyment, nor any other emotion.

Natalie kneels down before him, flips up the quilt, and undoes the bottom three buttons of his shirt, exposing his stomach. Between her fingertips, she wields the double-edged blade for a safety razor. She carefully nicks the skin above his father's belly button. She looks up at him, detects no reaction.

She makes intersecting six-inch-long slices into his stomach, then carves a large circle around the lines, working around the seeping blood. Upon finishing, she evaluates her work and nods.

"I'm going to bring you back, daddy," Natalie says to him, kissing his knuckles. "I promise."

After stanching the wounds with a washcloth, she rebuttons his shirt to cover the pentagram, one almost identical to her own.

AFTER HELPING OUT at his stepfather's lighting store—he and Rick had scarcely said three words to one another the entire three hours he was there—Derry picks Natalie up at four p.m. as planned. She has dressed up for the occasion in a black velvet microskirt with black rose lace stockings, thigh-high dominatrix boots, and a skull-bone brocade bustier that boosts her small breasts as much as possible. Derry notices, but tries not to look like he's noticing.

They go to Cal's house. Accepting sodas offered by Cal's mom—Derry and Cal have Cokes, Natalie a 7-Up—the three teens sit out on the slated front stoop, their gazes fixed across the street.

"What about his parents?" Natalie asks.

"He used to live with his mom down in Florida," Cal answers, "but she died a couple of years ago. So now his dad takes care of him. He usually lets him play by himself outside."

"And he sticks around your block?"

"Yeah. Never goes off it. His dad yells at him if he even sees him at the corner."

"Your folks leaving soon?"

"Should be."

"And you said they won't be home until after midnight?"

"Yeah. They're visiting friends in Ravenwood Hills."

"That's where all the rich assholes live," Derry adds. "They probably do that wife-swapping stuff. Bet Cal's mom is a first-prize piece of ass at their parties."

"Fuck you," replies Cal.

"Let's get something straight," Natalie says adamantly. "We're in this together. We are eternally united in the eyes of Satan. There's no backing out. Agreed?"

Derry and Cal pledge themselves.

"Good." Natalie returns her focus onto the house across the street—Tony's house. "Y'know, we're actually doing him a favor. He can never reach his full potential as a mortal, so he can't ever be immortal. Can't be any more than he is now. What kind of life is that to live? At least this way, he won't be a total waste of an existence."

The boys nod, trusting her logic.

"We got a date-date-date with the d-d-devillll!" Derry sings, bopping his head. "That's a Trigger Mortis song."

"Hope he shows," Cal says. "After we do all this, it would suck really hard if Satan stands us up."

"He'll come," Natalie assures them. "'Cause he'll know we truly love him. And he'll reward our love with everything we've ever dreamt of. We can crush anyone who defies us. We'll be invincible."

"I wanna be a metal guitar god," Derry proclaims. "And Cal can be the most insane thrash drummer ever. We're gonna be the most famous band of all bands in all of history. Kings of the fuckin' world." He guzzles his Coke and belches. "Not a bad deal, right?"

"It's more than a deal," Natalie says. "More than a pact. It's a gift from him. A gift for proving we're worthy."

"What if we're not?" Cal asks.

"We *will* be," Natalie replies.

"Sure we will," Derry says, echoing her confidence.

HALF AN HOUR later, Cal's parents pull out of the driveway in their silver Volvo. They've dressed up for the night out, she in a royal blue chiffon blouse, he in a pinstriped sports jacket. They pause at the apron, Cal's mother rolling down the passenger's window.

"Are you kids hanging out here all evening?"

"Maybe," her son answers.

"If you do, don't make a mess."

"Yeah. No *Night of the Living Dead* re-enactments," Cal's father hollers over his wife's shoulder. "And no headbanging the furniture."

"And if you go out tonight," his mother continues, "make sure you leave some lights on."

"And lock everything up," his father adds.

"Okay," Cal says.

Cal's parents rattle off perfunctory goodbyes to them—Cal's father jokingly calls Natalie "Vampira"—then depart for their get-together.

The three teens go inside Cal's house and descend the stairs to the unfinished basement. The concrete-enclosed space accommodates a wooden workbench, an old sofa, an exercise bike, and several storage boxes stacked along the wall.

They clear assorted tools and a broken blender off the workbench, then Derry and Cal move it to the center of the floor. They spread Natalie's black satin blanket over it. Cal rubs his hand across the sheet, sweeping up a tuft of white dog hair.

"It's got fur all over it."

"Doesn't matter," Natalie says. She rocks the workbench. "That leg's too short. Shove a book or something under it."

Cal hunts through the boxes, fetching a couple of *Choose Your Own Adventure* paperbacks from one of them. He slides the books under the stubby leg.

Natalie wobbles the workbench with more stable results. She nods, satisfied.

"Are you sure this table's gonna hold him?" Derry asks.

"It should," Cal answers. "My dad once fixed our big-ass lawn-mower on it."

"Better test it out to be safe," Natalie says. "Derry, hop on."

Derry boosts himself up onto the workbench and lays back. The wood creaks, but does not crack. He fidgets.

"It's not very comfortable."

"It doesn't have to be," Natalie tells him patronizingly. "It's a sacrificial altar."

AFTER COMPLETING PREPARATIONS, the teens wait outside smoking cigarettes on the stoop as dusk creeps over the neighborhood. Above the houses they're able to see the flashing lights of carnival rides—the Ferris Wheel and Pirate Ship—while small bats flit by the orange-tinged clouds.

"There he is," Cal says.

Across the street, Tony exits his house in gray sweatpants and a *Teenage Mutant Ninja Turtles* shirt. Licking a grape popsicle, he stops by an oak tree to watch a colony of ants scurry up and down its trunk.

"Hey, Tony!" Cal shouts.

Tony looks up at him and waves. "Hi Calvin!"

"Come here a sec!"

Tony bustles toward them and halts at the curb, checking the street in both directions for oncoming traffic.

"It's okay, Tony. No cars are comin'."

Tony dashes across the road, joggling his popsicle off its stick.

"How ya doin', Tony?" Cal asks.

"I dropped my ice pop."

"Don't worry about that," Derry says. "We got something better for ya."

"What?"

"We wanted to know if you wanna hang out with us," Derry continues. "If you're not too busy playin' with bugs or whatever."

"I don't know," Tony says.

"What's wrong?"

"It's getting dark."

"So? Ya scared of the dark?"

"No I'm not scared," Tony insists. "But my daddy says I gotta be home before it gets dark out."

"That's too bad, Tony," Natalie says. "We wanted you to join our club."

"You got a club?" Tony says, intrigued.

"Yeah. It's called the Cool Club. We do all these cool things, and we thought since you're a cool guy, you might wanna be part of it."

"What do I do?"

"You just have to come hang out with us right now," Natalie says. "We're having a real important meeting and if you miss it, we can't let you into the club."

"You do wanna be in our cool club, don't you Tony?" Derry asks.

Tony nods. "Uh huh."

Cal drums his fingertips on his jeans, his eyes darting all around him.

"The meeting won't last long," Natalie continues. "And we're only going to be over here at Cal's house, so you won't be far from home. After it's over, we'll walk you back."

"So what d'ya say, buddy?" Derry asks encouragingly. "You in?"

Tony ponders a moment, staring down at his sneakers. "Okay," he says excitedly. "Let me just go tell my dad—"

Natalie shakes her head. "It's getting late. We won't have time for the meeting if we wait up for you."

"Don't worry," Derry says. "We'll call your dad from Cal's house and tell him where you are. Okay?"

Tony grins and agrees. Together they go inside.

TONY SITS IN a plush suede armchair in the den. Derry lies on the couch staring at him. Cal stands across the room near the TV.

Each holds a Dixie cup with a butterfly design.

Natalie approaches with her own cup and a full bottle of Jack Daniels whiskey. She pours all of them a shot, filling Tony's last.

"Here you go, Tony," she says. "This is the official cool drink. It's club tradition for new members to finish off a bottle."

"We share the first cup with you," Derry adds, "then the rest is all yours."

"My daddy drinks that," Tony says, recognizing the label.

"So not only will you be cool," Derry says, "your dad will be proud of you, too."

Tony smiles.

"Now this is strong stuff, Tony," Natalie warns. "So it's best to swallow it quick without tasting it. Okay?"

Tony nods.

"Awesome." She raises her cup to her lips. "Ready..."

The others imitate her.

"Set... and down we go."

They swig their drinks, each flinching as the whiskey hits their throats like a fireball. Tony coughs harshly, his protruding tongue still stained purple from his popsicle.

"It only burns like that for a few sips," Natalie explains. "Then it'll make you feel all warm and fuzzy and won't sting anymore."

"It hurts," Tony rasps, tears streaming down his cheeks.

Natalie refills Tony's cup. "C'mon. Have another."

This time, Tony wavers, crimping his mouth.

"Don't be such a baby, Tony," Derry chides. "We've all done this before. It's just a drink. Right, Cal?"

"Yeah," Cal says. "It's no big deal."

"You have to prove you can be cool like us." Natalie softens her tone. "You don't want to fail the club initiation, do you?"

Tony shakes his head earnestly.

"Of course not. You want to be one of us."

"You can trust us, Tony," Derry says. "We're your friends."

Natalie and Derry begin chanting, "Go, go, go..." After Derry shoots him a look, Cal joins in.

Spurred on, Tony gulps his whiskey, promptly launching into another fit of coughing.

The teens clap for him.

"Alright, Tony!" Derry cheers. "You're the man!"
Tony smiles. "I'm cool!"
Natalie refills his cup.

DERRY AND CAL help carry the highly intoxicated Tony down to the basement, each boy supporting a limp arm over their shoulders, dragging Tony's feet across the concrete floor. They gracelessly hoist him onto the makeshift altar.

Natalie lights several candles throughout the space, then turns off the floor lamps in the farthest corners. She slaps Tony on the cheeks. He responds with soft groans, his eyes remaining closed.

"He's out," Derry says.

"He's heavier than he looks," Cal comments.

"You're just weaker than you think you are," mocks Derry.

"Go suck a duck."

"Stop," Natalie snaps at them. "Now let's get started."

"Should we strip down for this?" Derry asks.

Natalie shakes her head. "We can stay clothed. This invocation is powerful enough. Plus I look really good."

The boys agree.

"How about having another drink?" Cal suggests. "There's still a little JD left."

Derry nods.

"Okay," Natalie says.

Cal retrieves the three-quarters empty bottle from upstairs. They each take a turn knocking back the whiskey, finishing it off. They then lock eyes with one another, summoning their collective courage.

"Alright," Natalie says. "Where's the knife?"

"Here," Cal answers. He hands her a steak knife.

"Really?" Natalie says critically.

Cal and Derry both give her puzzled expressions.

She places the tip of her index finger on the point of the thin blade and jiggles it. "See? This won't cut it. It's got to be sturdier, more like a butcher knife."

"We got one of those in the kitchen," Cal tells her. "I'll go get it."

He rushes toward the stairs, tripping on a couple of steps as he climbs them in his semi-drunk condition. He reaches the kitchen and slides open a drawer, taking from it a bulky-handled, stainless steel chef's knife.

The doorbell rings.

Cal hesitates for an instant, then tiptoes across the kitchen to peer out the window. He sees Tony's father outside on the stoop. Mr. Harrison likewise spots Cal at the window and beckons him to come to the door. Cal walks over and opens it. Mr. Harrison appears sickly in the yellow porch light.

"Hello, Calvin."

"Hi, Mr. Harrison."

"Have you seen Tony?"

"No," Cal answers, acting as clueless as possible. "Why?"

"He hasn't come home yet. And he knows he has to be in before dark."

"Sorry. I haven't seen him... I mean, I saw him playing across the street before, but that was a couple of hours ago. Maybe he got lost?"

"Tony's never wandered off before."

Cal spots a mother escorting her two pre-teen children on the sidewalk by his house. Each child holds a star-shaped Mylar balloon. Their mother hugs a stuffed panda toy under her arm.

"Maybe... he's at the carnival?"

Mr. Harrison considers this. "That's possible. I took him there yesterday. He really loved it. Too much maybe." He expels a nervous chuckle. "He might've remembered the way there. Tony's a smart boy."

"Well... hope you find him."

"Thank you, Calvin."

"No problem." Cal offers a faltering smile.

Mr. Harrison hustles off, heading up the block toward the carnival.

Cal shuts the door, grabs the chef's knife he had placed on the foyer table, and returns to the basement.

"Who was at the door?" Natalie asks.

"Tony's father."

"What'd he want?" Derry asks anxiously.

"He was looking for Tony."

"Shit," Derry says.

Natalie purses her lips, concerned. "So what did you tell him?"

"I said I hadn't seen him for a while, and that maybe he was at the carnival."

"You don't think he suspected anything?"

"Nah. He bought it."

"You sure?"

"Yeah. Definitely."

"Good." Natalie releases a relieved breath. "Then we can get down to business."

NATALIE GRIPS THE knife with two hands above Tony's chest, the blade aimed at his heart. Derry and Cal wrap their hands around hers.

"We recite the invocation three times, then we do it when I say 'now,'" Natalie says over Tony's nasally snores. "Ready?"

Cal nods mechanically. Primed with anticipation, Derry also nods, cracking his neck and wetting his lips.

"Okay." Natalie stiffens her jaw. "Let's begin."

Thrice they incant, "The power of Satan impels us."

"Now!" yells Natalie.

Balking at the very last moment, Cal swiftly retracts his hands. Natalie and Derry plunge the knife into Tony's chest.

Tony's eyes bulge. He bolts upright and emits a piercing, agonized scream.

The teens recoil from him.

Tony slowly reclines again on the altar bench, his scream trailing off.

"Jesus!" Derry blurts.

Natalie glares at him. "Shhhh!" she says, sternly raising her finger. "Don't you utter that name again. Especially right now. Let's not forget what we're doing here."

"Sorry," Derry replies. "It just came out."

The teens stand a few feet away from the altar, staring at Tony. He lies motionless, the knife stuck halfway in his chest, his mouth gaping.

Cal cups his palm over his own mouth and puffs out his cheeks, then bounds up the stairs.

"Where's he going?" Natalie asks.

"Think he's gonna ralph," Derry answers.

Minutes later, Cal kneels before his toilet, heaving into the bowl. Natalie and Derry watch him from the threshold of the bathroom.

"Well, this is great," Natalie says, exasperated. "We now know Cal can't hack human sacrifice."

Cal withdraws his face from the bowl and leans against the mint green tub.

"I'm fine," he wheezes. "Think it's just something I ate before... this."

Derry examines the contents of the toilet. "Is that chicken?"

"Just hurry and get your shit together," Natalie barks at Cal. "Might've fucked things up by now."

Natalie storms away from the bathroom. Derry stays with Cal as he recovers.

"You all right, dude?"

"We're gonna get in so much trouble for this."

"No, Cal, we won't," Derry tells his friend confidently. "After this, we'll never get in any trouble again."

THE TEEN TRIO, led by Natalie, head back downstairs. Once her eye re-adjusts to the dim candlelight, it widens.

The altar is empty.

"Where'd he go?"

"Shit. He was dead," Derry remarks. "...Wasn't he?"

They dither a moment, baffled. Then they begin searching the basement.

"Tony," Derry calls. "Where are ya, buddy?"

Natalie switches on the floor lamps to see better. They inspect around the storage boxes, probe behind the sofa, and peek beneath the altar blanket to no avail.

"Hey," Cal says. "Over here."

He points to droplets of blood speckling the floor, leading to the stairs.

"Shit," Derry says.

The teens find Tony outside, lumbering through Cal's yard toward the driveway. They race up behind him. The knife is still embedded in Tony's chest, his shirt soaked with blood. Mucous runs from his nose, collecting on his jutting lower lip. Natalie and Derry clamp their hands onto his arms and shoulders, slowing him down.

"Whoa, Tony," Natalie says. "Where are you going?

"I wanna go home," he croaks.

"What are you talking about? The meeting's not over yet."

"I don't... don't feel good."

"We'll take care of ya," Derry assures him.

Tony continues to feebly, futilely resist. "You... hurt me."

"We don't have time for this," Natalie growls.

She spots a potbellied man in a bathrobe exiting the backdoor of the house adjacent to Cal's, toting a couple of bloated garbage bags.

"C'mon, Tony," Cal pleads. "Let us help you."

"Nooo!" Tony screams.

Natalie grabs him by the nape of his neck and, with all her might, slams him face forward against the wall of Cal's house. The knife sinks deeper into him, almost to its hilt.

Tony gasps and gags. Blood bubbles from his mouth, dribbling down the white vinyl siding. Natalie and Derry hold him up as his life drains from him.

They keep stone still until the neighbor is done noisily dumping the garbage bags into a trashcan. He returns into his house, oblivious to the atrocity occurring only a few feet beyond his property line.

The teens lie Tony on the ground. For leverage, Natalie places her foot on his collar bone and yanks the knife out of him.

"Let's get him back inside," she says.

Derry and Cal lift Tony's body and lug his dead weight into the house, Natalie vigilantly following on their heels.

AFTER RESETTING TONY on the altar bench, Natalie works rigorously on carving open his chest with a box cutter while Derry sops up the blood with a bath towel. Cal aims a trembling flashlight on the messy operation.

"Grab me the scissors," Natalie instructs Derry.

He wipes the perspiration beading on his forehead with his knuckle, leaving a smear of Tony's blood there. He then picks up a pair of culinary scissors from the array of other nonsurgical household implements fanned on a folding tray table.

Derry waits to pass Natalie the scissors as she uses both her hands to pry apart the flesh of Tony's chest in order to expose the ribcage.

"You're pretty good at this," Derry says.

"Dissected a baby pig in my old school," Natalie replies. She wiggles the middle finger of her left hand. "Cut through that bone next to this finger."

"Me?" asks Derry.

"Yeah. I have to hold this open."

Derry warily pinches the thick bone with the scissor and, with some effort, snips it off.

"And that one below it."

He repeats the procedure. Flinching, Natalie jerks her hand away and squints at her ring finger.

"Damn it! You nipped me. Be careful."

Derry nods. "Sorry."

She re-splays Tony's cleaved chest. "Take those pieces out."

Derry puts the scissors down on the tray table and reaches into Tony to pluck out the two bloody rib bones. He drops them onto the floor.

"Now give me the paring knife," Natalie says.

"Which one is that?" asks Derry.

"That small one."

He passes it to her. She inserts the sharp blade into the ribcage and spends some time slicing through fibrous tissue and blood vessels. She then sets the knife aside and dunks her hands into the cavity, gets a secure grip on Tony's heart, and raises it from his chest.

Cupping the organ in her palms, she elevates it up above her head.

Cal switches off the flashlight. He and Derry silently, solemnly observe Natalie in the candlelight. She shuts her eye and rolls her head on her shoulders, as if in a trance.

"Master," she recites, "we honor you with this sacrifice. May you feast upon its energy, and accept us as your faithful servants, and grant us all the powers of your dominion so we may serve you here on Earth. We declare you our lord and protector. Hail Satan!"

"Hail Satan!" Derry and Cal parrot.

"We summon you, o Master. Reveal yourself to us—"

"Oh my God!"

The teens immediately redirect their attentions to Cal's father, standing frozen at the bottom of the stairs.

"Shit... Dad?"

"What the hell are you kids up to?" He focuses on his son. "Calvin?"

"Uh," Cal fumbles to explain. "We're just... pretending..."

His father's expression of discomposure and disbelief does not wane.

"You're... home early?"

"Your mother wasn't feeling well." He scans the gory scene. "So then, this is all... another fake thing of yours?"

Cal nods.

"Yeah, Mr. Virgil," Derry affirms. "We're just, like, making a movie. Y'know? Like we did last summer."

Cal's father nods, moves closer. "Where's the video camera—"

THE LOUD *POP!* next to him makes Cal jump. He pivots his head to see Natalie now aiming a silver pistol like a TV cop. A wisp of smoke issues from its barrel.

Cal looks back at his father. A dark stain spreads across his shirt from the center of his chest. He flumps against the wall and sinks to the floor.

"Dad!"

Cal sprints to his father, his body quivering, his eyes glazing over. Cal kneels down beside him. Cal's father reaches out and firmly grasps his son's wrist, his mouth trying to form words that never come.

"Burt?" Cal's mother calls from the top of the steps, her voice brimming with concern. "Is everything okay? What was that noise?"

Brandishing the gun, Natalie charges toward the stairway. She slips in Tony's blood coating the floor. With a yelp, she collapses onto her knee, twisting her ankle.

"Shit!" she huffs through gritted teeth. She struggles to rise to her feet, wincing.

Cal comprehends her mien—determined, deranged.

"Mom, get out of here!"

"Calvin? What's happening down there?"

Natalie, her clothes sopping with blood, whips her head toward Derry.

"Derry, get her!"

"No!" Cal yells.

"Go Derry!" Natalie commands. "Before she ruins everything!"

Derry hesitates before hastily making a decision. He races to the foot of the stairs and looks up at Cal's mother, clutching a can of ginger ale in her hand.

She sees his frenzied, blood-smeared face.

"Derry?"

"Mom!" Cal screams. "Run!"

Fear envelops her face. She hurls the aluminum can at Derry. It strikes him squarely in the forehead, sloshing soda all over him. He reels backward.

"Owww... goddamnit!"

Cal's mother flees. Rubbing his head, Derry clumsily bounds up the stairs after her.

Natalie, holding the pistol rigid against her thigh, limps toward Cal.

Cal sobs as he watches his father draw his final breaths.

"Had to be done, Cal," Natalie says. "You know that."

"You fuck!" Eyes wild with rage, Cal lunges and pushes her into the altar bench. Together they tumble to the floor, toppling the tray table of sacrificial instruments. He furiously punches her in the head, knocking off her eyepatch.

Her own anger-fueled adrenaline spiking, Natalie shoves Cal off her, sending him sliding across the slick floor into the storage boxes. She snatches the paring knife from the floor, scrambles toward him, and stabs him in the throat. She then slashes at his face, creating crisscrossing rivulets of blood. Her accompanying shrieks sound inhuman, bestial.

CAL'S MOTHER RUNS from the house, her hysterical face bleached in moonlight.

"Help!" she bawls to anybody who might hear her. "Help me!"

She beelines for a neighbor's house, banging on the front door with both her fists. Nobody answers.

"Please," she cries. "Someone help me."

"Mrs. Virgil!"

Cal's mother whirls toward Derry as he emerges from the shadows a few feet away from her, his hands outstretched in a reassuring gesture.

"Relax," he tells her, panting and sweaty. "Everything's cool."

"Stay away from me!"

"Mr. Virgil's hurt. He wants you." Derry inches toward her. "Come on, Mrs. Virgil. You gotta come with me."

He strides further into the porch light of the house. Beholding his blood-smirched face again, she bolts across the lawn away from him. Derry leaps at her, tackling her down. She screams and scratches at him.

"Hey!" A burly neighbor in plaid pajamas rushes toward the fray. He puts Derry in a headlock and wrests him off Cal's mother. Derry flails his legs and tugs at the neighbor's muscular arms, but cannot free himself from his vise-tight hold.

"Calm down!" the neighbor demands. "Y'hear me? Just calm the hell down!"

Derry continues to writhe, his strength ebbing. Cal's mom lies curled on the grass, weeping. Somewhere a dog yowls.

NATALIE LOOMS OVER Cal, lying lifeless against the boxes, his face resembling a patty of chopped raw meat. She studies him emotionlessly. In a puddle of his blood rests the crinkled photo of her father in his racing uniform. She picks it up, then the pistol, leaving her sodden eyepatch on the floor.

Natalie's glassy eyes drift to the altar. In her blurred, rippling vision, she perceives a hulking, angular shape on the altar bench—the manifestation of her winged demon child, now the size of a full-grown man, perched formidably over Tony's body, its glowing ruby eyes fixed on Natalie.

She hears the wail of approaching sirens.

"Take me, Master."

Natalie places the barrel of the gun beneath her chin and pulls the trigger.

"OUR GUEST ON today's program," announces a crisply coifed, sharply dressed talk show host, speaking into a handheld microphone in front of a studio audience, "appearing live via satellite from Longrow Prison, is eighteen-year-old Derrick Rhodes..."

The host saunters across the stage to a large screen, on which is a police mugshot of Derry.

"...the young man convicted in two of the most brutal murders in the state's history. Murders that were part of a grisly, Satanic ritual. Murders that scarred his town and shocked our nation. When we return, we'll meet Derrick and talk about what led him down this dark path of violence."

The host then sweeps his arm toward three attractive women seated on the stage.

"And we'll learn why these three successful, sexy ladies want to marry him!"

The audience whoops in approval.

"All this and more, comin' at ya. Stay with us!"

Wearing an orange jumpsuit, Derry, his hair now cut short, sits at a table in a prison conference room, bathed in portable halogen lights, a lavalier mic clipped to his collar. He smokes a cigarette while watching the small monitor near him airing *The Barry Palmer Show*'s opening credits.

A suntanned middle-aged man wearing headphones operates the tripod-mounted Betacam, behind him an armed guard posted at the room's single door.

"We got ninety seconds before we go live," the cameraman says.

Derry nods.

"So, how old are you again?"

"Eighteen."

"Jeez, you're the same age as my daughter. Actually, she just turned nineteen. Goes to college in Los Angeles. Studying art and abnormal psychology. She'd love you... I mean, I'm sure she'd find you interesting... to talk to."

Displaying zero interest in having this discussion, Derry takes another drag of his cigarette.

The cameraman fishes his wallet from his jeans pocket and produces a small photo of a girl in a high school graduation gown.

He holds it up for Derry to see. He glances at the picture.

"That's my daughter. Megan. Most people call her Meg."

Derry, still disinterested, studies the smoke swirling from the tip of his cigarette.

The cameraman replaces the photo into his wallet. "Ever been to L.A.?"

Derry shakes his head.

"Well, I'm sure you'll get a chance to someday. You still got a lot of life ahead of you. Plenty of time to straighten yourself out, get your act together."

"Y'think?" Derry says.

"Sure you will," the cameraman replies, not catching Derry's snark. He hears a voice broadcast through his headphones. "Ten seconds."

Derry has a final hit off his cigarette and crushes it out in a foil ashtray.

"Ready to be famous, kid?"

With his cuffed hands, Derry brushes his hair from his brow, looks directly into the camera, and presents his most superstar smile.

A MANY SPLENDID THING

BY PATRICK THOMAS

The cop thought I was a jackass. I felt the same way about him.

"So, you just happened to come across a dead body? Sounds fishy to me."

"I don't see why it's so hard to believe," I said, beginning to think calling the cops had been a bad idea. The only way my dad would even notice I was missing was if I wasn't home to make dinner.

"You said you lived over on Denmark Avenue," Officer Myers said. "That's over two miles away. What are you doing all the way over here on Wire Street?"

"I was going to see a friend about some homework." Which was mostly true.

"Can your friend verify where you were?"

I looked at the flatfoot and shook my head. "I hadn't gotten there yet." That part wasn't exactly true. I had been by Jenny's house three times. I just hadn't got up the nerve to ring her doorbell yet. She was the most gorgeous girl in the senior class. I had the hugest crush on her, but she didn't feel the same way. Yet.

The cop wrote in his pad. "And how did you find the body?"

"Just like I told you. I was riding by the woods and saw the sun shining off something metal. I went to check it out, and when I got to the edge of the woods, I smelled something awful. I was expecting it to be a raccoon or some animal, but instead, it was a body. The metal was the belt buckle. I went down to the gas station to call the cops and here you are."

"You know what stinks?" Officer Myers said. "This story of yours. I think that you better come down to the station to answer some more questions."

"I don't know what else I could tell you," I said.

"Ease up, Myers. Jethro is a good kid. I was at his Christening." My Dad's pal, Sergeant Phil Hansen, had walked up behind me. "Give him a break. From the looks, our stiff's been dead for weeks and he had a bottle of rum in his pocket. Probably snuck out to get drunk then fell in the reservoir over there and drowned. The corpse eventually floated down to the drainage gully over here."

Officer Myers made a face like he had sucked on an especially sour lemon. "Maybe, but the simplest answer is not always the right one."

A Studebaker pulled up. A man in a black suit and fedora stepped out holding a matching black leather bag.

"Myers, take the coroner down to the body and I'll finish this interview."

"Sure, Sarge." Myers glared daggers at me then double-timed it away, leading the coroner into the drainage gully.

"Jethro," Sergeant Hansen said, "don't let Myers get to you. He thinks everybody's guilty, but sometimes it makes him a good cop. How ya holding up? Can't be easy finding something like that. Especially when the dead guy looks to be a kid about your age."

I shrugged. "I'm okay I guess."

"Good. Did you notice anyone nearby?"

I shook my head. "No."

Sergeant Hansen put a comforting hand on my shoulder. "That's enough for now. You remember anything else, call me, okay?"

"Sure."

"Jethro, you want me to give you a ride home?"

"Naw. My dad'll kill me if he saw me coming home in a police car, even yours. Besides, I have my bike."

Sergeant Hansen laughed. "Don't let your old man kid you. Back when we were about your age, we did a few stupid things that got us in a bit of trouble, too. How's he doing?"

He was doing lousy and had become a drunk, but I couldn't exactly say that to his friend. "He's still upset about Mom."

"Can't say I blame him. If my woman ran off with another man, I'd find something he was guilty of and send him off to jail for a long time."

That'd be nice, but Dirk Earls was a ridiculously large man, like six-five and three hundred pounds. My dad's maybe five-nine and one-eighty. Still, that never stopped Dad from rumbling with a guy twice his size, and even winning.

Dad's a scrapper and Dirk might have lost, but Dad couldn't bring himself to do it. He just didn't have the heart to make the woman he loved sad by beating the crap out of her new boy-friend, even though she broke his heart. In Dad's mind, if he couldn't pound the guy, that left one other option—crawl inside a bottle.

Problem was, he had forgotten to crawl back out. He manages to stop boozing just long enough to go to work.

"Jethro, tell your old man I said hi and that he and I need to go for drinks."

That was the last thing Dad needed, but I nodded and said, "Sure."

"And I know this won't be a problem, but I have to tell you not to leave town until we finish the investigation. I know you just found the body, but the detectives have to clear the case and if you disappear, it would look awfully suspicious."

"You don't need to worry about me. I ain't never been out of Montague Falls and I doubt that's going to change anytime soon."

"You sure about that ride?"

I nodded. "I'm good.

I thought about going past Jenny's house again. If I rang her bell now, I'd have a pretty cool story to tell. Maybe she'd be impressed. Maybe she might go out with me or even to the dance. Unfortunately, she lived in the opposite direction, and Myers was still glaring at me from down in the gully like he thought I'd killed this guy. Better not give him any more reason to suspect me for something I didn't do.

By the time I got home, Dad was already there, plopped down in his easy chair with a bottle of Ballantine beer in his hand and an empty shot glass on the table beside him. He was watching Uncle Milty on the flickering TV screen. Our reception wasn't the best.

"Hi, Dad."

My father's eyes darted from the television screen to the door, realized it was only me, then went right back to watching Milton

Berle selling the virtues of a new 1955 Buick.

"How was work?" I asked. That got me a grunt. In a normal father-son conversation, I might've waited a couple of beats for him to ask me about my day, but I knew if I did that I'd be waiting 'til the cows came home and we didn't own any so that was never going to happen unless some lost cow wandered by.

"I found a dead body today."

Amazingly, that tidbit made Dad turn his full attention from Uncle Milty to me.

"You did what?"

"Found a dead guy in a drainage gully."

"You sure he was dead?"

The question seemed more than a bit insulting, but I answered anyway. This was the longest conversation I've had with my father in weeks. "Yep."

"How? You poke it with a stick or something?"

"Didn't need to. It was bloated and stank like death itself. There were maggots all over him."

It must have been a good enough answer for him because Dad took a long swig of beer. "You call the cops?"

"Yep. Phil Hansen says hi."

"You tell him I said hi back."

I wasn't likely to see the cop again so I don't know how Dad figured I could pass along his message, but if I pointed that out, he'd smack me for cracking wise.

I miss the days when he was sober and had a sense of humor. Since Mom ran off, he's been nothing but drunk, miserable, or angry. Usually all three.

When it first happened, he couldn't hit Mom because she was a woman, or Dirk because it would make Mom sad. Unfortunately, Mom didn't care enough about her only son to be upset if I got hit, so I was fair game.

One night after a pretty impressive bender, Dad even blamed me for her cheating and leaving. It was my fault because them having a kid had taken all the fun out of their marriage. He figured if they'd never had me, she never would've left. He told me just looking at me sometimes reminded him of all the nasty things Mom did.

"You made sure the cops know you didn't do it, right?"

"Why would I have to do that?"

"Phil Hansen's always telling me how the DA wants the cops to hand him open-and-shut cases. Being actually guilty is just a bonus."

"Guy named Myers came right out and asked me. I told him 'no'."

"Good. I guess your head ain't a total waste of space after all. Now go make dinner." His attention shifted back to Uncle Milty's antics. "After you bring me another beer."

I was no dummy, so I brought him a brew from the ice-box first and then went back into the kitchen to make dinner. Although making dinner might've been an overly generous description. I preheated the oven, then took a couple of frozen TV dinners out of the freezer and put them in. I didn't bother to ask my father which kind he wanted. Just about the only thing my mother could make well was meatloaf, so that was always his choice. I don't think he could enjoy a dinner that didn't hit him in the emotional gut.

I placed our dinners on the coffee table and settled on the couch to watch television.

Dad ended up passing out in his easy chair and I took myself up to bed.

Dad woke up the same time every morning without any alarm clock and made it to work without any sign of a hangover. The drinking didn't affect his job at all, just every other aspect of his life, including his relationship with his son.

He yelled once for my feet to hit the floor. Beyond that, if I was late for school, it was on me.

High school wouldn't be so bad if it weren't for the other students. Not all of them. Mainly just the self-entitled jerks like Pete Charles and his gang. He came from a little bit of money and was of the mind that this was basically his world and everyone else was trespassing.

I ain't going to grovel to some prick because some accident of fate made him rich and me poor. The conflicts between us stopped short of him laying hands on me these days, but I can't lay claim to being the reason for that.

Back when we were freshman at Van Buren High, before my mom abandoned us to shack up with a Neanderthal, Pete and two of his buddies—Dean Wright and Stumpy Brown—beat the crap out of me and stole my cash. When I got home, my dad saw what happened and hit the roof.

I'd been in fights before. Some I won, some I didn't, but my dad had no issue with those. What my dad did have a problem with was three of them beating on me at the same time. So he threw me in his Packard and we drove over to Rocko's Bar on Essex Street, where the fathers of all three boys were known to toss drinks back.

Turns out all three of them had bellied up to the bar that night. Dad asked what they were going to do about their sons' behavior. The three fathers were unified in telling my blue-collar dad to buzz off. It was always a bad idea to talk down to my dad or tell him what to do.

Dad spun Mr. Charles around and socked him in the jaw. He went down like it was made of glass. Next, he went after Stumpy and Dean's fathers. I just stood and watched.

I've never been so impressed by my father. He beat all three of them until they looked as bad as I did, maybe even worse.

"Make sure your sons play fair with my boy, catch my drift?"

"They're just boys being boys," Pete's dad said. "Let your son fight his own battles."

"That's what I'm trying to do. They fight him one at a time or not at all. They come at him like that again and I'll have to step in."

"You're going to beat up high school kids?" Mr. Charles said.

"Nope. That would be wrong. They're just boys." Dad squatted down and grabbed Pete's dad by the collar of his fancy shirt and lifted him off the floor. "I'll come after the three of you. Whatever they do to my boy, I give each of you twice as bad."

"I'll have you arrested," Mr. Charles said.

Which is when Phil Hansen stepped up from the back of the bar and looked down at the three beaten men.

"Well, well, well. What do we have here? Looks like the lot of you must've fallen down the stairs. I know that's what must have happened because my good friend here has been with me the whole evening."

Pete's father glared daggers at the sergeant but didn't say a word. Phil Hansen's family was richer and better connected than the Charles' were. The mayor was his uncle and the DA his cousin, so going up against Hansen would have been a bad idea even if he wasn't a cop. I heard he might be in line for Chief of Police.

"You look like you've already had too much to drink," Hansen said, "so why don't you head home and keep a leash on your own children. I'm rather partial to Jethro here myself, you get me?"

All three men nodded then scowled and cursed under their breath as they helped each other limp out the door.

Pete, Stumpy, and Dean were very careful not to lay hands on me after that. That didn't mean they stopped making my life miserable.

"Hi ya, Jethro," Dean said in science class, right before the starting bell rang. The three of them leaned against their desks. "How's your mommy?"

Pete's laughter mocked me like an eagle would a rat that was trying to fly. "Come on now. You know perfectly well she's out whoring around instead of being poor Jethro's mother. Of course, who can blame her? Anything is better than looking at that puss every day."

"True, but she's with just one guy," I said. "The way I hear it, your mom sluts it up with the gardener, the mailman, the paper boy, and your dad's boss to make sure he doesn't get fired. Which I suppose is a bit better than Dean and Stumpy's moms. They've given up on anyone ever sleeping with them again ever since that drunk hobo ran off terrified because they tried to seduce him."

Jenny, who was wearing a knee-length skirt and Bobby sox which drove me wild, actually chuckled in the corner and I stood up a little straighter. I still hadn't talked to her since I found the body. Wonder if I could get her alone after class to tell her about it.

Stumpy got up in my face. "Why I aughta…"

He shut up mid-sentence. We all stopped what we were doing because Mrs. Carmine had entered the classroom and was slinking toward her desk. Every guy in the room turned and tried to look like we weren't staring or drooling.

Today her skirt rose up above her knees and her sweater made her chest look like it belonged on the far side of perfect. She had a face that would make movie stars jealous and golden curly hair so pretty that it hurt not to be able to reach out and touch it. Mrs. Carmine's blue eyes shone like pools that any guy would happily drown in. If the school caught fire, we wouldn't notice unless the fire got too close to her.

"All right, everyone, in your seats," Mrs. Carmine said, stepping behind her desk and sadly hiding the best gams in town. "Time to learn some science. Today we are doing chemistry."

"I'd like to teach her some chemistry," Pete whispered. Stumpy and Dean chuckled.

Truth was, all the guys I knew in the senior class felt that way. Mrs. Carmine was the unobtainable perfect woman. But a guy can dream, can't he? Still, my science grade was higher than it ever was before, just because I wanted to make Mrs. Carmine happy.

"We are going to be going over the reactivity of an alkali metal with water," she said. "Remember, a good scientist controls all the variables."

Mrs. Carmine lectured us on how to be careful, then handed out beakers filled with warm water, then gave each of us a piece of sodium metal about the size of a pea which she pulled out of a bottle of mineral oil with a tweezer. We were supposed to use tweezers to put it in the water when she told us to. When she went past her desk, her hip knocked a paper on the floor. I couldn't take my eyes off her curves as she bent over with her back to the class to pick it up. That's why I didn't notice Pete and his gang all dump their sodium metal chunks into my beaker.

My beaker erupted like a volcano, producing a flash of light and shooting water all over my desk and the floor.

I realized what Pete, Stumpy, and Dean had done as soon as I heard them laughing.

I'd never been so mortified. Not that I was brainy, but to look like I screwed up in front of Mrs. Carmine was unbearable.

"I'm so sorry, Mrs. Carmine. It was an accident. I'll clean it up."

She walked over and placed her palm on the back of my hand. From that moment on, the rest the world ceased to exist. The only thing that mattered was her skin touching mine.

"It's okay, Jethro. Mistakes happen. The important thing is to learn from them and don't make them a second time. Have you learned from this?"

I nodded, not trusting my mouth to be able to speak words instead of goofy sounds. And then she took her hand off of mine and the real world came back into focus.

"Do you think you'll make the same mistake again?"

"No, ma'am."

"Do I look like a ma'am to you?"

"No, ma'am. I mean, no, Mrs. Carmine."

"And that, class, is what happens when the chemical reaction sprays out molten sodium metal and hydrogen gas ignites." She looked at my beaker and my desk. "How interesting. There are three pieces of sodium metal in your beaker, yet the piece I gave you is still on your desk. I wonder how something like that could have happened?"

She turned to look at my tormentors who, in turn, focused their eyes on their shoes or the ceiling.

"Everyone else who still has their sodium metal, use the tweezers to put it in the water."

The others all got a nice fizzing reaction that stayed in their beakers.

The bell rang and everyone rushed out. Science was our last class of the day and, since it was Friday, of the week.

Mrs. Carmine stepped in front of me and the door. "Wait a second, Jethro. Would you stay and help me clean up this mess like you offered?"

I nodded. "I'd love to." Idiot. Play it cool. "I mean, sure."

It didn't take long. I even helped her pick up the sodium metal chunk remnants and put them back in mineral oil and then dump the water.

"We're pretty much done here. It's Friday, so I'm sure you want to go home and hang out with your friends for the weekend."

"There's not a lot waiting for me at home, and I can see my friends anytime. I'd rather help you."

She rubbed my back. It felt wonderful.

"Aren't you sweet? My husband is gone for the weekend, visiting his sick mother. I do have to do some grocery shopping and could use a hand with all the bags. If you could help me with that, I would be most appreciative."

"Sure," I said as I tried to control the goofy grin on my face.

I HONESTLY COULDN'T tell you how long the grocery shopping took. It was one of those rare moments in life when time didn't matter. Though Mrs. Carmine didn't really seem to need any help with her groceries. She wasn't some old granny who was having trouble carrying things. She could've easily handled them herself. And the market had bag boys who would have taken the bags to her car for her.

I tried to figure out why had she asked me to come along to do a task that didn't really need to be done. My mind was racing and settled on the idea that maybe the romantic feelings I had towards her were reciprocated. My crush on Jenny paled in comparison, but I figured with her I might have a chance. Not a good one, but it existed. Mrs. Carmine liking me was unthinkable, except maybe it wasn't.

Then my common sense chimed in. There was no way Mrs. Carmine would like a guy like me. I couldn't even get Jenny to pay attention to me and we were the same age and had known each other since kindergarten.

Why would a goddess like Mrs. Carmine feel anything toward me more than a teacher did for any student? Maybe she'd heard about my not-so-happy home and realized I didn't want to go there and was just giving me something to do.

Mrs. Carmine paid and I carried the groceries to her car and loaded everything in the trunk.

"Thank you, Jethro. I appreciate your help." She smiled, and I almost forgot how to talk.

I managed to say, "You're welcome. But…" Then my mouth stopped working.

"But what?"

I hadn't meant to give voice to what was in my head but since I'd already started I might as well finish. "Why did you ask me to help you? You're not some helpless, frail woman. You could have done all this by yourself. I don't get it."

Somehow her smile got even brighter, and she touched my shoulder. I had to make a conscious effort not to let my knees buckle.

The most beautiful woman I had ever met laughed and it sounded like sex. Or at least what I imagined sex would sound like. "Isn't it obvious? I enjoy your company." She looked down at her receipt. "Darn it. They forgot to give me my green stamps."

People loved collecting their green stamps. Save up enough and you could get all sorts of free stuff from the store's catalogs.

"I'll go get them," I said.

"No, I'll do it. I won't be a minute."

I hated that she left, but enjoyed watching her go.

Across the street, the Burger Dome parking lot was packed, the waitresses frantically zipping along on roller skates. I could smell the burgers from here, but I couldn't think about anything other than Mrs. Carmine and what she looked like underneath that tight sweater.

Until my daydream was interrupted by a Neanderthal.

"Well if it is isn't little baby Jethro."

I turned to face a guy who looked more ape than human. At six-feet-five inches he was at least a hundred pounds heavier than I was and his right arm was wrapped around the shoulders of the only woman I've known since before I was born.

I screwed up. Whenever I was in town, I was careful to keep an eye out to make sure I avoided Dirk and my mother, but I was so distracted by Mrs. Carmine that I forgot to look.

I glared at the pair.

"Aren't you going to say hi to your mom, little boy? Didn't she raise you right?"

"I like to say she did, but she taught me not to lie."

Dirk frowned and glared back. Even though he was a grown man, he slicked his hair back with enough grease to lubricate a new '55 Chevy.

"Are you trying to make your mom look bad?"

"I don't have to do that. She's done a great job of it all by herself. Well, maybe not all by herself."

"Trying to insult me now, boy? Maybe you get away with that fresh talk with your limp-dick daddy, but you ain't getting away with talking to me like that. But since you're her kid, I'd let it slide this once if you apologize to my Junie right now."

My mother giggled as Dirk grabbed her ass and gave it a squeeze. She did it back, right there in public. A class act, my mom.

"Start apologizing now, boy."

Mom giggled again. "The only thing I'm sorry about is that I had a child."

I couldn't take it anymore and lashed out. "And I'm sorry you didn't leave sooner."

My mom stopped laughing for a second. It almost looked like my words had hurt her. I hope they had, but a hammer smashing her hand wouldn't begin to be as painful as what she did to me and Dad.

"And I'm sorry the best you could find was a Neanderthal."

"Who you calling knee-ann-alcohol?" Dirk growled.

"You're right, Dirk. Calling you a Neanderthal is an insult to all the other cavemen. I'm just going to refer to you as a gorilla. So, Mom, when the two of you are done in bed, do you have to give him a banana for doing a good job?"

As soon as I said it, I knew I'd gone too far, but I was angry and I was hurt. I was doing my best to share those emotions with those who'd unleashed the pain on me.

Dirk charged at me like a rhino, only leading with his fist instead of a horn. I saw his punch coming and got out of the way. Problem was, Dirk knew how to turn and came at me again. This time his fist connected with my shoulder. It hurt, but gave me an opening.

I slammed my knuckles into his gut, but it only made him laugh. I think it hurt me more than it did him. I looked around, but nobody was nearby, although some people started to walk over to enjoy the show. None seemed in a hurry to stop it.

I did it again, but my punches left me open, and Dirk clipped my jaw and knocked me into the brick wall of the grocery. He yanked me back toward him with one hand and punched my stomach with the other. My belly exploded with pain and I tried to throw up, but his next punch caught me mid-vomit and stopped my lunch from coming up, but not me from crumpling to the sidewalk.

He'd obviously won the fight, but that wasn't enough for Dirk. He kicked me in my ribs. I moved my arms to block his boot and then he just kicked me somewhere my arms weren't.

People in the crowd finally told Dirk to leave me alone, but still, nobody stepped in. Then I heard a woman's mirth and looked up through the pain to see my own mother not trying to put an end to my misery by telling Dirk to stop. Instead she was laughing as her boyfriend kicked the crap out of her only son.

"That's enough. Back away from him now!" shouted a forceful voice.

It was Mrs. Carmine coming back out of the grocery store.

Dirk seemed shocked that it was a woman telling him what to do, which may be why he stopped kicking. I tried to stand up and get away but the best that I could manage was rolling in the opposite direction before more jolts of agony hurtled through me.

"Buzz off, missy. This ain't your concern," Dirk said.

"That's my son and as his mother. I'm allowed to beat him for misbehaving."

"Well, you aren't doing the beating. This monster is."

Dirk snorted and kicked me again, making me curl up in the fetal position.

"I said stop and I meant it, mister. Touch Jethro again and you'll have to deal with me," Mrs. Carmine yelled, stepping between me and Dirk.

"Lady, normally I don't hit dames, but you better get out of my face or I'll make an exception."

"Do that and I'll call a cop," Mrs. Carmine shot back.

Dirk stepped forward. "Assuming you can still talk."

A small crowd had gathered to watch, not that any of them tried to help.

"Oh, I'll talk," Mrs. Carmine whispered. "I'll tell them how you threatened to maul me, and Jethro tried to defend my honor."

"You wouldn't dare," Dirk growled.

Her voice still low, my teacher whispered, "Willing to bet your freedom on it?"

"You're a lying bitch and I'll tell the cops that!" my mom shouted.

Mrs. Carmine smiled. "Who do you think the boys in blue will believe? Me? Or a tired old hag, years past her prime who has to date an ape like this loser?"

"I'll claw your eyes out," Mom said.

"You try and I'll tell them how you said you wanted to watch me and your ape man go at it," Mrs. Carmine said, just loud enough for the four of us to hear, but not the crowd. "Walk away now."

"This ain't over," Dirk grumbled, pointing at me. I pointed back at him but used a different finger.

"No reason it has to be," Pete said, suddenly stepping out of the crowd. "Beat the prick some more."

"Excuse me, Mr. Charles?" Mrs. Carmine said in her angry teacher voice.

Pete went white as a sheet. "Mrs. Carmine? I didn't see you there." I guess he was too busy looking at my blood dripping onto the concrete.

"Peter, I expected more from you."

"I was just kidding," Pete said, then added in a voice loud enough for the crowd to hear, "Mind your own beeswax, mister, and don't be beating up a high school kid!"

Dirk snorted and rolled his eyes, but he and my mother left. Not only didn't she say goodbye or ask if I was okay, but mother dearest didn't even spare me a backwards glance.

Embarrassed that the prettiest teacher in history witnessed him being an ass, Pete headed for the hills in the opposite direction.

Mrs. Carmine bent down in front of me. From the worried expression on her face, I must have looked a mess.

"Jethro, are you okay?"

"I'm fine." Having the woman of my wildest dreams concerned for me made me high enough that, for a moment, I was feeling no pain.

"Can you get up?"

"Sure." I tried to stand, but stopped halfway up and sat back down. "It may take me a minute."

"Here..." She put her arm around me and pulled gently. "Let me help."

Together we managed to get me back on my feet.

"Let's get you back to my place and I'll take care of you."

That sounded like a slice of heaven.

MRS. CARMINE PULLED her Studebaker into her garage. It had one of those automatic door openers which she used to close the door behind us. There was a regular door on the side that led into the house, over on South Durant Street, a few blocks over from the Welcome to Montague Falls billboard overlooking Silver Peak Way.

"Let's get you inside and cleaned up."

I managed to get out of the car on my own and walked toward the trunk.

"What are you doing?" she asked.

"Bringing the groceries inside."

"Jethro, leave them there. You are more important than groceries. Let's take care of you first."

"But the milk will spoil."

"Don't worry about the milk." Mrs. Carmine led me into her kitchen. "I'll be right back."

She went into what I guessed was a bathroom and came out with some first aid supplies.

My personal Florence Nightingale sat on a chair opposite me, then opened a bottle of iodine and poured some on a cotton ball. She dabbed it on a cut over my eyebrow. I tried to be tough, but still flinched.

Mrs. Carmine's pupils got bigger. "Did that hurt?"

I shrugged. "Wasn't that bad."

"We have to clean out the cut so it doesn't get infected. On the plus side, I don't think it's bad enough that you need stitches. You got quite a beating."

My cheeks flushed from embarrassment. "I noticed."

"Jethro, don't feel bad. That man was a monster. You tried to fight back even though you had no chance. I like a man who's willing to fight, even when the odds are stacked against him."

Mrs. Carmine stopped and looked into my eyes. Like a deer in headlights, I had no choice but to stare back. We got lost in each other's eyes for what seemed like forever but was probably less than a minute.

Mrs. Carmine turned away first and put the iodine on the kitchen table. "Take your shirt off."

What was happening? "Why?"

"I want to make sure you don't have any more cuts that need to be tended to."

"Anything for a lady." I took the shirt off, debating about jokingly asking if she wanted to do the same. I just didn't have the nerve.

My shoulders and ribs were covered with bruises where Dirk had kicked me.

She reached out, gently placing her fingertips on my ribs. "Does that hurt?"

"Not so much when you're touching it."

"I guess I should touch you some more?"

Did I hear her right or did my daydream just seem real? I nodded and managed to get out an "Uh huh."

The prettiest woman I've ever seen put her right palm on me and rubbed my chest bruises. With her left, she rubbed those on my shoulder. She shifted forward in her wooden chair and her thigh brushed mine as both her hands moved down to rub my sides. She leaned forward until her sweater-covered breasts rubbed against my bare chest and she slid one hand around my back.

I couldn't be imagining this. It had to be really happening, but I couldn't leave well enough alone. I had to know for sure

"Mrs. Carmine…"

"I think you better call me Rosa."

"Rosa, I…"

Rosa placed her index finger over my mouth. "Hush. At times like this, words only spoil things. Understand?"

I started to say "yes," but Rosa silenced me with a press of her lovely finger on my lips, so I nodded instead.

"I think your lip looks swollen. I'd better kiss it and make it better."

She leaned over and brought her lips down to mine, which parted ever-so-gently as they touched.

My body felt like fireworks were going off in all my nerves.

Rosa pulled back and looked down at my trousers, which

were now raised up in the center. Rosa lifted her eyes back up to mine and smiled.

"Did that monster kick you in the groin?" Rosa said in the same tone she used when talking about my swollen lip.

Dirk didn't but, praying this was going in the direction I thought it was, I nodded anyway.

"I guess I'll have to kiss that and make it better, too. Although this does come with a bit of bad news."

"What's that?"

She moved her face close to kiss my lips again. This time her tongue touched mine and explored my mouth with an enthusiasm not even Columbus had searching for the New World.

She stopped and leaned back. "Figure out what the bad news is yet?"

I shook my head.

"The milk is definitely going to spoil."

"JETHRO, THAT WAS amazing," Rosa purred, lying naked beside me, her head on my shoulder and her hand stroking my bare chest.

I couldn't stop smiling if you offered me a million bucks. "Poets have yet to invent the words to describe how wonderful that was."

"You're so sweet," she said. "And enthusiastic. Was it your first time?"

Embarrassed, I pulled away. "Was it that obvious?"

"Not at all." Rosa smiled and lifted her hand from my chest to my cheek and kissed me. She took her time and when she stopped, we were both grinning like the happiest of idiots the world had ever seen. "I am very flattered that you chose me as the first woman you made love to."

Part of me wanted to say I would've chosen her months ago had I known that it was an option.

Rosa ran her fingertips up and down my chest. "My only regret is that our time with each other was so short."

I was suddenly more terrified than a man hanging over a cliff holding on by his last fingernail. "It doesn't have to be."

Rosa gave a small sniff that made her look sad, then stroked my cheek. "This was a once-in-a-million fluke. I'm married, Jethro.

Trust me, my husband would not understand."

"We could sneak around," I said. "Does he go on a lot of trips? I can see you then."

"Only occasionally. I think he'd notice if you were in the house."

"We can sneak into my house and use my bedroom. My father's drunk all the time. As long as I give him his TV dinner, he'll never even notice."

Rosa ran her fingers through my hair then shook her head.

"Our town's too small," she said. "People will eventually notice me going over to your house. We'll start the gossip mills, which will probably think I'm seeing your father. Or if they do think I'm seeing you, it could ruin my teaching career. I'd get fired and my husband would divorce me. I'd be broke and penniless with nowhere to live. What would happen to me then?"

"It's not long until graduation. I'll get a job and support us."

"That's very gallant of you, but we both know any job you'd be able to get wouldn't pay much to start. With the scandal, we'd both have to pick up and leave town and that would make it that much harder for either of us to find work. We just have to accept this for what it is and go on with our lives, even if they'll be much sadder because of it."

"You said your husband doesn't come back until Sunday night. I don't have to leave now. We can have tonight, tomorrow, and part of Sunday before we have to say goodbye."

Rosa was moving her head side to side as if looking for the right words. "Jethro, people can't find out. It would ruin me."

"They wouldn't. I could ride over here on my bike and put it behind the house. No one can even see your house unless they're driving right past it. Nobody would ever know I was here. My dad has no clue where I am most of the time, so it would work."

Rosa moved her face towards mine into until our lips were so painfully close it hurt not to kiss her. "I don't know..."

I brought my lips to hers and she responded with every bit as much enthusiasm as I did.

She pulled her mouth away from mine and whispered in my ear, "Jethro, I can't say no to you, but this can only happen until Sunday. Understood?"

Right then with her so incredibly close and so beautifully naked, I would have agreed to anything she asked.

"Of course," I said. "Whatever you want."

I WENT HOME long enough to feed my father and get to bed. I worked hard to stay behind him so he never noticed my swollen lip or the cut over my eye. Luckily, I had no bruises on my face, only the rest of me.

I woke up Saturday morning at the crack of dawn. My body ached from my beating and my exertions from the day before, but it was nothing a hot shower and some aspirin couldn't make tolerable.

I hopped on my bike and rode through the streets. They were almost empty except for me, a few paperboys, and a milkman.

I had to wait in the distance until the paperboy on Rosa's road disappeared around the bend and then rolled my bike up her driveway and behind her house, careful not to leave any tire tracks. I stashed the bike behind some bushes and knocked on the back door.

"Come in," said Rosa, her voice low and husky enough to pull a sled.

I opened the door slowly, careful not to knock the flowers I was holding in my hand. There would be some very unhappy gardeners waking up soon because I'd picked them from people's lawns on the way over.

I closed the door behind me and stepped into the kitchen and suddenly forgot how to breathe. Rosa stood waiting for me like some naughty sex goddess in the kind of black silk underwear that pin-ups wore.

Even though I'd had the pleasure of viewing her naked, seeing her in the lingerie was somehow more tantalizing. Rosa was more beautiful than Rita Hayward and Ava Gardner rolled into one.

Rosa smiled, looking proud of the fact that I had apparently forgotten how to move or talk. She strutted over to me in a pair of heels higher than any I've ever seen before, her hips keeping time like a finely crafted clock.

Rosa saw the flowers. "Are those for me?"

I stuck my arm out in front of me, stiff as a movie robot, while I nodded my head and managed to mutter, "Uh huh."

Rosa caressed my hand and then ever-so-gently took the bouquet from me, brought it up to her nose, and inhaled the fragrance of the petals. I found myself staring at the rising of her breasts.

"How can I ever thank you for such a lovely gift?" As she asked, she stuck her index finger in her mouth and gently nibbled on the tip.

"I might be able to come up with some suggestions," I said.

Rosa placed the flowers on the kitchen table. "I bet you could. How long do we have, my love? What time do you have to be home?"

"Not 'til tomorrow. I told my dad I was staying over at a friend's house."

"Good." Rosa smiled and threw me down on a chair then straddled me. "Then we can take our time."

WHEN MONDAY CAME, I was still walking on air. I'm the first one to admit that I haven't had a lot of experience with girls, but now I had been intimate with the most beautiful woman I'd ever seen. I know things were supposed to be over, but I didn't believe it. They couldn't be. A passion like the one Rosa and I shared only came along once in a lifetime, if ever.

We had to be together.

I'd already talked her into spending the weekend with me. Now I just had to figure out how to do that for a lifetime. Our love would find a way.

It had only been a few days, but things started to fall into place in my mind. I'd have to get a job to support us for when she divorces her husband and married me. Then after a few years there would be kids we would need to take care of.

I'd never really thought about getting married and having kids before. Sure, I figured I'd get around to it one day when I found the right woman. How was I to know I'd find her so early in life?

I knew I would have to bide my time and all we'd have for now was a few stolen moments, but with Rosa, a moment might as well be a lifetime.

And now the school day was almost over and I'd be able to see her again. I was feeling so good even Pete, Stumpy, and Dean couldn't bring me down.

"What's wrong with Jethro?" Dean said, crowding up behind my right shoulder as I walked down the hall.

"The loser looks like the cat who swallowed the canary," Stumpy said. "I've never seen him this happy before."

"Why you so happy, punk?" Pete asked me. "Did your mommy come visit you in the hospital after her boyfriend beat you up?"

I just kept on walking.

"He has the same look on his face you had the first time you got laid, Stumpy," Dean said.

"Did Jethro actually convince some blind girl to take pity on him?" Pete said. "Did our little loser finally become a man?"

I couldn't help myself. I smiled.

"Oh! He did get some," Dean said. "Who was desperate enough to let you touch them?"

"I bet it was Pizzaface!" Pete said. "Do her zits go all the way down her body? Did you have to put a paper bag over her head?"

The girl they rudely called Pizzaface was Lizzy and she was actually pretty. She just had some acne issues. To be honest, she's fun, nice, and a week or two ago was someone I would have considered going to the dance with if Jenny turned me down. That was assuming I got up the nerve to ask either of them.

But that was all before Rosa.

"Don't call her Pizzaface," I said. "Her name is Lizzy."

"It was her!" Stumpy said.

"It wasn't her," I said.

"What girl was it?" Pete said.

"It wasn't a girl," I said. "It was a woman."

"Then who was it?" Stumpy demanded.

"Probably your mom," Dean said.

"He probably snuck in and saw her after you left for school," Pete said. "Maybe the loser is going to be your new daddy."

I sped up and walked into science class.

My vision of beauty was standing behind her desk. "Good afternoon, Ro... Mrs. Carmine."

I'd say she gave me a glare over my almost slip of the tongue, but I couldn't tell for sure because she was wearing a big pair of sunglasses like the movie stars.

"Mrs. Carmine, is everything okay?" Pete asked, sounding genuinely concerned. "What's with the shades?"

"I'm fine. I had a little slip in the shower, " she said, brushing it off. "Let's get started with today's lesson."

I had trouble paying attention to what she was teaching because I couldn't stop staring at what looked like a black eye under the dark lens.

When class was over, I took my time collecting my books. Soon everyone else left. I waited a little longer until the hall outside was empty, then went up front to Rosa's side.

"Are you okay? Did you really fall in the shower?"

Without an answer, Rosa fell into my arms and started weeping.

I squeezed her tight to my chest, then stroked her blonde hair and whispered, "It's okay."

Rosa pulled back from my embrace and, with a handkerchief, wiped the tears from her eyes. "No, it's not and it never will be again. I didn't fall in the shower."

She took her sunglasses off and she had a huge shiner on her right eye.

"What happened?"

"Mike got back from his mother's early, barely half an hour after you'd left. Because of our time together, some of my household duties didn't get done. I didn't do the laundry or mop or vacuum. Dinner wasn't waiting for him when he walked through the door. Mike was furious."

I suddenly wanted to hurt this guy, beat him senseless. "Has he hit you before?

Rosa sniffled and nodded. "A few times when I hadn't done something exactly as he told me, but he was good to me the rest of the time, so I brushed them off. But this time was different. He never hit me before where other people could see the mark he left."

"He really blackened your eye just because you didn't do laundry and have dinner ready?"

Tears rolled down her cheeks. "Not just that. I thought I'd

have more time to freshen up the house. Mike said the house stank of sex and he accused me of cheating on him."

"Did you tell him the truth?"

"I'm not stupid or crazy. I care about you too much. If Mike found out for sure, he'd come after you. He'd kill us both."

Crap. I'd seen pictures of him in her house. He was a big man.

"I was weak, Jethro. I shouldn't have done what we did, but you made me feel so wonderful in ways I've never felt before. But everything between us is over forever. We have to be careful never to speak outside of school ever again."

"I'm not scared of him," I lied.

Rosa reached for my face. "He was a soldier and fought in the war in France and Germany. He could kill you before you could land a punch."

We both turned toward the door as we heard footsteps in the hallway.

"Oh, no, it's Mike. He can't find us together." Rosa put her sunglasses back on. "Hide!" Rosa rushed me toward her desk and shoved me under it.

I was ashamed to act like a coward in front of her, but my first instinct was to dive under that desk and cower.

"Principal Pappo, this is a pleasant surprise."

"Hello, Mrs. Carmine. I'd heard you had a black eye and just wanted to come check on you," the principal said. I could picture the overweight bald man and his constantly smug expression as I heard him close the classroom door.

"It was just a clumsy accident," Rosa said. "I slipped in the shower."

"Sorry to hear that. Perhaps you joining me for a drink might take some of the sting out."

"Thank you so much, Principal Pappo, but it's more embarrassing than painful."

"But there is still your tenure here to talk about and I'm sure you want to do everything possible to make sure you receive that job security."

I heard Rosa inhale deeply. "I'm so very flattered by your interest, but if the two of us were seen out in public at a bar, especially being married to other people... well, tongues would wag."

Pappo was hitting on Rosa? My Rosa!? He was old and fat. I didn't care if he was the principal, I was going to clean his clock.

It was as if Rosa sensed what I was thinking, because she sat down in her chair, blocking me in with the best legs this side of Hollywood.

"Mrs. Carmine, you make an excellent point. No sense in adding any grist to the rumor mill, is there? Fortunately, my wife is visiting our grandchildren and will be gone until the end of the month. We can have that drink at my place and no one will ever be the wiser."

Oh, hell no. I crawled forward to give that pig Pappo a piece of my mind and a bigger piece of my fists. Rosa's gams snapped out and pushed me back under the desk as she moved the chair to cover the sound.

"I don't know, Principal Pappo. My husband is expecting me home and Mike's a very jealous man. I'm not sure he'd understand."

"I see. However, it would really be in your best interest to meet with me. If you can't tonight, make arrangements for tomorrow. As you know, the next Board of Education meeting is coming up and I have to make my recommendation on whether or not you should continue in your current position. The board has never gone against my recommendation. If you want it, you best come see me about that drink."

I watched as Pappo reached down and grabbed Rosa's knee.

She slapped it away but still made sure I stayed pinned in place, pushing me back with her foot.

"Is that so? Why do you think I'm going to sleep with you to save my job? What do you think my husband will say when I tell him about your proposition?"

Principal Pappo's laugh sounded like a barking dog. "I'll tell him that you simply misunderstood what I was saying. It will be my word—that of a long-standing and respected member of the community—versus that of a young woman who has only been in town a few years. The fact that you are so beautiful will only help my case."

"How do you figure?"

"Any man who believes your outrageous story will undoubtedly side with me, as he would have done the same thing in my situation. With the exception of your husband, of course."

"That's the way you figure it, do you? I think that my beauty will hurt your lie, especially when I tell my side of the story." Rosa was speaking in the same tone she used when trying to calm down a rambunctious class.

Rosa pushed her chair back and stood. I assumed she was about to announce the fact that I was hiding under the desk.

Boy, was I wrong. Rosa took off her sweater. Was she actually going to go along with Pappo?

From my hidey hole, I could only see Pappo's shoes, but could see Rosa up to her neck. She was wearing a white button-down blouse with a white bra that you could make out underneath.

"Now you're getting the idea, Carmine. Keep stripping because I like what I see."

Rosa grabbed the top of her blouse and pulled it so hard that the thin material tore and three buttons popped off and flew across the classroom.

"You see, in my version of this story, I'll tell them how you attacked me, telling me I had to sleep with you to get tenure," Rosa said. "I'll run downstairs and through the school like this while screaming. Students are still here for sports and extracurricular activities. So are the custodians, a few teachers, and the office staff. Plenty of people will see me. They will tell the cops what they saw. When they hear my side of the story, who do you think they will believe? I mean, a dumpy old man like you only has a hope of getting a beautiful woman like me to sleep with him through force. They will figure you did it. After all, like you said, they all want me, so they'll figure you simply lost control."

"It's still your word against mine," Pappo said nervously.

"At first, maybe. But how long do you think it will be before the other women you pulled this on come forward to back up my story?"

"Forever. None of those women would want their families or husbands to know what they did. The shame will keep them silent."

"I wasn't talking about the teachers here. I meant the women who turned you down and got fired. They have nothing to be ashamed of. They did the right thing. We both know I can't be the first teacher who turned you down. The cops will interview all those women. Once I've blazed the trail, I bet at least a few of them will follow. If just one does, it's no longer your word versus mine. If two come forward, your position as principal is doomed. Sure, they might let you quit to keep it quiet, but word gets around. No one else will hire you. But what if three or more come forward? Then the police and the school board won't be able to sweep this under the rug. And what will your wife and those grandchildren of yours think about Grampa being a rapist? Think of the shame. Then you *will* be fired and go to jail. That's if my husband lets you live long enough for any that to happen."

"I'm still your boss and can make your life a living hell."

"You can certainly try, but do you really want to go against me when I'm not worried about using doing whatever it takes to win?"

The principal grumbled so deep in his throat it was almost a growl. "Fine, but we are not done here."

"I think we are," she said. "I will expect to see a copy of your letter to the board by the end of tomorrow, and I think it'd be best if it was the most glowing recommendation you've ever written."

Rosa pulled the edges of her blouse together to cover her exposed bra and breasts. "Now if you'll excuse me, I'm going to be busy in here for a while. I need to find a sewing kit to repair these buttons before I go home. I wouldn't want my husband to ask any questions that you wouldn't want me to answer."

Pappo's shoes moved out of my sight and I heard his footsteps as he opened then walked out the door, slamming it behind him.

Rosa dropped to the floor and crawled over to me under the desk. "I'm so sorry I made you hide, but I could never explain our relationship and who knows what Pappo would do with that information. I didn't hurt you when I kicked you, did I?"

I shook my head. "I'm fine, but I can't believe what you just did."

Rosa sighed and nodded. "I know. It was so unlike meek little me. But knowing you were nearby to protect me if anything happened gave me courage. Plus, I had to come up with a way to get rid of him so he wouldn't know you were here. If he knew about us and threatened to tell my husband, Lord only knows what he'd want me to do in exchange for his silence."

Rosa snuggled up in my arms and started to shiver. She squeezed my waist so hard I thought she might bust one of my bruised ribs.

"Jethro, I hate not being with you. I know we agreed not to see each other anymore so I wasn't putting you in danger, but I desperately need to be with you. To feel you loving me, to make this dark world go away for a little while. Will you do that for me?"

"I'd do anything you asked me."

And I meant it, knowing full well that her husband might try to kill me. Some people were worth dying for and Rosa was certainly one of them.

Her lips parted in a pout. "Take me now."

"Here? Under the desk?"

Rosa shook her head and took my hand. We stood and she led me toward a door. "This is my storage closet for all my chemicals and other supplies. It even has a lock. And I have the only key."

She opened the door and stepped inside. Her skirt dropped to the floor, followed quickly by her torn blouse and bra.

I quickly shut the door behind us.

I'D NEVER HAD such a good time at school before. Rosa's passion turned frantic as she let loose all the fear she was holding back. We both collapsed, exhausted, onto the closet floor. We lay tangled together for a moment, then Rosa gave me a quick peck on the lips, jumped up and started getting dressed. I watched the process with more than a bit of sadness. She saw me staring and smiled.

"I can't stay with Mike. I can't take the fear of when my next beating will come. And even if I could, I love you too much to not be with you."

Her words caught me off guard. I'd never heard anyone say that to me before, let alone mean it like Rosa did.

I was quick to respond. "I love you too, Rosa. Are we going to run off together?"

Rosa shook her head as she buttoned up what she could of her blouse.

"It's too risky. Mike might just come after us. Plus, we'd be setting ourselves up to fail. I don't want to end up penniless, struggling just to have enough to pay for food and a roof over our heads. I couldn't do that to you. When you weigh out all the options, there's really only one solution available if we want to be together. We've got to get rid of Mike."

I was confused. "You mean, like... scare him off? Somehow get him to join the Marines again?"

Rosa shook her head. Even though it was just the two of us in the locked closet, she leaned forward to whisper in my ear.

"I mean, we have to take Mike out of the picture. Permanently."

I jumped off the floor, still naked. "You mean kill him? We can't do that. That would be murder!"

Rosa put both her palms on my chest and looked up at me with big doe eyes.

"You can't think of it like that. We won't be murdering him. It would be self-defense, getting him before he kills me. Or heaven forbid, before he figures out that you are my lover and kills you."

"How does that help us with the money situation?"

"The house is in both our names. If he dies, I own it. I would still earn my salary as a teacher. Plus, Mike has a life insurance policy for twenty-five thousand dollars. That money would give us a lot of freedom."

Rosa leaned in and hugged me.

"We could travel and see the world. We'd make love on the beaches of Hawaii and on the balcony of a hotel room in Paris looking up at the Eiffel Tower. Our lives would be perfect if only Mike wasn't around."

"I get what you're saying, but I don't think I can kill a guy." Especially one so much bigger than me.

Rosa pulled herself away from me so fast it looked like my skin had burned her. She crossed her arms in front of her and hunched forward, turning her back to me.

"But Jethro, you said you love me."

I stepped forward and wrapped my arms around her, but she pulled away again.

"But I do love you."

"If you loved me, why won't you kill a monster who is going to kill me and rob you of my love?"

"First of all, I've never killed anyone before. How the hell am I going to beat someone who used to be a Marine for Christ's sake?"

Rosa stopped holding onto her shoulders and wrapped her arms around my neck. "You wouldn't have to kill him bare-handed, Jethro."

"I really don't know how to use a gun. Besides, gunshots bring people and cops. If I go to jail, that would rob you of *my* love so that wouldn't do either of us any good."

Rosa let go of me and stroked her chin as if she was deep in thought.

"What if there was something that would kill him without any-one being the wiser? Something you can give him that wouldn't kill him for an hour or so. That way you can be long gone by the time he dropped dead."

"You mean like poison or something?"

She raised a finger up in the air like I said something brilliant. "Exactly."

"I know even less about poison than I do about guns."

Rosa grinned. "But I know about them. I am a science teacher, after all. I could come up with something that would do the trick. You could slip it in his drink and that would be all she wrote."

"I can see a big hole in your plan right off the bat. You don't think your husband will be suspicious if I'm over your house and giving him something to drink?"

Rosa playfully swatted me on the shoulder, her smile back.

"Jethro, you're so silly. We wouldn't want to do it at *my* house. Why give the cops any reason to suspect his death is anything other than an accident? Mike goes out drinking a couple of times a week. You will just go to the bar and figure a way to slip it in his drink, then leave. Maybe he drops dead while driving the car on the way home and the cops blame it on his drinking. There won't be any suspicion of foul play."

I had to admit it made sense before the realization hit me that I was actually considering murdering another human. It made me sick to my stomach. I wanted to puke.

"Rosa, as much as I love you, I can't kill somebody. There has to be some other way."

Rosa went from smiling to bawling in less time than it took to blink. I pulled her in and held her against my bare chest. She pounded my ribs with her closed fists.

"Why won't you understand! There is no other way! If we don't kill him soon, you'll come to school one day and find that he killed *me*. How are you going to feel then? Especially if he figures out that you're my lover! You would follow me to the Pearly Gates."

"Rosa, this talk of killing is crazy."

She pushed herself back and slapped me hard across the face.

"You think I'm crazy? You said you loved me! Do you think you could love a crazy person? You're the crazy one if you're willing to risk us both being killed instead of grabbing the brass ring for our one chance at happiness together."

The blow stunned me into shocked silence for a few moments. "I wasn't calling you crazy, just the idea."

"When the world's gone insane, sometimes the only sane thing to do is something crazy. I realize I sprung this on you suddenly. It will take some time for your mind to adjust to what has to be done. I mean, in a choice between someone killing you or you killing them first, the smart move is the one that lets you live. Better him than me. I know once you have a chance to mull everything over you'll see that. Go home and think about it. I'm sure you'll see reason by morning."

I didn't think so but I nodded just to make her happy.

"It's a real pity," Rosa said. "I was going to tell you to come home with me. My mother-in-law took another turn for the worse and Mike ran up to check on her again. It would still be too dangerous for you to stay the night, but we could've gotten a couple more hours of 'us' time in."

I ran my fingers down her arms softly, from her shoulders to her wrists. "There's no reason we still can't."

Rosa shoved me back.

"Oh, no. If you think I'm going to make love to someone who called me crazy and who is willing to let me die rather than man up, then you're living in a dream world, mister."

Her words stung as bad as the slap.

"Can I at least walk you to your car?"

Her eyes glared, and her lower lip stuck out as she pouted, but she said, "Fine. You can carry some books for me. But I think you better get dressed first, don't you?"

Rosa didn't seem anywhere near as broken up when I put on my clothes as I did when she got dressed. She put her sweater back on over her torn blouse and we left the closet. I picked up a stack of books and lugged them downstairs to the parking lot.

Principal Pappo was nowhere in sight, but Pete was. He saw me walking with the prettiest woman in town and made a bee-line to cut us off.

"Hi, Mrs. Carmine," he said, ignoring me.

"Hello, Peter."

Pete grabbed the books out of my hands.

"Jethro, you look like you're straining. These books are probably too heavy for you. I'll take them from here."

All signs of Rosa's tantrum were gone and she beamed at my tormentor.

"Thank you, Peter. That's very thoughtful of you. Would you mind putting them in my car for me?"

"I'd be happy to, Mrs. Carmine."

Pete walked to the driver's side, opened the door, and put the books in the middle of the front seat.

"Thank you for helping me with those heavy books," Rosa said. "Hopefully I will be able to get them in by myself when I get home."

"I can go home with you and carry them in," Pete said, turning his head to give me a sneer and a wink. It took all my self-control not to sucker punch him in the face.

"That would be very kind," Rosa said, "but I couldn't impose."

"No imposition at all. I'm happy to do it."

"Mrs. Carmine," I said. "I'd be happy to do it, too."

"I appreciate that, Jethro, but I think it's best if you go home and think about our conversation. I'm sure Peter will be more than adequate for this task."

Pete ran to the passenger side of Rosa's car and got in.

I moved close to her and whispered, "Pete's not a nice guy. You shouldn't be alone with him."

"So not only do you think I'm crazy, but you think I can't handle myself with one of my own students?"

"That's not it at all."

"Are you willing to change your answer? Because if you are, then you can take Pete's place."

I wanted to tell her what she needed to hear worse than anything else I'd desired to do ever. I wanted to have those few more stolen hours, but I just couldn't lie to my Rosa.

"I can't," I said.

"Then toodles."

Rosa climbed into the driver's seat, started the car, and drove away. Pete leaned out his window and made an obscene gesture with his middle finger, making sure he used his body to block it so Rosa couldn't see him doing it.

I wanted to hit something, to break something, but I didn't.

Instead, I went home.

I'D ALREADY SERVED our fine foil-covered cuisine and Dad and I had polished off the TV dinners when the phone rang.

I watched Dad not move and keep staring at the TV screen.

"Don't worry," I said "I'll get it."

Dad didn't acknowledge either my sarcasm or my existence. His beer, on the other hand, got treated with tender loving care as he drank it.

"Hello," I said, picking up the receiver.

"Jethro, it's me." Rosa's voice was no louder than a whisper and it sounded like she'd been crying.

"Rosa, what's wrong?"

"I feel like such a fool. I'm sorry for pressuring you and not listening to what you said about Peter. You were right. He carried the books in my house but then he wouldn't leave. Now I fear he will have his way with me, whether I want to or not. You have to do something! Come over and help me!" Her voice was frantic.

"He's coming. I have to go. Hurry, Jethro!"

She hung up.

I put down the receiver and ran in front of the TV.

"Dad, can I borrow the car?"

"Hell, no. You don't need to be driving my car. You want a car, then do what I did. Go and get a job and buy your own."

"It's an emergency!" I said.

"Then call the cops."

That would be the worst idea possible. "It's not that kind of emergency."

"I guess you better get walking, then."

Rosa's house was too far for that, so I got my bike and peddled like a bat out of hell. At some points, I actually passed cars, but it still felt too slow. Pete was alone with Rosa and she needed my help. I prayed I wouldn't get there too late.

I finally arrived at her house and sped into the backyard. I didn't bother to hide the bike behind the bushes. Instead, I rushed in the back door and heard a woman's screams and a man's grunting. I stepped into the living room.

I was too late. Rosa's hands were tied with a man's leather belt above her head and her skirt was hiked up above her hips. All the buttons on her blouse were torn off now and her breasts were hanging out of her bra.

Worst of all, Pete was on top of the woman I loved, acting like he was king of the world.

"Get off of her!" I screamed, yanking Pete by his hair and throwing him to the ground. His pants were down around his ankles, with no belt.

"Jethro? What the hell are you doing here? This is none of your business!"

"It is my business when Rosa called me for help, saying she was worried you were going to attack her and I walk in and find you raping her!"

"Rape? Man, you're nuts. She wanted me. Hell, she begged me for it. Mrs. Carmine even got me all liquored up before she seduced me."

"If she seduced you, then why are her hands tied and her blouse torn?"

Pete stood up and stumbled, then pulled up his trousers. "She asked me to tie her up. As for the blouse, she told me she liked it rough and begged me to rip it off. Our teacher is a sex freak."

"You're a liar!" I barely recognized the screaming voice as my own.

Pete grinned and then stepped backwards. "Wait a sec. Mrs. Carmine is the woman who popped your cherry? Oh man, that's rich! And you were so bad at it she had to come and get me to do her right."

"Shut your lying mouth!"

Pete raised his fists, but was blinking hard, like he was having trouble seeing. "Make me."

I lunged forward and swung at his face. I guess I was so angry I was faster than I'd ever been before because I clocked him right in the nose. Pete stumbled back, then swung at me, but it went wide, missing me. I must have hit him real hard because he seemed barely able to stand up.

I gave him a couple of quick kidney punches in the side, then another sock to the jaw.

Pete fell over backwards, his head hitting a coffee table and knocking over two empty wineglasses.

I waited for him to get up, but my tormentor wasn't moving.

"Pete?" He didn't answer.

"You knocked him out." Rosa ran into my arms. "Thank you for coming so quickly, Jethro. I'm so sorry…"

"Rosa, you have nothing to apologize for. Everything bad that happened was Pete's fault."

"I know. I told him to stop but he wouldn't listen. He just came at me like an animal." She held her wrists out towards me. "Would you please untie me?"

"Of course."

I undid the belt. Rosa then wrapped me in a hug that threatened to crush my rib cage.

"I'm here," I said. "You're okay now."

"I know I'll always be safe with you to protect me, Jethro."

"What do we do now? Things will get complicated if we call the police. Pete figured out that we slept together. If they arrest him, he'll tell the cops. Then your husband will find out."

"I'll make up something," Rosa said. "We can say you heard my screams from outside as you were riding by and came in to save me. I'll make you sound like the hero you are. My husband will have to accept that. I'll tell the cops Peter is lying to try to get out of paying for what he did."

I looked back at Pete. He still hadn't moved. "I never knocked a guy out before. How long does it take for someone to wake up?"

"I don't know." Rosa went over and looked at Pete. "Oh, my God. I don't think he's breathing."

She bent down and put her hand in front of his mouth and nose, then her ear to his chest.

"He's not breathing and I can't hear a heartbeat." Rosa sat and looked up at me. "I think you killed him."

I FELT NAUSEOUS, like I was going to throw up every meal I've ever had all at once. My legs trembled so hard I thought I might fall.

"I couldn't have killed him. I didn't hit Pete that hard."

"He must have hit his head on the table when he fell. That must be what killed him."

"That will be tough explaining to the cops," I said.

"We can't call the cops now. They'll arrest you for murder."

I felt so much of the blood from my head dive down into my feet that I could've passed out.

"But it was an accident. I was defending you."

Rosa was weeping openly now.

"Some bumps and bruises they might understand, but he's dead. They'll want someone to pay for that and they will make sure it's you."

"What can we do?"

Rosa looked frantically around the room. "We'll have to get rid of the body."

"How?"

I had no idea how to do something like that. I barely took out the trash at my house.

"The two of us can carry him into the garage and put the body in the trunk of my car."

"That gets it out of here, but where would we dump it?"

"I don't know. Maybe in the woods?" Like a flash of lightning,

Rosa's eyes lit up. "No, not the woods. I have the perfect place! We'll get two birds with one stone. We make sure that the police investigation never comes anywhere near you and you get revenge on that monster for beating you up."

"You mean Dirk?"

"Yes. Have you been to his house?"

I nodded. "Once, when I brought some of my mom's stuff over there."

"Does he have a pool or shed?" Rosa said.

"He has a shed."

"We dump the body there and then I can make an anonymous call to the police and let them know where to look. They'll do an investigation. Enough people saw Peter go up to Dirk after he beat you up and yell at him. When they interview us, we tell them Pete also called him an idiot who couldn't punch his way out of a paper bag. That would give Dirk a motive for going after Peter."

I was mentally and physically numb, so I just nodded. Then I helped Rosa put Pete's dead body into the trunk.

"WHAT IF THEY'RE home?" I whispered, lying on the floor of the backseat of Rosa's car. I don't know why I was whispering. The windows were shut, so it wasn't as if anybody outside was going to hear me.

"Don't worry. They won't be."

I was amazed by how utterly certain she sounded. "How can you be sure?"

"Woman's intuition."

"I thought that was only to figure out if a guy likes you or something, not for being able to predict if someone's going to be home or not."

"Jethro, you worry too much."

"We have a dead body in the trunk!" I said, my voice cracking a little. "Can you blame me for being a little worried?"

"Instead of asking me so many questions, perhaps you should be focusing on the fact that I obviously love you more than you love me."

Even though I couldn't see her, I could tell by her tone of

voice that Rosa had a pouty face and was sticking her bottom lip out.

"How do you figure that?"

Rosa harrumphed. "When you found out my life was in danger and you could save me by killing my husband, you showed me a yellow streak a mile-wide running down your back. I watched you kill a man and here I am now. Not only am I helping you hide the body, but I came up with a way to make sure you won't be blamed for it."

"I didn't kill Pete on purpose. It was an accident. And I did it to save you."

I only saw the back of her head from my position on the floorboards.

"Which is exactly why I acknowledged that you do love me. Just not as much as I love you."

The vibration of the tires changed. The car had moved off the pavement and onto a dirt road. "Where are you going?"

"It's still light out," she said. "We can't pull up on their block and unload the body from the trunk in front of the neighbors, now can we?"

"No." The answer seemed kind of obvious but the solution didn't. "So how exactly are we going to get the body into Dirk's shed?"

"The property behind their house is undeveloped, so I'm pulling up in the woods behind it. That way you'll be able to carry the body, hopefully without anyone seeing you."

"Aren't you going to help?"

Rosa laughed and I didn't much care for the way it sounded this time.

"I'm not the one who killed him. I know you love me enough that if you get caught you won't bring me into this. Besides, you're so big and strong, it's not like little old me would really be all that much help in the carrying department."

The car stopped.

"We're here. As near as I can figure, if you go straight through these woods, you'll end up in Dirk's backyard."

I sat up onto the backseat and looked out the window. I couldn't see any houses through the trees.

"How exactly did you figure that out?" I said. "Woman's intuition again?"

Rosa chuckled. "No, silly. I have an excellent sense of direction."

I looked down and saw a small bit of cardboard sticking out from under the seat where my feet were. I bent down and picked it up. It was a library card.

"Who's Jeff Swanson?"

The name sounded familiar. I thought he might've been a freshman at my school who had run away a couple months ago.

Rosa's face seemed to freeze for a second before a smile exploded all the way from her lips to her eyes. "Why do you ask, my darling?"

I held up the cardboard rectangle. "I found his library card under your seat. How did it get there?"

Rosa reached back and plucked the card from my fingers and tucked it inside her sweater.

"He's a boy I used to tutor. I gave him a ride home once. He must have dropped it then. It was such a shame he ran away. He showed such promise."

"You do tutoring?"

"Only a few times at the beginning of the year, but Mike got upset once when I wasn't home in time to have his dinner ready as soon as he walked in the door, so he forbade me from doing it after that. Now come here and give me a kiss."

She leaned over and grabbed my cheeks between her hands and kissed me in such a way I thought we were going to do it right there in the car, but then she broke it off.

"Go dump the body. When you're done, just follow the dirt road to get home."

I got out and opened the trunk. We hadn't wanted to leave my bike at her house in case her husband came home before I could go back to get it. We didn't need him getting suspicious. My bike was on top of Pete. We had wrapped him in an old blanket that had slid off his face. His eyes were open and seemed to be staring at me accusingly.

I did my best to ignore the corpse's stare and lifted the bike out. I walked it a little ways into the woods and hid it behind a shrubbery so it couldn't be seen from the dirt road.

I came back and covered Pete's face with the blanket, then hefted the dead body over my shoulder in a fireman's carry. Rosa had insisted we wrap him in the old blanket. She didn't want it to look like I was carrying a body. I don't think it accomplished that. I still looked like I was carrying a body, just one wrapped in a blanket.

Pete wasn't as heavy as I thought he'd be. I walked to the driver's window.

"As soon as you're on your way," Rosa said. "I'll leave."

"I still don't see why. No one saw me on the way over to your house or here. I can ride back to your place the same way, so we could spend more time together."

"Jethro, think about what I've just been through and how insensitive what you're suggesting is. And even if I was in the mood, as I said, it's not worth the risk of someone seeing us together. If they did, it wouldn't be long before word got around town and Mike ended up coming after you. I'll see you in school tomorrow."

Rosa blew me a kiss and drove off.

I DID MY best to make it through the woods without making a sound, but failed miserably. I've never been much of an outdoor person. It sounded to me like I was stepping on every leaf and twig in Montague Falls.

A branch snapped nearby, startling me. I spun around to see what it was, dropping Pete's corpse into a pile of fallen leaves and brambles. I expected to see another person there and was wracking my mind for an excuse to explain the human-shaped blanket I was lugging. To my relief, it turned out to be a squirrel jumping between trees.

I leaned against a tree for support and realized I might now have some idea what a heart attack feels like.

I bent to pick up the body. It was a lot harder getting it off the ground than it had been lifting it out of the trunk of the car, but I managed and got moving again.

I'll be damned if Rosa wasn't right. The woods led me right to Dirk's backyard.

I stopped twenty feet from the yard and stashed the body

behind a tree before I made my way closer, crouched down on my belly.

Luck was with me because Dirk had fences along the sides of his yard, but not the rear. I guess he just wanted to block the view of his neighbors.

I watched the house, looking for some sign somebody was home, but saw none. No light was on and Dirk's beat-up Rambler wasn't in the driveway. Dirk didn't have a garage, and I hoped he hadn't moved the car to the front of the house instead of the driveway because I couldn't see the street from where I was.

Laying on my stomach in the woods wasn't going to help me get away with murder. I crept into the yard, then to the wooden shed and opened the door with my hands inside my sleeves so I wouldn't leave fingerprints.

The shed was a bit of a mess, so I cleared a spot on the floor. Leaving the door open, I crept back to where I had left Pete. Once again, I threw his lifeless body over my shoulder and very quickly raced to the open shed.

I'd meant to bend over and gently lower the corpse onto the shed floor, but lost my grip and the body crashed with a loud bang. The shed was right next to one of the fences. A dog on the other side started barking.

A man's voice from farther away in that yard yelled, "What is it, boy? Is someone back there?"

I quickly unwrapped the blanket from around Pete's body, then replaced it with a dirty tarp that was in the shed. The dog kept barking and was now scratching at the wooden fence.

The man spoke again. "Okay boy, I'm coming. Let's see what's got you so riled up back there."

Upon hearing that, I did what any sane man would do. I exited the shed and used the blanket to close the door, then tossed it over my head and ran for the woods like the devil himself was chasing me.

I got home fine, although I halfway expected a cop to jump out and arrest me.

I realized I was acting paranoid. I kept staring out the windows.

Dad was too drunk to notice. I went to bed at my normal time, but couldn't fall asleep.

About one in the morning I got up and poured myself some of Dad's whiskey and then some more. He never had a problem falling asleep, so I figured the booze wouldn't hurt. It didn't, at least until I woke up the next morning.

My mouth felt like I was sucking on cotton balls. Every light hurt my eyes and the slightest noise made my head feel like it was in a vise. I was actually impressed that my dad was able to get up and go to work every day feeling like this. I drank a bunch of water, took two aspirin, and forced myself to eat breakfast.

I got to school expecting everyone to know Pete was dead. They didn't, but apparently Stumpy and Dean knew he was missing.

Besides the two bullies, no one else seemed to care, so I did my best to get through the day.

Everything else hit the fan right before last period. The halls were buzzing. The cops had gotten an anonymous phone call and found Pete's body in Dirk's shed. They had arrested him. Even as hungover as I was, the thought of that Neanderthal in jail made me smile.

As I walked by the main office, I saw Phil Hansen in his cop uniform bringing Rosa to one of the conference rooms and shut the door.

When I got to science class, the lecherous Principal Pappo was there.

There was no fooling around today. Everyone was very quiet and took their seats without being asked. When the bell rang, Pappo stood up in front of the class.

"As some of you may have heard, we have received some tragic news. Our very own Peter Charles was found dead today. The police haven't revealed much about what happened, but they are investigating the matter. Right now, they're talking to Mrs. Carmine and she may not make it to this class, so I'd like you all to open up your textbooks and read chapter nineteen to yourselves. If Mrs. Carmine has not returned by the time the bell rings, you may all leave and go home."

Principal Pappo then left and the entire class turned toward Stumpy.

"What happened to Pete?" Jenny asked.

Stumpy looked a little teary-eyed and very angry.

"We don't know exactly," he said. "His parents called my parents last night when he didn't come home. They didn't know where he was and neither did we. We just heard about it ourselves when the cops called us in and asked when the last time we saw Pete was. He stayed after school for detention. We have no idea what happened to him after that."

That set off a lot of talk and speculation. Nobody read the assigned chapter or even opened the textbook.

The bell rang and Rosa still hadn't come back to class. Hanging around to wait for her would only look suspicious, so I left. You'd think with their friend dead Stumpy and Dean would have other things on their minds besides continuing their harassment of me, but you'd be wrong.

"You must be thrilled by this, huh Jethro?" Stumpy said.

"Thrilled by what?"

"That Pete's dead," Dean said.

They couldn't be more wrong. If anything, I was probably more upset about it than they were, but it's not like I could tell anybody why.

"Look, Pete's pretty much the biggest jerk I know, but that doesn't mean I want him dead."

Stumpy give me the once-over from head to toe.

"If I thought you had a spine or a set of balls, I'd say you probably were the one who killed him."

"Actually, when the cops asked me about anybody I thought would want Pete dead, I gave them your name, Jethro," Dean said with a nasty grin, showing his crooked teeth.

"Nice to see you're a jerk to the end, Dean." When I turned back toward my locker, Officer Myers stepped in front of me. "All right punk, come with me."

I froze. Did Rosa rat me out?

"What's the matter?" Myers said. "You got water between yer ears? Get moving to the main office. We got some questions for you."

We got to walk right past Stumpy and Dean, who looked like cats who ate then crapped out a canary.

"First we find you with a dead body…"

"Because I called to report it," I said.

"Did I say you could talk?" Officer Myers growled at me. "No, I didn't, so keep your yap shut. And now we find you right smack in the middle of another murder." Myers stared. "What's the matter, punk? Cat got your tongue? Are you scared that we finally caught on to you?" I kept quiet as he stopped outside the main office door. "Why aren't you talking?"

"Because you told me not to speak unless you told me to."

"Well, I'm telling you to speak now. Tell me why you killed Peter."

"I didn't kill anybody." It was amazing the ease in which the lie slipped from my lips.

"The evidence says different," Myers said. He opened the door and motioned with his chin for me to go inside the main office. The conference room door opened and Rosa walked out, dabbing her eyes with a frilly handkerchief.

I looked at her for some sign that she hadn't ratted me out. What I got was a brief glance as she walked by, otherwise ignoring me almost entirely.

"Get in there and sit down."

I did as he told me, hoping to see Sergeant Hansen inside. Instead there was a guy in a suit who I didn't recognize.

"Jethro, thank you for taking the time to come in and answer some questions." I wanted to say I wasn't given much of a choice, but was smart enough to keep my trap shut. "I'm Detective Reynolds. It seems your name had come up a couple of times in our investigation into the murder of Peter Charles."

A couple of times? If one of them was Dean, who was the second? Rosa wouldn't have ratted me out, would she? I mean, people who love each other don't do that kind of thing.

Do they?

Detective Reynolds didn't say anything else and I tried to sit there and make like I was tough, but the quiet was driving me nuts. I finally broke.

"How exactly did my name come up?"

"One of your classmates mentioned that you and the deceased had an adversarial relationship."

"If you mean, did he torment me relentlessly, I have to answer 'yes'."

"I appreciate your honesty," Reynolds said. "You'd be surprised how rare I get that in my line of work. What's your relationship like with your mother?"

I shrugged. "Almost nonexistent since she left me and my dad. I've seen her maybe twice."

Reynolds nodded and wrote something in the notebook on the table in front of him.

"What kind of relationship do you have with Dirk Earls?"

"We really don't have much contact, but what little we do have is pretty horrible."

There was more writing in the notebook.

"When was the last time you saw Dirk?"

I looked up at the ceiling like I was thinking. "After school last week. I think it was Friday."

Reynolds nodded and gave me a compassionate smile. "Did anything unusual happen during this meeting?"

"Yeah. He beat the crap out of me."

"Why did he do that?"

I sighed. "He wasn't happy with the way I was talking to my mother."

"You weren't being respectful?"

"She left me and my dad to shack up with some other guy. I can't think of any reason to be respectful towards her."

"And how did this fight end?"

"Because..." I caught myself before I used her first name. "...Mrs. Carmine stood up to Dirk and told him if he didn't stop, she'd call the cops."

I figured it was best to leave out the rest of the details because no one but Dirk, my mom, Rosa, and me knew them

"You're lucky to have a teacher who cares that much," Reynolds said. I nodded. "And she's a real dish, too."

I worked hard not to defend her honor. After all, as far as everyone else knew, we were just teacher and student, so I just nodded again.

"Was the deceased involved in this fight at all?"

"No."

"Was he there?"

I nodded. "At the end." The detective jotted something else in the notebook.

"I guess with the two of you being adversaries, he must've been cheering Dirk on, right?"

I took a deep breath and prayed Rosa stuck to the plan about our story.

"You'd think that," I said, "but he didn't. He actually told Dirk he was being a jerk for beating up a high school kid."

Reynolds raised his eyebrows. "Why do you think he stuck up for you after having tormented you for so long?"

"I tried to figure that one out myself, because he was the same way Monday that he always was. As near as I can figure, maybe he felt territorial. Like it was okay for him to torment me, but not someone else. That's just my guess because I really don't know." My heart had slowed a bit and I tried to think how I would act in this situation if I were anybody else. "Why are you asking all these questions about my mom and Dirk? Is he trying to get me arrested for fighting with him?"

Reynolds put down his pen and shut his notebook, staring at me all the while. He tilted his head and didn't take his eyes off me, like he was trying to look into my soul. I guess he must not have seen the blackness I was hiding within because he said, "Normally, I wouldn't discuss an ongoing investigation with a witness, but the story will be in all the papers in the morning. We found Peter's body in a place that Dirk had access to. That's all I can say right now."

"So, Dirk is a suspect? Is my mom?"

"I'm sorry, son, but I simply can't answer those questions. Thank you for your help."

"Can I go now?"

The detective nodded and gestured toward the door. I took a couple of steps.

"Jethro, wait a second. You told me that Dirk beat you up. Why didn't you call the cops like your teacher suggested?"

I turned back and shrugged.

"Because it was my word against grown-ups. I didn't know if the cops would have believed me. Unfortunately, I was pretty sure my mom would side with Dirk over me. She laughed while he punched and kicked me."

Reynolds had a slight downtick of his face, which could've been a frown. Felt sorry for me, I guess.

"Did you tell your dad about it?"

"No way."

"Why? Because you lost?"

"No, it's not that. If I told my dad, he might go after Dirk and end up in jail. Or that jerk might have hurt him. Or even worse, my mom would side with Dirk against my dad. I didn't want to break my dad's heart a second time."

Reynolds nodded. "Makes sense. But you could have called us. It wasn't just your word. Mrs. Carmine and Peter would've backed you up."

I just nodded. It seemed like we were done talking, so I turned and walked right past Myers, who watched me until I left the office.

I WENT STRAIGHT home, though I didn't want to. It was driving me crazy that I couldn't talk to Rosa and find out what she actually told the cops, but right now there was no way to tell if someone would be watching her or me, in case we were suspects.

I actually got home before my father so I sat and waited for him to walk through the door.

I was torn between hoping he'd gone out for drinks with the guys or decided to come home and drink alone.

Apparently, he opted for drinking solo.

I was sitting on the couch when Dad came through the door. He gave me a strange look, sitting there without the TV or radio on.

"Jethro, are you all right?"

"Not exactly." I told him what the cops told me, being careful not to add any details.

"Hope they lock that bastard up for the rest of his life. They arrest your mother?"

I shrugged. "Detective Reynolds didn't say he'd arrested anybody."

My dad got a goofy grin and his face lit up for the first time since mom left us. I thought it was just joy over Dirk's situation, but it was worse than that.

"You know what this means, don't you Jethro?"

"Dirk is probably going to jail for a long time?"

"Exactly. And that means your mother is going to come back to us."

I was stunned. I'll admit that at first, I wanted her to come back, but not anymore. I didn't feel the same way about her. I didn't trust her.

"But why would we want her back after what she did to us?"

"I know that's a logical reaction, son. You're a little young to realize this, but sometimes when a man falls in love, it's forever. Doesn't matter what the woman does. He'll always be miserable without her. I think we can get another shot to make it work." Dad did a little jig and spun in a circle, which was weird because my dad didn't dance. "Isn't this wonderful?"

I didn't point out that it wouldn't be wonderful and that she would just probably leave and hurt him again.

"Do you think I should give her a call and tell her she's welcome to come home?" Dad said.

"Dad, that's a horrible idea. First off, we don't know if she even wants to."

My dad stopped looking happy. Instead his face turned dark as a storm. "Why wouldn't she want to?"

"I don't know. Maybe because she left us to shack up with another guy."

"We were having some rough times."

"Dad, stop making excuses for her. Rough times aren't an excuse to cheat on somebody. You would never have done it to her. You shouldn't be so quick to forgive her for doing it to you. And she didn't just do it to you. She left me, too. She hasn't bothered trying to talk to either of us except to get her stuff or to laugh at her boyfriend beating me up."

I instantly regretted not keeping my mouth shut and wished I could take it back, but it was too late. The cat was out of the bag.

"That bastard laid hands on my son? I'll kill him!"

I put my hands up and got between Dad and the front door he was trying to walk out of.

"Dad, stop. The cops are going to arrest him soon and going

to jail is worse than whatever you could do to him. Why don't you just sit down and relax. I'll get you a beer."

I imagined the struggle going on inside Dad's mind. Fortunately, he needed a drink more than revenge, so he planted his butt in his chair.

"Okay. And as far as your mother laughing at the beating, I'm sure Dirk was lying about that to piss you off."

"The jerk didn't tell me about it."

"Then how do you know she laughed about it?"

"Because she was there and I watched her do it."

My dad's face went crimson with rage. "You're lying. Don't talk that way about your mother!"

"But Dad, it's true."

"No, it's not! Go to your room right now."

"Dad, I'm eighteen. I'm too old to be sent to my room."

"You're not too old for me to lay you over my knee and whip your ass. Move it!"

I did as I was told and ended up going without dinner. I didn't feel so bad because Dad did, too. Not because he didn't want it, but because he let it go up in smoke. I could smell the frozen dinner burning all the way from my room.

I WAS HOPING to steal a moment to talk to Rosa before school started, but there was a substitute teacher in her room, so she must've called out sick. I went to my first period class and was surprised to see Detective Reynolds waiting outside.

I nodded in greeting and went to step around him, but he put his hand on my chest.

"Sorry, sport. I got good news and bad news. The good news is you get to miss school today. The bad news is it's because you're coming downtown."

I think the detective was trying to sound tough, like he was on TV, because our town wasn't big enough to have a downtown. We just had town.

"Why?"

"To answer some questions," Detective Reynolds said.

"I answered your questions yesterday."

"Well, today I got some new ones. Now, are you going to stop flapping your gums and come with me under your own steam, or are we going to do this the rough way?"

My entire body felt like it'd been dropped in ice water. Was Rosa already at the station? Is that why she wasn't in school?

"I'll come with you. Am I under arrest?"

The detective frowned. "Why would you think you were being arrested?"

"Well, maybe it's because you threatened to rough me up if I didn't come with you. I didn't think cops did that."

Reynolds chuckled. "We try to keep it to a minimum. Once a month, although I do get a free pass on my birthday, which is why I love working on my birthday."

The detective motioned with his hand and I started walking one step behind him.

"You still didn't answer my question," I said.

"No, Jethro, you're not being arrested. But the day is young."

THE INTERROGATION ROOM at the police station was brutal. They gave me a painfully uncomfortable chair, and like you see in the movies, positioned a desk lamp so it shone directly in my face.

"Comfortable?" Reynolds said this from a well-padded chair.

"Extremely," I said in protest, although as I leaned backward, I soon realized one of the rear legs was shorter than the other three, so my back pinched near my hip. "It's so comfortable, in fact, that you'll have to forgive me if I doze off."

"I'll try to keep your attention. Although maybe the reason you're ready to fall asleep is you didn't get much sleep last night. Maybe a guilty conscience kept you up?"

"Nope. Slept like a baby."

"That statement never made any sense to me. What grown man sleeps like a baby? Did you wake up crying because you wet or crapped yourself in the middle the night?"

I was nervous, which was bad because I tended to mouth off before I could stop myself. I was probably more nervous than I've ever been, which goes to explain what I said next.

"Why? You have trouble controlling your bladder?"

"Real wise guy, huh? Little high schooler thinks he's tough? I fought Nazis in dubya dubya two, so listen to me, Jethro. Don't

nobody think you're tough. Most of the people in your school—
teachers and students alike—think you're a wimp. Three guys
torment you for years and you don't do squat about it except tell
your daddy on them?"

I guess I must've looked surprised.

"Yeah, we know about your daddy having to stick up for you
so you didn't get beat up every day of your miserable life. One of
the guys beating you up was Peter, wasn't it?"

"I pretty much told you that yesterday."

"Maybe you did," Reynolds said. "But maybe you left out the
part about how you snapped and decided to put an end to the
bullying once and for all."

"I can't tell you about something that didn't happen."

"I hate liars but, in the end, liars always get caught. You
know why?" Reynolds really didn't want me to answer as he
kept on talking. "'Cause they ain't smart. They're dumb and can't
keep their stories straight. Sooner or later, they slip up. In your
case, you did that by not coming clean the first time you talked
to me. I could have worked something out with you then. Talk
to the DA and have him go easy on you, take into account that
you're practically a kid who has had to deal with being tortured
for years. With good behavior, you might have gotten out before
your thirtieth birthday, but now you won't see the outside of the
jail cell for the rest of your days. And that's assuming they don't
go for the death penalty."

"You can't put me in the electric chair for something I didn't
do."

"Keep thinking that," Reynolds said. "See, this morning I had
a second interview with a woman close to you. From what we
know, she is arguably the woman who is the closest to you in the
world. Do you know what she told us?" Again, he didn't want me
to answer, at least not yet. That or he liked hearing the sound of
his own voice. "She says she saw you kill Peter with her own eyes."

At that moment, I probably looked like I was cool as a bliz-
zard. I was too numb to care or cry. My eyes didn't blink, my face
didn't react because my heart was too busy breaking.

After all that talk of love, Rosa sold me down the river. My life
was over. The part that hurt the most wasn't going to jail, it was

knowing Rosa and I wouldn't be together anymore.

Still, maybe Reynolds was bluffing. "Detective, I truly have no idea what you're talking about."

Reynolds fished out a cigarette, lit it, and took a long drag. "That's not how your mother tells it."

"My mother?"

"Yes. The woman who brought you into this world couldn't stand what you did. She told us she saw the whole thing and even watched you hide the body."

I relaxed. Either Detective Reynolds was lying through his teeth or my mother was. I was sure she wasn't home. I'd bet my life on it.

"That's nonsense," I said, upping my innocent act. "First off, I was nowhere near Pete's house the night he disappeared. And why would my mom be at his house? She doesn't live anywhere near that neighborhood."

Reynolds leaned forward and blew smoke across the table at me. "Why do you say she couldn't have been near there?"

"I didn't say she couldn't, only that it made no sense."

"And who said he was killed there?"

I shrugged. "Nobody. I guess I assumed."

"The murder could have occurred at any number of places. Where exactly were you when Peter got killed?"

"I guess that all depends on when he was killed, doesn't it?"

"According to our coroner, somewhere between four and ten pm Monday night."

"I was probably home."

"Why only' probably'?"

"I don't clock in. My best guess is I was home. Look, I know you've got no reason to believe me, but you have even less reason to believe my mother."

Reynolds put the cigarette in his mouth, leaned back in his comfortable chair, and folded his hands across his gut.

"And why is that? What reason would she have to lie?"

"From what you were asking me yesterday, I think it's safe to assume your first suspect was my mother's new beau. She's crazy and stupid enough to do anything to protect her new meal ticket."

"Even sell out her only child?

"She's already written off my dad and me. In her new world, we don't matter. The only times I've seen her since she left is when she had asked me to bring her stuff and then again when Dirk kicked the crap out of me." I lifted up my shirt to show the bruises. "I didn't do this to myself. Do you really think a woman who would laugh at her only son being beaten to a pulp would really care one bit about making up a story about him? I have no idea what made you think Dirk might have been involved, but if he was, maybe there's a chance she was, too. Or she's covering for him."

Reynolds took a long pull on his cigarette, then stared at me from across the table. "You're a real piece of work, aren't you, Jethro? Willing to sell out your own mother and say she murdered a guy just to not have to face the consequences for what you did."

Turnabout is fair play.

"I'm not saying she killed anybody. I'd like to think that my mother wouldn't do that, although I have to admit, I really don't know who she is anymore. Maybe she found out about the murder and just wants to cover it up so her boyfriend doesn't go to jail and leave her all alone. What I do know is I haven't done anything wrong. So ask me all the questions you want, check out my whereabouts for whenever this horrible crime happened. Everything you find will only prove to you that I'm telling the truth."

Reynolds blew out a smoke ring. "You own a gun?"

I forced myself not to think about the question. I knew damn well that's not how Peter died, so maybe Reynolds was trying to gauge my reaction to the question.

"No. Is that how Peter got killed? Somebody shot him?"

"You tell me."

I shrugged. "What else could I possibly tell you?"

"You have a gun in your house?"

"My dad has a rifle he hunts with."

"You wouldn't mind if we tested the rifle?"

"I guess not, but you'd have to ask my dad."

Detective Reynolds nodded and pointed his cigarette at me.

"It seems Dirk and your mother's stories about what happened during the fight outside the grocery store differ a bit from yours.

They claim Peter started by cheering Dirk on, then changed his tune when your teacher scolded him."

"That's not the way it happened at all."

"They also said your teacher, Mrs. Carmine, threatened to tell the cops Dirk was mauling her."

"That's ridiculous. Like I said, Peter told him to lay off. And Mrs. Carmine said to Dirk if he was the kind of man to hit a kid, he'd probably also hit a lady, and that she would tell the cops he threatened her, too."

Reynolds nodded and laid his cigarette in the ashtray. "Mrs. Carmine's story matches up with yours."

"There you have it. Unless you think a teacher is going to lie to the cops to protect a student."

"Maybe she would."

I wiped sweat from my brow.

"You nervous?" Reynolds said.

"Sure."

The detective put his forearms on the table and met my eyes without blinking. "What do you got to be scared of?"

"That should be a no-brainer. You think I shot a guy who's been bullying me for years, because my own mother lied to you and said she saw me do it. So now I might go to jail for something I didn't do. I figure I got the right to be nervous, don't you?"

"I do."

"So," I said, "you believe I shot Pete?"

Reynolds grinned like the Cheshire cat. "I never said Peter was shot."

"Yes, you did."

The big man shook his fedora-covered head. "No, I just asked you if you had access to a gun. I never said that's how the victim died."

"Then why bring it up at all?"

"The reaction. You'd probably be really good at poker with a face like yours, kid. I listen to what people say and what the evidence tells me. Right now, I'm not sure who is lying, you or your mother and her boyfriend. At the moment, you got one point in your favor and it's the same one you brought up. There is no reason why a dish like Mrs. Carmine would lie for somebody like you. For the moment, we're done, but I may drag you back here at any time, so don't leave town. Some more evidence could come in and then it's a whole new ballgame."

My mouth felt as dry as desert sand when I tried to swallow. I nodded.

"So I can go?"

Reynolds stood up. "Go on, get lost before I change my mind."

REYNOLDS HAD DRIVEN me from school to the police station but didn't offer me a ride back. I certainly didn't want to call my dad.

However, there was someone I did want to call. I found a pay phone a few blocks away. Maybe it was creepy, but I had looked up Rosa's number in the phone book and stared at it so long I memorized it. She picked up on the third ring.

"Hello?"

"Rosa, it's me."

She didn't sound happy. "Are you crazy? You can't call me here! What if my husband answered?"

"I figured he'd be at work. And I had to talk to you."

I heard her sigh. "Are you playing hooky?"

"I only wish it was something that simple. I spent all morning being questioned by a detective about why I killed Peter. He told me that the woman closest to me in the world ratted on me."

"Jethro, honey, I didn't tell them anything. You have to believe me." She sounded upset.

"I do. Turns out my mom says she saw me kill him."

"Did she see you dump the body?"

"No. She was making it all up to protect Dirk." I told her everything that happened.

"What kind of a bitch tries to pin a crime on her son to save her boyfriend?"

"My dear old mom, that's who."

"You didn't tell them anything, did you?"

"Nope, but I still think they figure I might be good for the murder. They told me not to leave town."

"Could they get any more cliché? Look, it's great to hear your voice and I appreciate you calling to let me know what's going on, but right now we have to be real careful about being seen together. At least until after my husband's dead."

"Rosa, we already talked about this..."

"And this is us talking about it again. I'm scared my own husband is going to kill me. The cops won't believe me, I've got no family to run to. If something doesn't happen to him, I'm a dead woman. And..."—her voice suddenly purred like an evil kitten—"...apparently, the only thing keeping you out of jail is me backing up your story."

"Rosa, you wouldn't tell them, would you?"

"I wouldn't want to. I'd hate to. It would break my heart to. But I don't want to die, Jethro. Better him than me. Can't you understand that?"

"If this poison works so good, why can't you just give it to him at home?"

"Because if he dies here at home, there might be an investigation."

"Why don't you put it in his morning coffee so he dies on his way to work?"

"Because he wouldn't be drunk at that hour. There'd be an investigation. If he's coming home from a bar, the cops will smell alcohol on him and write it off as a drunk crashing his car. That means I get the house and the insurance payout and, most importantly, you and I get to live happily ever after."

"You could go to the bar and do it," I said.

"Jethro, use your head, my love. If I show up at the bar and don't go home with him, a lot of questions would be asked. I need someone else to do it and that someone has to be you."

Rosa had me over a barrel. To avoid jail for one murder, I was going to have to commit another.

"How exactly am I even supposed to recognize him?"

"Oh, give me a break. I saw you staring at the pictures of me and Mike around the house when you and I had our heavenly weekend together. I watched as you tried to size him up on the sly. You'd be able to pick him out of a lineup without any problem at all."

Damned if she wasn't right. "And how exactly am I supposed to get him to take the poison?"

"Easy. Pour it in his beer when nobody's watching."

"Doesn't sound so easy to me. It's not like I can ask someone to go with me and be a distraction, now can I?"

"We'll set up a time that you'll make sure you're there. I'll call Clancy's Bar and ask for Mike. I'll make up some story. When you hear the phone ring, you know it's time to move."

"How am I going to get the poison?"

"I'll be back at school tomorrow. You stay after class for a minute and I'll slip it to you. And then you go to the bar tomorrow night and slip it to my husband. Then after the funeral, you get to slip it in me again. So, my valiant lover, are you going to save this damsel in distress?"

"Or go to jail when you change your story."

"Sweetheart, I'd hate to do that, but I'd hate even more to die."

"I could tell the cops where it happened and that you helped me hide the body."

"And I'll tell them you threatened me to tell them that story. They already suspect you're guilty, so who do you think they're going to believe, some high school student or a teacher?"

Dammit yet again if she didn't have a point.

"Fine, I'll do it. But after I graduate you and me go public with our relationship, you got me?"

"Nothing would make me happier, Jethro. Now get back to school."

I hung up and stomped off.

WHEN I GOT home, I told my dad what happened. Not only did he hit the roof, but he kept on going so it looked like he might be the first man in space.

Dad tried to get hold of Phil Hanson, but he was on patrol.

I got a lecture not to talk to a cop again unless he was there.

The next day at school, things were weird. I've never been the most popular kid, but I wasn't a pariah either. Now everyone seemed to be either avoiding me or trying not to look like they were staring at me.

I guess it was true what they say about girls liking bad boys, because a lot of the ladies in my school seemed to be checking me out. That had never happened before, at least to the point where I was able to notice.

Turns out even Jenny liked herself a bad boy, because the girl I'd had a crush on for most of high school came over and touched my elbow and held her hand there. She'd never touched me before.

"Jethro," she said, "how you holding up?"

I shrugged. "As well as could be expected."

"I'm glad to hear that." Jenny tilted her head and tossed her hair over her shoulder. "Is it true the cops took you in for questioning and grilled you?"

"Like a steak."

"Did they try to beat a confession out of you?"

I smiled and lifted my eyebrows and made what I hoped was a cool face. "I'm not really at liberty to discuss the details of what happened, if you get my drift."

Jenny's head bobbed up and down like a cork in the ocean. "Of course. I definitely get it." She nibbled on her bottom lip, bent her head forward and batted her eyelashes. "You heard about the dance next Friday, right?"

She wasn't actually about to ask me, was she? "Sure."

"I thought if you were going, that you and I might go together. You could pick me up at six thirty and my curfew is not 'til ten. We could leave the dance early and drive up to Lookout Point."

Had this happened two weeks ago, I might've fallen to my knees with my arms outstretched to Heaven, screaming *Thank You*!

Not only had my crush finally noticed me, but she actually asked *me* out! No girl actually asks a guy out. But a lot had changed. Making out with Jenny might be fun, but it wouldn't compare with being with Rosa.

Still, a bunch of people knew about my crush on her, so it would be weird if I said no.

"Well, they told me not to leave town, so I should be around. Unless the cops take me in again."

Her hand reached out and touched me again, this time moving up to my shoulder. I swear she looked like she was practically puckering her lips, and I had to admit her touch felt nice.

"Do you think that will happen?"

I lifted my shoulders toward my ears and brought my hands

out to my sides. "I hope not. But you never know," I said. If she wanted a bad boy, I was happy to oblige. "Once the cops get onto you, you never know when they'll make their play."

Her hand slid from my shoulder up to my neck.

"Then maybe we should go up there sooner. I'm free tonight. I could tell my folks I'm going over to a girlfriend's house and we can meet up instead."

Before I could answer, I spotted Rosa marching double-time right toward us, fury burning in her eyes.

"All right you two, break it up," she barked. "This is a high school, not make-out point."

Jenny pulled her hand away from me so quick it was like she'd been burned. "Yes, Mrs. Carmine." She turned toward me and gave me a wink, then wiggled her hips as she walked away.

I didn't even realize I was staring until I noticed Rosa glaring at me.

"This is how you prove your love for me?" she whispered in a way that felt worse than yelling. "Practically making out with some trollop right in the halls of the school?"

"I'd be happy to make out with you, but that's against your rules," I whispered back. "And Jenny came on to me. Before you and I were a thing, I had a crush on her. She just asked me to the dance. Too many people know I used to like her. I thought it would look weird if I suddenly turned her down for no good reason, so I said 'yes'. But you don't have anything to worry about. You're the only woman for me."

"Good. You better make sure it stays that way. I'm getting rid of my husband for you. Don't do anything to make me regret that decision. Now get to class."

She said the last sentence loudly and pointed the way with her left arm.

I tried to look suitably chastised. "Yes, Mrs. Carmine."

THE REST OF the day was more of the same. Well, the staring and being avoided, not so much being asked out by pretty girls.

Rosa glared at me throughout science class then asked me some bizarre question about the half-life of uranium that no high school student who wasn't some sort of genius could be expected to answer. She used my wrong response as an excuse to keep me after class.

I waited at my desk until everyone else had left the room. Jenny winked at me on her way out.

Rosa didn't notice because she was too busy looking down and grading some papers.

When she finally looked up at me, I smiled hopefully. "Boy, you're really steamed."

Rosa didn't smile, but crossed her arms over her chest. "Now what would make you say that?"

"The way you're running hot and cold. Giving me angry stares and then mixing it with the cold shoulder."

"Why would I be doing that?"

I wiggled my eyebrows. "I think you're jealous."

Rosa's arms swung down to her sides. "Can you blame me if I am? I broke my marriage vows for you, helped you cover up a murder, and then chose you over my husband. Then I find you flirting with some schoolgirl! How do you think that makes me feel?"

"Maybe it makes you realize just how lucky you are to have me." It sounded cocky, but that's how I was feeling. I'd never had one woman interested in me and now I had the only two women I've cared about wanting me. That sort of thing gives a guy more than a little bounce in his step.

I wasn't sure if my words would set her off again, but instead they did the opposite. Rosa smiled at me for the first time in what seemed like forever and all was right with the world.

"I am lucky... I've mixed up what you need."

"What is it?"

"A little something I made from water hemlock. You just put it in his drink and then leave my husband to his fate. It's inside a lipstick case on the red box in the closet. Now remember, I will call the bar at ten to seven. You need to be in place by then."

"Is there a clock in Clancy's?" I asked.

Rosa crinkled her eyes and looked right into mine. "Why?"

I shrugged sheepishly. "Because I don't own a watch."

She rolled her eyes and opened her desk drawer and pulled out a fancy watch with a blue band. "Here, wear this."

Rosa put it on my left wrist.

"Is it your husband's?" I was worried he might notice it.

"No. It was left behind by a student. Now go get the water hemlock out of the closet."

"Why don't you get it?"

"I already mixed it up and gave you a watch. I'm your lover, not your mother."

That comment was a bit insensitive, but I ignored it and opened the door just enough to fit through. Remembering what happened the last time I was in here, I looked back at Rosa.

"Aren't you going to come in with me?"

I reached out to take her hand, which she promptly snatched away.

"No. Not until after the funeral."

Part of me wanted to point out that I had a perfectly good offer for Lookout Point tonight but thought, it might make me sound petulant and really piss off Rosa. I couldn't afford that. She could still get me sent to jail, but I figured after I helped her off her husband, I'd have the same thing to hang over her.

I would be able to tell the cops that she used the poison and they'd have no choice but to believe me. I mean, how would I possibly know anything about mixing up some weird poison? But a high school science teacher on the other hand, that they'd believe.

Although it was weird she didn't just hand it to me. I found it right where she said it would be. When I picked up the lipstick case with my handkerchief, I could feel it was filled with liquid. I put the wrapped tube in my pocket.

I turned to go back out, but stopped when I heard Principal Pappo's voice.

"Hello, Rosa."

"That's Mrs. Carmine to you, Principal Pappo. What are you doing here? I thought our business was concluded."

The classroom door closed, followed by what sounded like the click of a lock.

"I thought you might, but I can't let a woman dictate what I can and can't do at my own school." I could hear the smirk in his voice. "Here's my letter for you."

I peered through the opening and saw the principal hand

Rosa a sheet of paper. She looked at it and the fury was back in her eyes. "You're firing me!?"

"I am. I'm going turn in this letter at the school board meeting tonight along with my recommendation that you be terminated."

"I'll tell them what's really happening."

The principal smirked. "You are welcome to try, but it's a closed-door meeting and your accusations might make a couple of members of the school board nervous. I'm not the only one who has taken advantage of this type of situation. You'll just assure they vote to fire you."

"I'll tell my husband. I'll go to the papers."

"Go ahead. I had my secretary type up this letter the day you threw me out of your classroom. I have no doubt the gossip mill has already heard all about the pending loss of your job. You tell your story, I'll tell mine."

"What do you mean 'your story'?"

"About how you found out you're going to be fired and you offered to sleep with me to save your job. But being the good upstanding and moral married man that I am, I turned you down, and in anger you started spreading these vicious lies about me."

"No one will believe you," Rosa said.

"I think you're confused about who they will and won't believe, my dear. Looks like you'll have to seek gainful employment elsewhere, which will be difficult without a recommendation from me. Of course, there's still one way to make all this go away. Luckily, my wife is still away visiting our grandkids until the end of the month."

Rosa took a step back, but Principal Pappo took three steps forward and wrapped his arms around Rosa so that one hand was on her shoulder blade and the other one was on her ass. Pappo put his mouth on her neck and kissed it. Rosa tried to pull away and pushed on his chest, but at only five-foot-four she couldn't get out of his grasp.

I stepped out of the closet. "Principal Pappo, take your hands off Mrs. Carmine."

Pappo jumped back like a little kid who'd been caught with his hand in the cookie jar. "Jethro, what are you doing here?"

"I didn't do so good in class today, so Mrs. Carmine made me stay after to rearrange her shelves."

"This isn't what it looks like. Mrs. Carmine was choking and I was trying to help her."

"How?" I said. "By squeezing her ass?"

"Fine. The truth is she's being fired and came onto me trying to save her job. I was just trying to get her to stop," Pappo said, taking a handkerchief out of his jacket pocket and dabbing the sweat from his brow.

"I heard the whole thing. I saw you maul her."

The principal narrowed his eyes and gritted his teeth. "Then I guess you saw too much for your own good. You leave me no choice but to expel you for being disrespectful."

"What?"

"Expelled. I'll make up some story. The cops already think you may have murdered Peter. No one will doubt me when I say you became aggressive, leaving me no choice but to kick you out of school."

"Mrs. Carmine will back up my story," I said.

"Not if she wants to keep her job."

Rosa took a step forward. "But you've already fired me. I have no job to protect. I'm going straight to the papers and the police. I have a witness now. And I'm going to press charges. The cops will have no choice but to arrest you."

"Again, who do you think they're going to believe?" the principal said with a smirk, but his confidence sounded forced.

"Your word against either of ours," Rosa said, "I'd bet on folks believing you. However, with both of us against you, that's a whole other story. I think they're just as likely to believe us. And when I tell them that you told me you fired women who didn't go along with your little sex scheme, they'll question them all. Are you willing to bet your career that one of them won't crack and sell you out? I'm willing to bet they will. Jethro and I can go straight to the police station. Better yet, we'll go to the office and I'll call the police from there, weeping and sniffling. That should add to our believability, wouldn't you say?"

The principal stroked his chin and started pacing. "I see your point. So we have to come up with a way for us to come out of this unscathed."

"Here's how we'll do that," Rosa said. "At tonight's board meeting, you'll recommend I be given tenure. Right now, I'll go down to the office crying but refuse to tell them anything. Jethro will come with me. We'll make enough of a scene to make sure people remember. Tomorrow, if I get a letter from the board saying I've been given tenure, I don't go to the police."

"Fine, but the boy's still expelled."

"No way," I said in a raised voice, stepping toward Pappo. Rosa pulled me back.

"Guess we'll see which is more valuable to Mrs. Carmine," the principal said smugly. "One of her students, or her job.".

Rosa looked at me, pleading with her eyes, so I pulled a trick from her playbook and opened up the classroom window. There were kids on the field practicing.

I took a deep breath and leaned out. "Which do you think sounds better? Pappo is raping Mrs. Carmine? Or should I say 'Principal Pappo' when I scream out this window?"

Pappo turned a deep shade of crimson. "You son of a bitch! I'll ruin you. I'll tell the cops you confessed to killing Peter."

"Bet I can shout faster than you can get to a phone and dial," I said, sounding tougher than I ever had in my life. "Wanna play chicken?"

Pappo looked at me, then at Rosa. She shrugged and smiled. "I'm backing Jethro."

Pappo's face and neck were bulging like a balloon about to pop. "Fine. No expulsion."

"Then we can put this all behind us," Rosa said.

"If you cross me, you're out of work." Pappo then grabbed my arm and pulled me away from the window. He stooped to whisper in my ear. "You're safe for now, but once she has tenure, Carmine ain't going to care about you anymore. Then I'm going to make your life a living hell for the rest of the school year."

I was all out of comebacks, so I just glared at him and pulled out of his grip.

"Now excuse me," Rosa said. "I have some crying to do. C'mon Jethro."

I WAS FREAKING out.

"You gotta do something!" my dad shouted. "He's treating Jethro like he's some commie."

Phil Hanson put a hand on Dad's shoulder in an effort to get him to calm down.

"Reynolds is just doing his job. He had a report from somebody who said they saw your son kill the Charles kid. He has to check it out. It's his job."

"Who's the bastard who was lying about my boy?" Dad said.

The police sergeant and I exchanged a covert look. I hadn't told Dad it was Mom who ratted me out because it would mess him up. Looks like Hanson felt the same way.

"It's an ongoing investigation. I'm not allowed to share that information. Even my talking to you about this could cost me my job. What I can tell you is, while Jethro is *a* suspect, he's not the *main* suspect. Right now, there's nothing you or I can do about it but wait. Try to relax."

"I don't like any of this," Dad said. "I feel so helpless. Jethro wouldn't kill anybody, would you Jethro?"

And that was the real reason I was freaking out. I was planning to sneak out to Clancy's Bar in order to kill a man. I spent the last day justifying it in my mind that if I didn't kill him, he'd kill Rosa. And if I didn't do it, Rosa would recant her story and I'd end up going to jail for killing Peter. And even if I didn't go to jail, I was going to get kicked out of school. I had to be at Clancy's before six-fifty, which is when Rosa said she would call.

I looked down at the watch on my wrist. I wasn't going to make it, even riding top speed on my bike.

"Maybe if I go down and talk to Reynolds, I can make him see reason," Dad said.

Phil Hanson shook his head. "That would be a bad idea. One, Reynolds doesn't like anyone telling him what to do, so he tends to do the opposite just to piss people off. Two, when you're like this, you don't so much act reasonably as punch people. You punch a detective, you're going to jail and you're not going to be able to help anybody then, are you?"

My dad let out a sound that was equal parts shout and growl.

"You're having a rough time," Hanson said. "How about we

go hoist a few brews like in the good old days? It'll take the edge off."

"I could do that. Maybe some screwball'll start a fight," my dad said with a grin.

"Oh no you don't. You getting into a fight is going to do nothing to help Jethro. If you are going to be that stupid, you better stay home."

I expected my dad to get pissed, but he took a deep breath and nodded.

Phil looked over at me. "You're having a pretty tough time, too, Jethro. How about you come out with a couple of old men and have your first beer?"

I didn't have the heart to tell either of them that it was hardly going to be my first beer.

Before I could answer, Dad said, "No way. Jethro's too young."

Phil chuckled. "Sam, I don't know how to break it to you, but your little boy is eighteen. In this state, he can go out and drink if he wants to."

My dad nodded, then punched me in the shoulder. "Yeah, I guess he can."

"So, Jethro, where do you want to go?"

This is the lifeline I'd been praying for. I heard the story from my dad of the first time he went drinking and got drunk, and where it was. I had to play it just right.

"Where'd you guys go for your first beer?"

"Clancy's," Dad said.

"If it was good enough for you guys," I said, "it's good enough for me."

Dad slapped my back. "Clancy's it is."

CLANCY'S BAR WAS nothing special, just some wooden tables and chairs scattered around and a jukebox in the corner. But it did have what I was looking for—Rosa's husband, Mike Carmine, sitting at the bar with a couple of other guys. Luckily, he had a few empty stools to his left.

My insides were swirling with emotions.

One, he was pretty damn big. Scary big. Not in height, like Dirk, but in muscles.

Two, I was jealous because he was married to Rosa and got to come home to her every night. The guy must have been an idiot to be out drinking when he could be home with her.

Three, I was pissed that this guy had the nerve to beat a woman as wonderful and sexy as Rosa, to the point where she was afraid for her life.

Despite all that, deep down in my gut I really didn't want to kill him. Rosa should have just gone to the police, but it was too late for that now. If I didn't do what Rosa wanted, I was going up the river for accidentally killing Pete.

I looked at my new watch. We'd gotten there with time to spare. Cars were much faster than bikes. Hopefully, Rosa's idea would work. I found myself fingering the poison-filled lipstick case in my pocket for the fourth time to make sure I hadn't lost it.

"First round's on me," Dad announced and motioned me and Phil to sit at one of the wooden tables, then walked up to the bar, shook hands with the bartender, and ordered drinks. He was standing to the left of Mike Carmine. To my great relief, the two of them ignored each other.

Dad brought three filled mugs over to the table and put one in front of each of us. He then raised his glass in a toast.

"To my boy's first beer."

Choosing not to correct him, I raised my mug and clinked it against Dad's and Phil's glasses.

It wasn't long before we had no reason to contemplate whether our glasses were half-full or half-empty, because we'd drained them dry. I glanced down at my watch. I needed to be at the bar next to Rosa's husband in the next two minutes.

"I'll buy the next round," I said.

"Whoa, look at the big spender," Dad said.

"Well, if you're buying, Jethro, make mine a Jamison," Phil said.

Dad drained the last drops from his mug. "Mine, too."

Great. I may have outsmarted myself. I only had two bucks but was pretty sure that would cover three beers with a couple dimes to spare, but I doubted it would be enough for two shots and a beer.

I looked down at my new watch. Crap. I had a little over a

minute until the phone was supposed to ring, so I walked over to the bar, making sure I stood up alongside Mike.

"What can I get you?" the bartender asked.

"Two shots of Jamison and another beer." I took a deep breath. "How much?"

"Two and a quarter."

The bartender grabbed a couple of shot glasses and reached behind him for a whiskey bottle.

Mike looked over at me staring at the two bucks in my hand then back at my table.

"Your pop taking you out for your first drink?" Mike said.

The idea of the man I was about to murder speaking to me made my vocal cords go numb, so I just nodded.

"Let me guess, you offered to buy the second round and he and his buddy upgraded the quality of their booze, since they weren't paying."

Shrugging, I admitted, "Pretty much."

"When you offered to buy, you figured it would be beer and you don't have enough to cover the more expensive drinks."

"Exactly."

"Give most guys a chance at free booze and they're going to go for the good stuff."

"I guess so. Now I have to go over and ask my dad for a quarter."

"Save yourself the walk."

The man I was about to poison used his index and middle fingers to push a pair of quarters from a pile of change toward me.

How could a man who beats his wife be such a nice guy? "I can't take your money."

"Sure, you can. I was young once too and somebody helped me out. I'm just helping you like someone helped me," Mike said, seeming nothing at all like the monster Rosa portrayed him to be. He must be a great actor.

"Thanks, but I only need one quarter."

Mike laughed. "Then let me impart some hard-learned wisdom on you, my young friend. Never stiff a bartender on his tip or you will get slow service and spit in your drink."

The bartender poured the shots in front of me and went to

pull out a mug when the phone rang. He walked down to the other end of the bar and picked it up.

"Clancy's... Mike? Let me check." The bartender covered the mouthpiece with his hand and mouthed, "It's your wife."

Mike nodded and walked down to the phone. I already had the lipstick case open and made like I was yawning and dumped the contents in his beer. I waited for the bartender or somebody else to yell at me that they'd seen what I did, but it didn't happen.

The bartender came back and put the beer in front of me. I paid him the two fifty and returned to our table as I heard Mike say into the phone, "Sure honey, I'll pick up some bread on the way home. Love you."

When I sat down, my drinking partners grabbed their shots. We toasted again and they downed the whiskey in one gulp while I sipped my beer, trying to pretend like I wasn't looking back at Mike to see if he was drinking his.

He was.

Dad and his buddy tried to goad me into buying the next round, but I told them I was flat busted. They bought a bunch more and we closed down the place.

Mike left about twenty minutes after I poisoned his beer.

I didn't hear until the next day that he died in a car accident on the way home.

And that wasn't the only thing I heard. Turns out they finally, through his dental records, identified the body I'd found in the gully.

"The funeral service was so beautiful," Rosa said. Not that I went. She insisted it would be too risky. I even had to sneak into her house, like always. "And I guess I never really realized how many people in this town loved Mike until it was too late."

Part of me wanted to point out that the only reason it was too late was because she'd blackmailed me into poisoning him, but I kept my trap shut. I was more than a little distracted by the form-fitting black dress she wore, because she was supposed to be in mourning. Even the little black hat with lace covering her eyes and nose only increased Rosa's allure.

She gave me a smile that made my stomach do flips.

"Now in just a few short months we can announce our love to the world and won't be forced to hide our passion like a couple of criminals."

Again, I wanted to point out that, technically, since we had been involved with the killing of two people, we certainly qualified as criminals, but instead Rosa leaned in to kiss me. I kissed her back. It was long, gentle, and slow.

Rosa pulled back, her face aglow.

"I can't tell you how much you saving my life by getting rid of that monster means to me, Jethro, but I'm going to try to show you. But first, a little celebration. You wait here."

She strutted into the kitchen, her hips swinging side to side, keeping time like the sexiest metronome in the world. I watched as she opened a bottle of red wine. She turned her back to me so I couldn't see her pour it into two glasses.

She strutted back and put a glass in front of me and the other in front of her.

"Don't drink yet. I want to make a toast first, but I have one more surprise for you. Wait here."

Rosa practically ran out of the living room into her bedroom. She was gone a few minutes, leaving me to my own devices, so I did a little rearranging of our beverages.

When she returned, Rosa was the most amazing sight I've ever viewed in my life. I wouldn't have been surprised if my tongue was hanging out of my mouth. I'm pretty sure I was panting.

She had changed out of her black mourning outfit into a red silk negligée that put her black one to shame. It didn't start until it was above her hips and only went up halfway to her armpits before cutting around her perfectly shaped bosom to push her breasts up even higher than they stood on their own. She topped it all off with a red lace robe, red stockings, and a pair of red high-heeled shoes.

She stopped to pose in the doorway. "Like what you see?"

"Very much."

I stood, planning on meeting her and then going into the bedroom, but instead, she rushed over to me, put her hands on my chest and pushed me back down onto the couch.

"What's the rush, handsome? We have the rest of our lives to spend together."

Rosa picked up the glass closest to her by the stem and handed me the other.

She raised her wine. "To the truest of loves and a lifetime of happiness. I promise to fill the rest of your life with ecstasy and joy. Cheers."

I clinked my glass with hers. "I promise to do the same for you. Cheers."

Rosa was sitting on her knees and leaning forward, showing off her best assets. She snaked her little arm around mine for us to drink the wine. I moved my glass toward her mouth, but she reached up with her other hand and gently pushed it away.

"No, silly. We each have to drink our own. We down all of it quickly and then head into the bedroom."

I waited until she had drunk about a third of her glass before I started on mine. We finished at the same time.

I rose and picked her up in my arms, then carried her over the threshold of her bedroom where we did the things that men and women who love each other do. And some that had nothing at all to do with love.

Somewhere between all the joy and ecstasy, I found myself wanting to weep for all I'd done, but was unable to stop myself from feeling the pleasure Rosa not only offered, but delivered in spades.

WE LAY IN the rumpled covers of the bed she had shared with her late husband. My left arm was around her and her leg was draped over my pelvis. She was smoking a cigarette and grinning.

"Jethro, that was our best time together. Hell, it was my best time ever. No one's ever made me feel so much like a woman before. How was it for you?"

"You have to ask?"

Rosa giggled and passed me the cigarette. I'd never smoked before, but when a beautiful naked woman gives you a cigarette, it would be rude not to take it. Of course, the coughing fit that followed might have been even ruder, but it made her laugh, each note sounding like it came from the angels themselves.

I handed the cigarette back to her and she put it in the ashtray on what had been her husband's nightstand.

"We can just drift off to sleep. I've never known a man who didn't want to go to sleep right after making love."

"Oddly enough, I'm not tired."

"So, you want to go again, do you? I forgot what teenage boys are like," she said as she grabbed hold between my legs and stroked me.

Despite myself, I could feel myself hardening at her touch.

"I was wondering if you'd heard the news," I said.

Rosa leaned in and planted kisses along my neck. "What news?"

"They identified that body I found. It was Jeff Swanson. Turns out he didn't run away, which is odd, since he supposedly left a note telling his parents he was leaving town with a woman. Wasn't he the student you were tutoring?"

Oh, how the tables had turned. My words made *her* stiffen.

"That's terrible. His poor family."

"I know what you mean. But the real shocker is the coroner did some sort of blood test. It turns out the Swanson kid had rum and water hemlock in his system. Isn't that the same stuff you gave me to put in your husband's beer?"

Rosa slid to the edge of the bed and stood up, her face a mask of fear.

"But that's impossible. There's no way they could know enough to test Jeff for that. How the hell could the coroner know? Did you spill it to the cops?"

"Actually, the coroner didn't know. I made up the stuff about the poison. I wanted to see how you'd react." Plus, I had seen he had a bottle of rum in his pocket, which lent the lie just enough credibility. "I thought it was awfully strange that the kid's library card was in your car. Did you tell him you loved him, too, before you convinced him the two of you were running off together?"

I practically saw a switch flip in Rosa's head as her expression and body language changed. The alluring vixen had been replaced by a cunning killer who knew she didn't have to hide who she was anymore.

"Sure. Boys and men are all too willing to believe it when a woman tells them how great and sexy they are. How they make her feel things no one else ever had. Your egos are the perfect way to manipulate all of you."

"So, if he was so easily manipulated, why'd you kill the guy?" I said, putting my hand on my gut like it was hurting. Rosa saw that and smiled.

"Same as you in the beginning. Balked at a little murder. Wouldn't kill my husband, even after I made him a man. Several times." Rosa stared into my eyes. "Does it hurt knowing you're not special? That you were just a tool to me?"

"It don't feel good, that I can tell you. So the guy didn't want to become a killer for you. Why'd you off him?"

"Idiot said he was going to the cops. I said he showed me the error of my ways and I would let Mike live, and he and I could run away together. Back then, Mike's ma wasn't sick, so we made love in my car. We drove out to the woods, drank some rum, and after I gave him a great sendoff, I dragged his body to a gulley. Stupid flooding from the storm dredged up his body and screwed up my plans."

"Seems only fair," I said, "as you seem to be screwing everybody else."

Rosa perked up at that. "So, you *are* jealous you weren't my only." She preened at her naked reflection in the wall mirror, running her hands along her curves, and then turning so she could view herself in her glory from every angle. "Can't really blame you. Or Jeff. Or even Pete."

I could feel my jaw clench and teeth grind.

"Yes, Pete was telling the truth. I seduced him willingly."

"I'd already figured that out. It was too odd that Pete fell over so easily from just a few punches. Then I remembered he said that you gave him wine and there were two glasses on the table. You said the water hemlock takes about an hour to work. That certainly gave you enough time to get the poisoned booze into him before you called me and I made it here. Turns out I didn't kill Pete. You did."

Rosa tilted her head back and laughed hysterically, like she was some crazy dame in a gangster movie.

"I guess you're not quite as dull-witted as I took you for. But you're still not all too smart if you realized all that, yet still drank the wine. I figure you've got less than twenty minutes before you shuffle off this mortal coil and then there's nothing left that can trace me to Mike's death."

"That does seem really stupid of me, huh? I mean, you told me you loved me so much, so why would I ever think you would ever poison me?"

Rosa stopped looking at her reflection and turned toward me. "Jethro, you're a sweet kid and an enthusiastic lover, but I'm certainly not willing to tie myself down to you for the rest of my life. In a choice between you and my dearly departed husband, you would've always come in second. If I'd let you both live, that is."

"So, you loved Mike?" I asked.

"Not really. He was handsome and good in bed. And he was a way out of the Podunk town I grew up in."

"Did he really beat you?"

"Nope. Well, he hit me once during an argument, but I made him sleep on the couch for a week and it never happened again,"

"So how did you get the black eye?"

Rosa laughed, but it didn't sound like sex anymore. It sounded like betrayal. "Hit myself with a can of succotash."

"You really are crazy, aren't you?"

"I'm determined. I made sure Mike got both of us twenty-five thousand dollars of life insurance. The house is already paid off. I'm now a tenured teacher. I'm going to be sitting pretty."

"You still could have had all that and me, too," I said.

"I'm fine with just the money, thanks. Aren't you curious about what I'm going to do to get rid of your body without help?"

I shook my head. "Not really. I took a peek in your garage when I got here. I noticed a new red wagon. I figured you'd bring it in here, roll my corpse out of the bed into the wagon, pull me out to the garage, and put me in the trunk of your car. Then you'd wait until the middle of the night and dump me somewhere in the woods, like you did with Jeff. Except this time you'll work harder to make sure my body won't be found."

"Remember what I taught you. A good scientist controls all the variables in an experiment. Jethro, I'm very impressed you were able to figure all this out, but I still can't get past the fact that you wanted to get laid so much that you drank the poisoned wine, anyway."

"And I'm amazed that someone as devious as you hasn't realized yet that I wasn't the one who drank the water hemlock wine." Now that I had the real story, I allowed myself a grin and couldn't have stopped myself from chuckling, even if I'd wanted to. "You are."

Rosa's brow furrowed and her eyes darted out the bedroom door toward the living room.

"No, you're wrong," she said. "I put the poisoned wine in front of you. I *handed* it to you! I wouldn't even sip it when you tried putting it to my mouth."

"That's when I was pretty sure I was right about you being a murderous bitch. A good scientist does control all the variables, but you were so cocky you weren't a good scientist. When you went into the bedroom to change into that lovely red lingerie, I switched our glasses. Once I watched you drink it willingly, I drank mine. To be honest, I was hoping I was wrong about all this."

"Why?" Rosa shouted, doubling over as she grabbed at her gut.

"Because even though you didn't really love me, I loved you."

And I guess Dad was right, that a man in love will overlook most anything.

Rosa started to twitch from her face to her feet. "Then why would you poison me?"

"Better you than me. Isn't that what you said about Mike?"

"No, this can't be happening. I had everything figured out. There's no way some idiot kid like you could trick me…"

Rosa collapsed forward onto the bed. Her twitching became convulsions, then she went still. I waited a bit and got dressed, then checked her for breathing. I even put my head on her chest. No heartbeat. Rosa must have measured out the poison for someone my size and weight, so it killed her small self even faster.

I went out to the kitchen, dumped the rest of the bottle of wine down the sink, and put it in the trash. I cleaned the glasses and wiped every surface in the house that might have my fingerprints. Then I went out to the garage, got the red wagon that Rosa had planned to use with me and wheeled it into the bedroom. I slid Rosa, still naked, into it. There was no sense in dressing her.

Rosa turned out to be an evil teacher, but I still learned a few things from her.

I loaded the corpse of my first love into the trunk of her car.

I HAD A plan. And I do have to say my solution for getting rid of Rosa's body was inspired. It was a special delivery to someone else who thought he could screw with me and get away with it.

I waited until the dead of night, then drove to Principal Pappo's house. It was so kind of him to let Rosa know that his wife was going to be gone. Headlights off, I parked her car in his driveway. I wore one of Mike's fedoras and his long coat so I wouldn't be recognized. I'd left my bike a couple of blocks away. I snuck through the backyards to reach it, then ditched my disguise. I got home and into bed, my dad none the wiser.

By lunchtime the next day, it was all over school that Rosa's nude body had been found in Pappo's yard. It didn't take long for the police investigation to reveal what he had been doing to make sure lady teachers got tenure. They charged him with Rosa's murder. His wife left him, he was fired from his job, and ultimately ended up being convicted.

So did Dirk. Everyone assumed that because Pete's body was found on his property that he must've done it. He got life. My mom didn't get charged, but she did try to get back with my dad. I was surprised he had the good sense to tell her to go to hell and slammed the door in her face. At least the first time. By the third, he let her move back in.

Jenny and I went to Lookout Point and did more than make out. She wasn't Rosa, but she was pretty fantastic and soon she helped heal my heartbreak.

A happy ending, right? You probably think I'd gotten away with murder, but you'd be wrong.

Oh, I got away with Mike's murder. And Rosa's. Even though I really didn't kill Pete and only hid his body, I got away with that, too.

The funny part is, I ended up getting arrested for murder anyway and it was one I didn't even commit.

I got convicted for killing Jeff Swanson.

Rosa got her revenge from beyond the grave.

It turns out the watch she gave me belonged to Jeff Swanson. Someone noticed the blue band while I was wearing it and told the cops. They checked and found a serial number that proved it had been his.

Since I was wearing it, the police assumed I'd been the one who killed him and took his watch.

Of course, I denied it. My lawyer claimed I'd found it near his body and kept it, but the jury didn't buy it. The DA pointed out that the watch wasn't waterproof, and if it had been on the body during all the flooding, the water would have damaged it.

Unfortunately, the watch was in perfect condition. I could have told the truth then, but that would have tied me to two other murders. Better to keep my trap shut.

Jenny stuck with me until sentencing, then dumped me. I'm doing twenty years to life at Longrow Prison.

They say love is a many splendid thing, but don't you be sucker enough to fall for it like I did, because they are all a bunch of stinking liars.

ABOUT THE AUTHORS

RUSS COLCHAMIRO IS THE AUTHOR OF the rollicking space adventure *Crossline*, the zany sci-fi backpacking series *Finders Keepers*, *Genius de Milo*, and *Astropalooza*, editor of the sci-fi mystery anthology, *Love, Murder & Mayhem*, and contributing author for his newest project, *Murder in Montague Falls*, a noir novella collection, all with Crazy 8 Press.

Russ has contributed to several other anthologies including *Tales of the Crimson Keep*, *Pangaea*, *They Keep Killing Glenn*, *Altered States of the Union*, *Thrilling Adventure Yarns*, *Brave New Girls* vols. 3&4, *Camelot 13*, *TV Gods 2*, and *Footprints in the Stars*.

He is now finalizing the first in an ongoing SFF mystery series featuring his hard-boiled private eye Angela Hardwicke and has several other SFF, crime fiction, and children's book projects in the works.

Russ lives in New Jersey with his wife, their twin ninjas, and their crazy dog, Simon.

For more on Russ's works, visit www.russcolchamiro.com, and follow him on Facebook, Twitter and Instagram @AuthorDudeRuss.

SAWNEY HATTON IS AN AUTHOR, EDITOR, and screenwriter who has long loved playing in the dark. His published works include the dark comedy novel *Dead Size*, the YA noir novella *Uglyville*, and the dark fiction short story collection *Everyone Is a Moon*. He also edited the sci-fi horror anthology *What Has Two Heads, Ten Eyes, and Terrifying Table Manners?*

Other incarnations of Sawney have produced marketing videos, attended chili cook-offs, and played the banjo and sousaphone (not at the same time). As of this writing, he is still very much alive. For more semi-unseemly insights into Sawney, visit his website at www.SawneyHatton.com or find him on Twitter and Facebook.

PATRICK THOMAS IS THE AWARD-WINNING AUTHOR of the beloved Murphy's Lore series and the darkly hilarious "Dear Cthulhu" advice empire.

His 40+ books include *Fairy with a Gun, By Darkness Cursed, Lore & Dysorder, Dead to Rites, Startenders, As the Gears Turn, Cthulhu Explains It All,* and *Exile and Entrance.* His is the co-author of the Mystic Investigators series, *The Santa Heist,* and the Jack Gardner mysteries.

Patrick is the co-editor of *Camelot 13* (with John French), *New Blood* (with Diane Raetz), and *Hear Them Roar* (with CJ Henderson), co-created The Wildsidhe Chronicles YA series and is the creator of the Agents of the Abyss series.

He has had more than 150 short stories published in magazines and anthologies. As Patrick T. Fibbs, he writes YA and children's books including the Ughabooz books, the Undead Kid Diaries, the Joy Reaper books, and the Babe B. Bear Mysteries.

You can visit him online at www.patthomas.net and at www.patricktfibbs.com

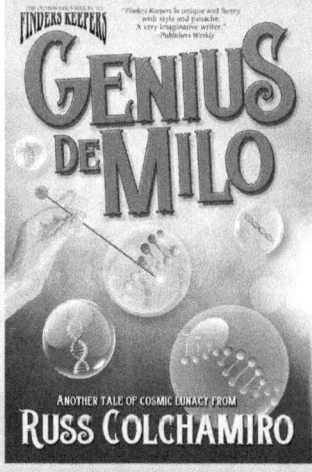